STARS & STRIPES TRIUMPHANT

BY HARRY HARRISON

FICTION

Deathworld

Deathworld 2

Deathworld 3

The Stainless Steel Rat

The Stainless Steel Rat's Revenge

The Stainless Steel Rat Saves the World

The Stainless Steel Rat Wants You

The Stainless Steel Rat for President

A Stainless Steel Rat Is Born

The Stainless Steel Rat Gets Drafted

The Stainless Steel Rat Sings the Blues

The Stainless Steel Rat Goes to Hell

Planet of the Damned

Planet of No Return

Bill, the Galactic Hero

Bill, the Galactic Hero on the Planet of
    Robot Slaves

Homeworld

Wheelworld

Starworld

West of Eden

Winter in Eden

Return to Eden

Plague from Space

Make Room! Make Room!

The Technicolor Time Machine

Captive Universe

The Daleth Effect

Montezuma's Revenge

Queen Victoria's Revenge

A Transatlantic Tunnel, Hurrah!

Stonehenge, with Leon E. Stover

Star Smashers of the Galaxy Rangers

The Lifeship, with Gordon R. Dickson

Skyfall

The QE2 Is Missing

Invasion: Earth

Rebel in Time

The Turning Option, with Marvin
    Minsky

The Hammer and the Cross, with John
    Holm

One King's Way, with John Holm

King and Emperor, with John Holm

Stars and Stripes Forever

Stars and Stripes in Peril

Stars and Stripes Triumphant

SHORT STORY COLLECTIONS

War with the Robots

Two Tales and Eight Tomorrows

Prime Number

One Step from Earth

The Best of Harry Harrison

Stainless Steel Visions

Galactic Dreams

JUVENILES

Spaceship Medic

The California Iceberg

The Men from P.I.G. and R.O.B.O.T.

ILLUSTRATED BOOKS

Great Balls of Fire

Mechanismo

Planet Story, illustrated by Jim Burns

Spacecraft in Fact and Fiction, with
    Malcolm Edwards

HARRY HARRISON

STARS & STRIPES TRIUMPHANT

BALLANTINE BOOKS · NEW YORK

A Del Rey® Book
Published by The Ballantine Publishing Group

Copyright © 2003 by Harry Harrison
Illustrations copyright © 2003 by Angela Tomlinson

www.delreydigital.com

Library of Congress Cataloging-in-Publication Data
Harrison, Harry, 1925–
Stars and stripes triumphant / Harry Harrison.— 1st ed.
p. cm.
"A Del Rey book"—T.p. verso.
ISBN 0-345-40937-X
1. United States—History—Civil War, 1861–1865—Fiction. 2. International relations—Fiction. 3. Great Britain—Fiction. I. Title.

PS3558.A667 S84 2003
813'.54—dc21
2002073618

Manufactured in the United States of America

Book Design by Ann Gold

First Edition: January 2003

1   3   5   7   9   10   8   6   4   2

STARS & STRIPES TRIUMPHANT

PROLOGUE

ABRAHAM LINCOLN, PRESIDENT OF THE UNITED STATES

The threat of war, and war itself, has plagued my presidency of these United States of America ever since my inauguration. Instead of a peaceful handing over of presidential power, a continuation of the rule of law with which this country is blessed, it has proved to have been an administration of strife. The dissension began even before my tenancy of the White House, when the Southern states attempted to break their bond with the Federal Union and organize a confederacy. Once this new alliance had fired on the Federal troops in Fort Sumter the die was cast. War was inevitable. There was no way to return to the path of peace. Thus began the Civil War in America that pitted brother against brother in deadly battle. I hesitate to think what the outcome would have been had these hostilities been allowed to run their course; surely it would have meant a nation sundered and brave men dead by the thousands. That is what would have happened in the very least. At worst it would surely have meant a national catastrophe, the destruction of this country as we know it.

But fate intervened. What began as a small incident, the capture of the British mail packet *Trent* by the American warship the USS *San Jacinto*, was inflated, blown up out of all proportion by the British government. As president, I would have been happy to release the two Confederate ministers who were taken from the *Trent* had the British government, Lord Palmerston and Queen Victoria in particular, shown any understanding of our position. Despite all of our efforts at peacemaking, they persisted in their intransigence. My government could not, would not, give in to threats and imprecations at the highest level issued by a foreign power. While we in America worked for a peaceful solution to our national differences, they appeared to want nothing less than a headlong confrontation. While my government was locked in battle with the Southern secessionists, we still had to deal with this militant foreign power.

Alas, international peace was not to be. Defying all logic, the forces of the mighty British Empire invaded this sovereign land.

The world knows what happened next. With our nation threatened from the outside, the Civil War, the battle between our government and the seceding states, was ended. The result was that a reunited United States fought back against these invaders, the common enemy. It was not an easy war—none are—but in the end the strength of our common cause was such that the invaders were repulsed and hurled back from our shores. Disheartened by our victories, the enemy was sent packing as well from Canada, when that nation declared its liberty from colonial rule.

Throughout this war I learned to depend on General William Tecumseh Sherman to fight and to win. He was respected and admired by our Northern troops, and it became a matter of the greatest importance that the officers of the Southern army regarded him highly as well. They appreciated his knowledge and attitude toward the South, as well as his warrior skills—respected the man so well that they were willing to serve under him in the battle against our common enemy.

Finally that invasion and war was ended and we were at peace. Or were we? Unhappily this was not to be the end of our struggle. The Lion of the British Empire had lost battles before—but had never lost a war. Try as hard as they could, it appeared that the British simply could not swallow this defeat. Despite all attempts at sweet reason upon our part, they persisted in their bellicosity to the extent that they attempted another invasion of our country, this time through the war-torn land of Mexico.

My generals, now more experienced and wise in the ways of war, devised a counterplan to contain this threat. Instead of our armies being

A PRESIDENT'S BITTER MEMORIES

bogged down in a war of attrition on our borders, it was decided to take the war closer to the enemy shores. Thus the American invasion of Ireland began. The proposed enemy invasion from Mexico was quickly terminated as the British realized that their forces were needed closer to home.

I am proud to say that not only did our forces prevail against the enemy in Ireland, but in fact succeeded in liberating that much-stricken nation.

I pray that this national rivalry between our two great countries will now end. These last months my mind has been occupied with domestic matters, not international concerns. During the past August of the year 1864, the Democratic National Congress nominated Judah P. Benjamin as their presidential candidate: a worthy man, without whose unstinting aid peace and reconciliation in the South would not have been attained. It was my pleasure to be nominated by the Republican Party for a second term, with Andrew Johnston of Tennessee standing for vice-president at my side.

It was a hard-fought election. I regret to say that my name is still anathema in parts of the South and the voters there voted *against* me rather than for the Democratic candidate for president. However, the soldiers— both those recently discharged and those still in the service—looked upon me as their commander in chief, and their votes carried the day.

But that is in the past. I began my second term in March of this year, 1865. Now it is May and Washington City was never more beautiful, with green leaves and blossoms everywhere. America wishes only peace in the world, but has perhaps become too used to war during the past four years. To provide weapons for our armies and iron ships for our fleets, a growing and successful manufacturing economy has evolved, one that we never knew before in peacetime.

I would be the happiest man in the world if I could preside peacefully over this prosperous land, to oversee that our cannons of war were beaten into the plowshares of peace. Where our native manufacturing genius has succeeded in wartime, it could surely succeed as well in a time of peace.

But will peace prevail? Our British cousins remain bellicose. They still take affront at being expelled from Ireland, after all their centuries of rule. They will not face the fact that they are gone from that green island, and gone for good. Their politicians still make warlike speeches and rattle their sabers in their scabbards. To counter this British exercise in ill will, our politicians are now busy on the European continent seeking trade agreements and attempting to strengthen our peaceful ties.

Will peace and sanity prevail? Can another disastrous war be averted? I can only pray with all my strength that it will.

BOOK ONE
A JOURNEY ABROAD

★

BRUSSELS, BELGIUM
JUNE 1865

The floor-to-ceiling windows were open to the warm sunshine, admitting the background hum of the busy Belgian capital. They also admitted the effluvia of horse manure, a smell unnoticed by anyone who had dwelled for any time in a large city. President Abraham Lincoln was seated on an ornate Louis XV couch, reading the document that Ambassador Pierce had just given him. He looked up when there was a tap on the hall door.

"I'll see who it is, Mr. President," Pierce said. He strutted a bit when he walked; this was his first political appointment and he was immensely proud of it. He had been a Wall Street banker, an old business associate of Lincoln's from the same law firm, until the President had nominated him for this position. Secretly he knew that he had been selected more for his knowledge of French, and his intimacy with international commerce, than for any political skills. Nevertheless it was still quite an honor. He held the door wide so that the two general officers could come in. Lincoln looked over the tops of his reading glasses and acknowledged their salutes.

"Sashes, swords, and ribbons, gentlemen, as well as festoons of gold braid. We are quite elegant today."

"Seemed appropriate for this morning's presentation at court," General Sherman said. "We were just informed about it."

"As was I," Lincoln said. "I was also told that it was most important, and was told as well that they particularly requested that you and General Grant be present."

"Did they say why, sir?" Grant asked.

"Not directly. But Pierce here, who has made many important contacts since his appointment, took a senior Belgian civil servant aside and managed to elicit from him the fact that the presentation of some honors would be involved."

"They will surely be a fine sight," Pierce said. "It seems that the smaller the country, the bigger the medals are. And I was assured by the same official that the past war between our country and the British would not be involved in this presentation. It seems that Queen Victoria is very touchy on that subject, and King Leopold, who, after all, is her favorite uncle and constant correspondent, has no desire to offend her on that score. The awards will be for heroic actions that you gentlemen engaged in during our recent civil war."

Grant smiled as he peered down at the plain blue cloth of his infantryman's uniform. "It could do with a bit of smartening up."

They all looked up as Gustavus Fox, the Assistant Secretary of the Navy, let himself in through a connecting door. He was a man who kept a very low public profile; only at the very highest levels of government was it known that he headed America's secret service. He nodded at them and held up a sheaf of papers.

"I hope that I am not interrupting, but is there time for a briefing, Mr. President?" he asked. "Some new and urgent information has just been made known to me."

Ambassador Pierce grunted slightly as he pulled his fob watch from the pocket in his well-rounded waistcoat. "More than enough time, I do believe. The carriages are not due to arrive here until noon."

"I hope that with a bit of luck you are bringing me some good news, Gus," the President said hopefully. "There never seems to be much of that."

"Well, I am forced to admit that it is somewhat of a mixed bag, sir. Firstly, just two nights ago the British raided the harbor at the port of

Kingstown in Ireland. This is the ferry port that is quite close to Dublin. They landed troops, and the attackers burned the city hall, as well as some of the harbor installations, then finished it all off by seizing and setting fire to some ships that were tied up there. The Irish believe that it was a terror raid, pure and simple, since it accomplished nothing but wanton destruction. It apparently was a clear reminder to the Irish that the British are still out there. As they left they exchanged shots with an Irish revenue cutter, but retreated back to sea before the troops from Dublin could arrive."

Lincoln shook his head with great unhappiness. "I feel that the timing of this action is deliberate, that there is no coincidence here since this intrusion occurred just as our delegation was arriving in Belgium."

"I concur, Mr. President. It is obviously a simple message to us," Sherman said, his face cold, his pale eyes deadly. "They are telling us that they can strike at Ireland, whenever and wherever they please. And they will let no international conference stand in their way. It appears that their losses and defeats in America and Ireland have taught them nothing."

"I am afraid that yours is the most valid interpretation," Lincoln said with a great weariness. "But you said it was a mixed bag, Gus. Is there no good news in there? Can you pull nothing from your bundle that will bring cheer to a weary old man?"

Gus smiled and shuffled through the papers, drew out one sheet, and passed it over to the President.

"This came in on the navy packet that tied up in Ostend this morning. It is a personal report made to your cabinet by Mr. John Stuart Mill. They have forwarded this copy to you. If you will look there, you will see that the Secretary of the Treasury has penned a personal note to you on the first page."

Lincoln nodded and read the opening aloud. "Yes, indeed, this will surely be of interest to all of you here. 'Mr. President. You will of course wish to acquaint yourself personally with the contents of this most valuable economic report. But permit me to sum it up in its entirety. I do believe that Mr. Mill's conclusions are not only very accurate, but inescapable as well. The American economy is booming, as it never has in the past. Our factories are working flat out, both in the industrialized North and in the new works that have been constructed in the South. It is evident now that everyone who wants a job is hard at work. The reconstruction and modernization of the railroads is almost complete. It is obvious what has happened. Due to the exigencies of war this country has been involuntarily changed from being a basically agrarian economy to one that is rich with industry. Exports are rising, the railroads are being modernized and extended, while shipbuilding is at an all-time record high. All in all, Mr. Mill is most enthusiastic about this country's economic future. As am I. Yours faithfully, Salmon P. Chase.' "

Lincoln skipped through the report. "Most interesting, gentlemen. Mr. Mill appears to have been comparing production figures right around the world. Great Britain, the powerhouse of industry ever since the industrial revolution, had always led all of the other countries in strength and output. But no more! He believes that when the final figures are compared at the end of the year, America will outstrip Britain on all fronts."

There were murmured agreements, and when they died away Fox spoke again.

"With this inspiring news, Mr. President, do you think you can spare a few moments to meet with a delegation?"

"Delegation? I made no appointments."

"They arrived at dawn this morning. I had the pleasure of their company at breakfast. It is President Jeremiah O'Donovan Rossa of Ireland. With him is his vice-president, Isaac Butt—accompanying them is General Thomas Meagher. They say it is a matter of some urgency, and they hope that you will grant them a few moments of your time. They were—how shall I say it?—greatly upset. I think it would be prudent if you could make the time to see them now."

"But you say that Tom Meagher is here? The last I heard he was stationed at Fort Bragg."

"No longer. Some months ago he was granted indefinite leave to go to Ireland, where he is advising the Irish army."

"We are pressed for time, Mr. President . . ." Pierce said, looking at his watch again.

Sherman's voice was icily cold. "We are not too pressed, I sincerely hope, to see the elected President of Ireland—and with him an old comrade who, in addition to his victories in Ireland, has fought long and hard for our country."

"Yes, of course, we must see them," Lincoln said. "By all means show them in."

"Shall we leave?" Grant asked.

"No—with Meagher here, this matter must surely be of some importance to the military."

Lincoln stepped forward when the three men came in and took Rossa's hand. "We haven't met since your inauguration in Dublin," he said warmly. "I must say that it was quite an occasion, as well as being one that I will never forget."

"Nor shall I, Mr. President—for you speak the very truth. Until the day I die I shall always remember with great warmth the events of that gorgeous day. If you will recall, it was the first day of a springtime that held out such great promise for our future. That promise is indeed being fulfilled. But, as you know, there have been many problems as well. There has been so much water under the bridge since that blessed occasion. But excuse me, sir, I digress. You remember Vice-President Butt?"

"Of course. I speak only the truth when I say, Mr. Butt, that yours, and the President's, is a most grave and important labor," Lincoln said as he took the Vice-President's hand. "I do marvel every day at the glowing reports I read of your unifying and modernization of Ireland."

"It has been a mighty task indeed—but well worth every effort," Rossa said. His expression darkened as he went on. "A task that has been made far more difficult by the continuing harassment by the enemy from the outside. Goodness knows that I, and the people of Ireland, have enough black memories. Our history has indeed been a long and dark one ever since the day when English troops first set foot in our poor country. Now, I am most sure that I speak for every man in the country when I say let bygones be bygones. Enough of painful memories and ancient crimes. We Irish tend to live too much in the past, and it is high time that we were done with that practice. The past is done with and shall not return. We must turn our backs on it and instead turn our faces toward the glowing sun of the future—"

"But they will not let us!" Isaac Butt broke in, cracking his knuckles resoundingly, so carried away was he by the strength of his emotions. "The recent raid on Kingstown was but a pinprick among our greater sorrows. Every day—every hour—sees its like. There are constant landings in remote Irish seaports, where innocent Irishmen are killed and their small craft, their only possessions, burned. Ships are stopped at sea as well, stopped and searched, and many times they have their cargo confiscated. It is as though we have a demon on our backs that cannot be removed, a curse from hell that cannot be lifted. The war was well won— yet it will not end. The British are indeed our demon possessor!"

General Meagher's quiet voice was in great contrast to Butt's impassioned plea, and the more damning because of that.

"And there is worse. We have had reports now of kidnapping and imprisonment in the city of Liverpool. We do not know the details—other than that something terrible is happening there. As you must know, there are many Irish resident in the Midlands, hardworking people who have been many years resident there. But now it appears that the British question their loyalty. In the name of security, entire families have been rounded up and taken away by armed guards. And the worst part is that we cannot find what has happened to them. It is as though they have vanished into the night. We have heard rumors about camps of some kind, but we can discover nothing factual. I do not deny that we have had agents among the Liverpool Irish, but that certainly cannot justify the arrest and detainment of innocent people. This is a matter of guilt by association. Are the women and the children guilty as well? They are treated as such. And we have unconfirmed reports that other camps are being built across the breadth of England. Are these for the Irish, too? I can only say, Mr. President, that this is a monumental crime against humanity."

"If what you say is true—and I have no reason to doubt you in the slightest—then I must agree with you," Lincoln said wearily as he found the couch and seated himself once again upon it. "But, gentlemen—what can we do about it? The American government can protest these crimes strongly—as indeed we have done in the past and shall do in the future. But beyond that—what can be done? I am afraid that I can read the British response already. This is only a civil matter, an internal one, of no concern to other nations." In the grim silence that followed, Lincoln turned to Meagher. "You, as a military officer, must recognize that this is not a situation that can be resolved by the military. Our hands are tied; there is nothing that can be done."

"Nothing . . . ?" Meagher was not pleased with the notion and worked hard to conceal his dismay.

"Nothing," Sherman firmly concurred. "I speak not for myself, but as general of the armies. The war has ended and the world is at peace. The British are now doing their best to provoke us, and they have certainly succeeded in stirring our rage. They know that after the recent war, we are concerned with Ireland and have a vested interest in Irish freedom. But does that mean that there is ample cause here to go to war again? I frankly do not think so. The British are careful to make this appear to be an internal matter—over which we, of course, have no providence. You must remember that this day we are embarked on a most important civil mission of peaceful negotiation. The major nations of the world are assembling here in Brussels, and one can only wish them the best of success. We can talk of war again only when our mission fails. None here wish that. But, with your permission, Mr. President, I can take a few moments with these gentlemen, and General Grant, to discuss what material assistance we can afford them. About the imprisonment of Irish people in camps in England— it is my frank belief that there is nothing officially that can be done. But the other matters, the raids, halting vessels at sea, I can see where an American presence night alleviate some of the problems."

"We must leave here in half an hour," Pierce said, worriedly, consulting his watch.

"I regret that we have taken up your time," General Meagher said. "Thank you for seeing us, Mr. President."

"I must thank you for making the effort to come here and present us with details of the current unhappy Irish problems. Be assured that we will do everything in our power to alleviate them."

Gustavus Fox showed General Sherman and the visitors into an adjoining room, then remained with them to take notes. When they had gone, Lincoln shook his head wearily. "I am beginning to feel like the feller that tried to catch the rainbow, and the faster he ran after it the faster it vanished away before him. I have had enough of war, yet I fear greatly for the peace. With men of strong will and determination in Britain, the matter of peace does indeed take second place."

"That is why we are gathered here in Brussels, Mr. President," Pierce said. "As the various delegates have arrived, I have taken the time to have many confidential talks with them. It is my fond belief that all of them are united in their desire for peace and prosperity. Europe has had too much political unrest in recent years, not to mention the wars that have always plagued this continent. The overall feeling appears to be that we must all labor together to bring about some lasting peace."

Lincoln nodded and turned to the silent Grant, who sat sternly on the front edge of his chair. The general's hands rested on the hilt of his sword, which stood upright before him.

"Is this the military view as well, General?" Lincoln asked.

"I can only speak for myself, sir. I believe in a world at peace—but I am afraid that not all men share that belief. The bloody history of this continent is mute witness to the ambitions and ancient hatreds of the countries here. Therefore he must consider the situation carefully—and must always be prepared for war, as little as we may desire it."

"And America is prepared?"

"She is indeed—at the present moment more so than ever before in our history. You read us Mr. Mill's letter. Certainly the manufacturers who supply and support our military strength are operating at full pace. But we should consider our military manpower as well. With the onset of peace many soldiers will find that their terms of enlistment are up. This is already beginning to happen. It is obvious that the lure of a return to their families will be great. If nothing is done we are going to see a dwindling away of our physical resources."

"Has not the regular army been expanded?"

"It has indeed. With enlistment bonuses and better pay and conditions, our forces have grown and increased greatly. But at the present time I must admit, in private to you gentlemen, there are not really enough divisions existing to engage in a major conflict."

Pierce was more interested in protocol than in world politics, worried about being late. While Lincoln sat bemused, trying to understand the ramifications of General Grant's summation of the military situation, Pierce kept looking at his watch and fidgeting nervously. He relaxed only when General Sherman rejoined them.

"I am afraid that we must leave now, gentlemen," Pierce said, opening the hall door and making small waving motions, stepping aside as they passed. He walked out after them. Fox remained behind, then closed the door.

The American mission with all their officials, clerks, and functionaries occupied the entire second floor of the Brussels Grand Mercure Hotel. When Abraham Lincoln and his party exited the rooms, they saw before them the magnificent sweep of the wide marble staircase that dropped down to the lobby. There was a growing murmur of voices from below as Lincoln and his party appeared at the top of the staircase.

"We are indeed expected," he said, looking down into the lobby of the hotel.

From the foot of the stairs, stretching away to the outside door, two rows of soldiers, to either side of a crimson carpet, stood at stiff attention. Silver-cuirassed and magnificently uniformed, they were an honor guard, all of them officers of the Belgian household regiments. Beyond them, outside the glass doors, a magnificent carriage was just drawing up. The soldiers themselves, standing to attention, their swords on their shoulders, were silent, but not so the crowd that filled the lobby behind them. Elegantly dressed men and women pushed forward, all eager to see the President of the United States, the man who had led his country to such resounding victories. A small cheer arose when Lincoln's party appeared.

The President stopped a moment to acknowledge the reception and raised his tall stovepipe hat. Set it back in place and tapped it firmly into position—then led the way down the stairs. Generals Sherman and Grant were close behind him, while Ambassador Pierce brought up the rear. They made their way slowly down the steps, then across the lobby toward the open doors.

There was a murmur from the crowd and a disturbance of some kind.

Suddenly, shockingly, apparently pushed from behind, one of the ranked officers fell forward onto the floor with a mighty crash. As he fell, a man dressed in black pushed through the sudden opening in the ranks of the soldiers.

"Sic semper tyrannis!" he shouted loudly.

At the same moment he raised the pistol he was carrying and fired at the President, who was just a few paces away from him.

AN ATTEMPTED
ASSASSINATION!

It was a moment frozen in time. The fallen Belgian officer was on his hands and knees; the other soldiers still stood at attention, still obeying their last command. Lincoln, shocked by the sudden appearance of the gunman from the crowd, stopped before taking a half step back.

The pistol in the stranger's hand came up—and fired.

The unexpected is the expected in war. While both of these general officers accompanying the President had had more than their fill of war, they were still seasoned veterans of many conflicts and had survived them all. Without conscious thought they reacted; they did not hesitate.

General Grant, who was closest to the President, hurled himself between his commander in chief and the assassin's gun. Fell back as the bullet struck home.

There was no second shot.

At first sight of the pistol, General Sherman had seized his scabbard in his left hand and, with his right hand, had pulled the sword free. In one continuous motion the point of the sword came up, and as he took a long step forward, Sherman, without hesitation, thrust the gleaming weapon into the attacker's heart. He drew it out as the man dropped to the floor. Sherman stood over him, sword poised and ready, but there was no movement. He kicked the revolver from the man's limp fingers, sending it skidding across the marble floor.

Someone screamed, shrilly, over and over again. The frozen moment was over. The officer in charge of the honor guard shouted commands and the uniformed men drew up in a circle around the President's party, facing outward, swords at the ready. Lincoln, shaken by the sudden ferocity of the unexpected attack, looked down at the wounded general stretched out on the marble floor. He shook himself, as though struggling to understand what had happened, then took off his coat, folded it, bent over, and placed it under Grant's head. Grant scowled down at the blood seeping from his wounded right arm, started to sit up, then winced with the effort. He cradled his wounded arm in his left hand to ease the pain.

"The ball appears to still be in there," he said. "It looks like the bone stopped it from going on through."

"Will someone get a doctor?" Lincoln shouted above the din of raised voices.

Sherman stood above the body of the man he had just killed, looked out at the milling crowd, which was pulling back from the ring of cuirassed officers who faced them with drawn swords ready. Satisfied now that the assassin had been alone, he wiped the blood from his sword on the tail of the dead man's coat. After slipping the sword back into its scabbard, he bent and rolled the body onto its back. The white-skinned face, the long dark hair seemed very familiar. He continued to stare at it even as one of the officers handed him the still-cocked assassin's revolver. He carefully let the hammer down and put it into his pocket.

The circle of protecting soldiers drew apart to admit a rotund little man carrying a doctor's bag. He opened the bag and took out a large pair of shears, then proceeded to cut away the sleeve of Grant's jacket, then the blood-sodden fabric of his shirt. With a metal pick he bent to probe delicately at the wound. Grant's face turned white and the muscles stood out on the sides of his jaw, but he said nothing. The doctor carefully bandaged the wound to stop the bleeding, then called out in French for assistance, a table, something to carry the wounded man. Lincoln stepped aside as uniformed servants pushed forward to aid the doctor.

"I know this man," Sherman said, pointing down at the body of the assassin. "I watched him for three hours, from the front row of the balcony in Ford's Theater. He is an actor. The one who played in *Our American Cousin*. His name is John Wilkes Booth."

"We were going to see that play," Lincoln said, suddenly very tired. "But that was before Mary was taken ill. Did you hear the words that he called out before he fired? I could not understand them."

"That was Latin, Mr. President. What he shouted out was '*Sic semper tyrannis.*' It is the motto of the state of Virginia. It means something like 'thus always to tyrants.'"

"A Southern sympathizer! To have come all this way from America, to have crossed the ocean just to attempt to kill me. It is beyond reason that a person could be filled with such hatred."

"Feelings in the South still run deep, as you know, Mr. President. Sad as it is to say, there are many who will never forgive you for stopping their secession." Sherman looked up and saw that a door had been produced and that Grant, his bandaged arm secured across his chest, was being lifted carefully onto it. Sherman stepped forward to take charge and ordered that the wounded Grant be taken to their suite of rooms on the floor above. He knew that a military surgeon accompanied their official party—and Sherman had more faith in him than he had in any foreign sawbones who might appear here.

It was silent in the bedroom once the servants left. The closed doors shut out the clamorous crowd. From the bed where he had been carefully placed, Grant waved to Sherman with his good arm.

"That was a mighty fine thrust. But then, you were always good at fencing at the Point. Do you always keep your dress sword so well sharpened?"

"A weapon is always a weapon."

"True enough—and I shall remember your advice. But, Cumph, let me tell you, I have not been drinking of late, as you know. However, I never travel unprepared, so if you don't mind I am going to make an exception just this one time. I hope you will agree that these are unusual circumstances."

"I can't think of anything more unusual."

"Good. Why then you'll find a stone crock of the best corn in that wardrobe thing in my room . . ."

"Good as done."

As Sherman stood up there was a quick knock on the door. He let the doctor in—a gray-haired major with years of field experience—before heading off to find the crock. While he was away, the surgeon, with a skill born of battlefield practice, found the bullet and extracted it. Along with a patch of coat and shirt material that had been carried into the wound by the ball. He was just finishing up rebandaging the wound when Sherman returned with the stone jug and two glasses.

"Bone's bruised, but not broken," the surgeon said. "The wound is clean; I'm binding it up in its own blood. There should be no complications." As soon as the doctor let himself out, Sherman poured two full glasses from the crock.

Grant sighed deeply as he emptied his glass; color quickly returned to his gray cheeks.

The President and Ambassador Pierce came in just as he was finishing a second tumbler; Pierce was flustered and sweating profusely. Lincoln was his usual calm self.

"I hope that you feel as well as you look, General Grant. I greatly feared for you," he said.

"I'm not making light of it, Mr. President, but I've been shot a lot worse before. And the doctor here says it will heal fast. I'm sorry to ruin the party."

"You saved my life," Lincoln said, his voice filled with deep emotion, "for which I will be ever grateful."

"Any soldier would have done the same, sir. It is our duty."

Suddenly very weary, Lincoln sat down heavily on the bench by the bed. "Did you get off that message?" he asked, turning to Pierce.

"I did, sir. On your official stationery. Explaining to King Leopold just what happened. A messenger took it. But I wondered, Mr. President: Would you like to send another message explaining that you won't be able to attend the reception tonight at the Palais du Roi?"

"Nonsense. General Grant may be indisposed, but he, and General

Sherman, have seen to it that I am fit as a fiddle. This entire unhappy affair must have a satisfactory end. We must show them that Americans are made of sterner stuff. This attempt at assassination must not be allowed to deter us, to prevent us from accomplishing our mission here."

"If we are going to the reception, may I ask a favor, sir?" Sherman said. "Since General Grant will not be able to attend, I would like to ask General Meagher to go in his place. He is not due to return to Ireland until tomorrow."

"An excellent idea. I am sure that no assassins will lurk in the palace. But after this morning I admit I will feel that much more comfortable with you officers in blue at my side."

Sherman remained with Grant once the others had left. The two generals shared a bit more of the corn likker. After years of heavy drinking, Grant had given it up when he resumed his military career. He was no longer used to the ardent spirit. His eyes soon closed and he was asleep. Sherman let himself out and the infantry captain stationed in the hall outside snapped to attention.

"General Grant, sir. May I ask how he is doing?"

"Well, very well indeed. A simple flesh wound and the ball removed. Has there been no official statement?"

"Of course, General. Mr. Fox read it out to us—I had one of my men bring a copy to the palace. But it was quite brief and just said that there had been an attempt on the President's life and that General Grant was wounded in the attempt. The attacker was killed before he could fire again. That's all it said."

"I believe that is enough."

The captain took a deep breath and looked around before he spoke again in a lowered voice. "The rumor is you took him with your sword, General. A single thrust through the heart . . ."

Sherman ought to have been angry with the man; he smiled instead. "For once a rumor is true, Captain."

"Well done, sir, well done!"

Sherman waved away the man's heartfelt congratulations. Turned and went to his room. Always after combat he was dry-mouthed with thirst. He drank glass after glass of water from the carafe on the side table. It had been a close-run thing. He would never forget the sight of Booth pushing forward between the soldiers, the black revolver coming up. But it was all over. The threat had been removed; the only casualty had been Grant being injured and left with a badly wounded arm. It could have been a lot worse.

That night a closed carriage was sent for the American party. And, not by chance, it was surrounded by a troop of cavalry as it made its way across the Grande Place and past the Hôtel de Ville. They drew up before the Palais du Roi. The two generals exited first, walking close beside the President as they climbed the red-carpeted steps; Pierce followed behind. Once they were inside, Pierce hurried ahead of the rest of the American party as they entered the hall, whispered urgently to the majordomo who was to announce them. There was a moment of silence when Lincoln's name was called out; all eyes were upon him in the crowded hall. Then there was a quick flutter of clapping and then the buzz of conversation was resumed. A waiter with a tray of champagne glasses approached them as they entered the large reception room. All of the other brilliantly clad guests seemed to be holding a glass, so the Americans followed suit.

"Weak stuff," General Meagher muttered, draining his glass and trying to see if the waiter was about with another.

Lincoln smiled and just touched the glass to his lips as he looked around. "Now, see the large man in that group of officers over there; I do believe that is someone I have met before." He nodded in the direction of the imposing, red-faced man, dressed in an ornate pink uniform, who was pushing through the crowd toward them. Three other uniformed officers were close behind him. "I do believe that he is a Russian admiral with a name I have completely forgotten."

"You are president, we meet once in your Washington City," the admiral said, stopping before Lincoln as he seized his hand in his own immense paw. "I am Admiral Paul S. Makhimov, you remember. You people they sink plenty British ships, then they kill British soldiers . . . very good! These my staff."

The three accompanying officers clicked their heels and bowed as one. Lincoln smiled and managed to extricate his hand from the admiral's clasp.

"But that war is over, Admiral," he said. "Like the Russians, the Americans are now at peace with the world."

As the President spoke, one of the Russian officers came forward and extended his hand to Sherman, who had, perforce, to take it.

"You must be congratulated, General Sherman, on a brilliant and victorious campaign," he said in perfect English.

"Thank you—but I'm afraid that I didn't catch your name."

"Captain Alexander Igoreivich Korzhenevski," the officer said, releasing Sherman's hand and bowing yet again. While his head was lowered he spoke softly so that only General Sherman could hear him. "I must meet with you in private."

He straightened up and smiled, white teeth standing out against his black beard.

Sherman had no idea what this was about—though he dearly wanted to know. He thought quickly, then brushed his hand across his mustache, spoke quietly when his mouth was covered.

"I am in room one eighteen in the Hotel Grand Mercure. The door will be unlocked at eight tomorrow morning." There was nothing more that could be said and the Russian officer moved away. Sherman turned back to his party and did not see the captain again.

General Sherman sipped his champagne and thought about the curious encounter. What had caused him to respond so quickly to the unusual request? Perhaps it was the officer's command of English. But what could it all be about? Should he be armed when he unlocked the door? No, that was nonsense; after this day's events, it appeared that he still had assassination on his brain. It was obvious that the Russian officer wanted to communicate something, had some message that could not go through normal channels without others being aware of what was happening. If that was the case, he knew just the man to ask about it.

The reception and the presentations, the bowing and saluting, went on far into the night. Only after the Americans had been introduced to King Leopold could they even think about leaving. Happily, the meeting with the King was brief.

"Mr. President Lincoln, it is my great pleasure to meet you at last."

"It is mine as well, Your Majesty."

"And your health—it is good?" The King's eyes widened ever so slightly.

"Never better. It must be the salubrious air of your fine country. I feel as comfortable here as I would at home in my own parlor."

The King nodded vaguely at this. Then his attention was drawn elsewhere and he turned away.

Once they had been dismissed, the President rounded up his party. It was after midnight and they were all tired. Not so, apparently, the Belgian cavalry officer commanding the troopers who accompanied their carriage back to the hotel. Spurred on by his shouted commands, they surrounded the carriage, sabers drawn and ready, warily on guard. The streets were empty, echoing the clattering hoofbeats of the mounted guards; a strangely reassuring sound.

As soon as he had left the others at the hotel, General Sherman went and pounded on Gustavus Fox's door.

"Duty calls, Gus. You better wake up."

The door opened immediately. Gus was in his shirtsleeves; lamps illuminated a table strewn with papers. "Sleep is only for the wicked," he said. "Come in and tell me what brings you around at this hour."

"An international mystery—and it appears to be right down your line of work."

Gus listened to the description of the brief encounter in silence, nodding vigorously and enthusiastically when Sherman was done.

"You have given this officer the perfect response, General. Anything to do with the Russians is of vital interest to us right now—or at any time, for that matter. Ever since the Crimean War they have had no love for the British. They were invaded and fought very hard in their own defense. But it is not only Britain that they see as the enemy—it is almost every other country in Europe. In their own defense they have a superb spy network, and I must say that they make the most of it. I can now tell you that a few years ago they actually stole the plans for the most secret British rifled hundred-pound cannon. They actually had the American gunsmith Parrott make them a replica. Now we discover that an English-speaking officer on the Russian admiral's staff wants to meet with you in private. Admirable!"

"What should I do about it?"

"Unlock your door at eight in the morning—then see what happens. With your permission I will join you in this dawn adventure."

"I wouldn't have it any other way—since this is your kind of game and not mine."

"I shall be there at seven, which is only a few hours from now. Get some sleep."

"You as well. And when you come, why, see that you bring a large pot of coffee with you. This has been a long day—and I feel that it is going to be an even longer one tomorrow."

The knock on the door aroused Sherman. He was awake at once; his years of campaigning in the field had prepared him for action at any hour. He pulled on his trousers and opened the door. Gus stepped aside and waved the hotel servant past him—who pushed a wheeled table laden with coffee, hot rolls, butter, and preserves.

"We shall wait in comfort," Gus said.

"We shall indeed." Sherman nodded and smiled when he noticed that there were three cups on the table. When the waiter had bowed himself out, they saw to it that the door remained unlocked. Then they sat by the window and sipped their coffee while Brussels slowly came to life outside.

It was just a few minutes past eight when the hall door opened and closed quickly. A tall man in a dark suit entered, locking the door behind him before he turned to face the room. He nodded at General Sherman, then turned to face Gus.

"I am Count Alexander Igoreivich Korzhenevski. And you would be . . . ?"

"Gustavus Fox, Assistant Secretary of the Navy."

"How wonderful—the very man I wanted to contact." He saw Gus's sudden frown and waved away his concern. "I assure you, I am alone in my knowledge of your existence and will never reveal that information to a soul. I have been associated with Russian naval intelligence for many years, and we have a certain friend in common. Commander Schulz."

Gus smiled at this and took the Count's hand. "A friend indeed." He turned to the puzzled Sherman. "It was Commander Schulz who brought

us the plans of the British breech-loading cannon that I told you about."
With a sudden thought he turned back to Korzhenevski. "You would not,
by any chance, be associated with that affair?"

"Associated? My dear Mr. Fox—at the risk of appearing too forward, I
must admit that I was the one who managed to purloin the plans in the first
place. You must understand that in my youth I attended the Royal Naval
College in Greenwich. Graduated from that admirable institution, having
made many friends there down through the years, I am forced to admit that
I am fairly well known throughout the British navy. So much so that old
shipmates still refer to me as Count Iggy. Someone not too bright, but very
rich and well known as an ever-flowing font of champagne."

"Well, Count Iggy," Sherman said. "I have only coffee to offer you
now. Please do sit and have some. Then, perhaps, you will enlighten us as
to the reason for this sub-rosa encounter."

"I will be most delighted, General. Delighted!"

The Count took the chair farthest from the window and nodded his
thanks when Fox passed him a cup of coffee. He sipped a bit before he
spoke.

"My greatest indulgence these days is my little boat, the *Aurora*. I
suppose you would call her more of a yacht than a boat. A steam launch,
since I never could master all of those ropes and lines and sails and things
that most sailors are so fond of. It is really quite jolly to fool about in.
Makes traveling here and there and everywhere most easy as well. People
admire her lines, but rarely query her presence."

Sherman nodded. "That is most interesting, Count, but—"

"But why am I telling you this? You are wondering. I do have my
reasons—first I must bore you with some of my family history. History
tells us that the Korzhenevskis were glorious, but impoverished Polish
nobility until my great-grandfather chose to join the navy of Peter the
Great in 1709. He had served with great valor in the Swedish navy, but was
more than happy to change sides when the Swedes were defeated by the
Russians. He was still in the service when Peter expanded the Russian
navy, and my reading of our family history reveals that his career was a
most distinguished one. My great-grandfather, who was also very much a
linguist, learned English and actually attended the British Royal Naval Col-

lege in Greenwich. Very much the anglophile, he married into a family of the lesser nobility, who, impoverished as they were, considered him a great catch. Ever since then our family, in St. Petersburg, has been very English-orientated. I grew up speaking both languages and, like the eldest son of each generation, attended the Greenwich Naval College. So there you have it—you see before you an Englishman in all but name."

His smile vanished and his face darkened as he leaned forward and spoke in a barely audible voice. "But that is no more. When the British attacked my country, I felt betrayed, wronged. On the surface I still amuse and entertain my English friends, because that role suits me best. But deep inside me, you must understand, is the feeling that I loathe them—and would do anything to bring about their destruction. When they attacked your country—and you defeated them—my heart sang with happiness. May I now call you my friends—because we are joined in a common cause? And please believe me when I say that I will do *anything* to advance that cause."

Deep in thought, Gus rose and put his empty cup on the table, turned, and smiled warmly.

"That is a very generous offer, sir. Do you think you might consider a little ocean cruise?"

The Count's smile mirrored his. "I might very well indeed. I was thinking of tootling up the Thames to Greenwich. I have some classmates still stationed there. Might I invite you to join me? *Aurora* is getting a refit in Hamburg just now. I intend to join her in a week's time. I shall then sail her to Ostend. Please think about this, and when you make a decision, please leave a note for me at the desk sometime today, since I will be leaving at dawn tomorrow. A yes or a no will suffice. And I do hope that you will say yes. And in addition, you must excuse me, I do hate to be personal— but I must tell you that there are almost no redheads in Russia."

He rose and put down his cup, turning once again to Gus. "If I could bother you—to look down the hall. It is important that we not be seen together."

The hall was empty. With a cheery wave, the Count was gone and Gus locked the door behind him. Sherman poured himself some more coffee and shook his head.

"I'm a simple man of war, Gus, and all this kind of thing is beyond me. Would you kindly tell me what that was all about?"

"It was about military intelligence!" Gus was too excited to sit and paced the room as he spoke. "By revealing himself as an intimate of Schulz, he was letting us know that he has experience and training as— well, not to put it too fine—as a spy. He also believes that Britain and America may go to war again and has offered us assistance in preparing for that eventuality."

"So that's what all that strange talk was about. He wants you to join him in snooping around the British Isles?"

"Not me alone. Remember—it was you he contacted. He wants to give you an opportunity to see for yourself what the British defenses are like. If another war is forced upon us, we must be prepared for anything. An intimate knowledge of the coast defenses and major waterways of that country would be of incalculable aid in planning a campaign."

"I begin to see what you mean. But it sounds pretty desperate. I don't think that I would relish going to sea in the Count's ship. We would have to hide belowdecks during the daylight hours and emerge like owls after dark."

"That we will not! If we go, why, we are going to be Russian officers. Swilling champagne on deck and saying 'Da! Da!' Of course, you will have to dye your beard black. The Count was very firm about that. Do you think you can manage that—*gospodin?*"

Sherman rubbed his jaw in thought.

"So that's what the bit concerning red hair was about." He smiled. "*Da,*" he said. "I think I can manage almost anything, if it means that I can take a look at the British defenses and wartime preparation."

With sudden enthusiasm Sherman jumped to his feet and slammed his fist down so hard on the table that the plates and saucers bounced.

"Let's do it!"

THE ULTIMATUM

The rain was streaming down the glass lobby doors. Barely visible through them were the horses, hitched to the carriage outside and standing with lowered heads in the downpour. Abraham Lincoln stood to one side of the lobby talking with Ambassador Pierce and General Sherman. Pierce was upset and very apologetic.

"That is all I know, Mr. President. A servant brought me a note from Mr. Fox, saying that he would be slightly delayed and we should not wait, but should go on without him."

"Well, if truth be known, I'm in no rush to go out in this rain. We'll give him a few minutes in the hope that the weather might ameliorate. I am sure that we still have plenty of time once we get to the assembly."

"Here he comes now," Sherman said, then turned and looked out at the waiting carriage; he turned his uniform coat collar up. "At least, considering the time of year, it will be a warm rain."

"Gentlemen, my apologies," Gus said, hurrying to join them. "I was delayed because I was getting a report from an agent. It seems that the British *are* coming after all. A goodly sized party was seen already entering the palace—and it was headed by Lord Palmerston!"

"Well, there is no end to surprises," said Lincoln, "as the man said when he first saw the elephant. I believe that we shall meet at last."

"For good or ill," Pierce said, mopping his sweating face with his kerchief.

"We'll know soon enough," Lincoln said. "Well now—shall we brave the elements and finally get to meet Lord Palmerston?"

The carriage was still accompanied by the Belgian cavalrymen, now looking damp and miserable, the elegant plumes on their helmets drooping and wet. King Leopold had taken it as a personal responsibility that the American President had been assaulted in his country. He was determined that there would be no reoccurrence. There had been unobtrusive guards in the hotel, most disguised as employees, and others now waited along the route that the carriage would take. The King believed that the honor of Belgium was at stake.

It was a short ride to the palace, but when they reached it they had to stop and wait until the occupants came out from the two carriages that had arrived ahead of them. The men who emerged had to brave the rain to enter the building while servants with umbrellas did their best to shield them from the elements. The cavalrymen did not like the delay, and transmitted their unease to their mounts, which stamped and pulled at their reins. They were relieved when the other carriages left and they could take their place at the foot of the steps.

Once inside, the Americans were ushered to the great chamber where the conference would convene. Even on this dark day, light streamed in through the ceiling-high windows. Ornate gas lamps abolished any traces of gloom, illuminating the ornately painted ceiling where centaurs pranced around lightly clad, very large women.

But Abraham Lincoln had no eyes for any of this. Across the floor and opposite their table (with the neatly lettered sign ÉTATS-UNIS upon it) was that of GRANDE BRETAGNE. One seated man stood out sharply from the dark-clothed delegation. His foot propped on a stool before him, his hands clasped around the head of his cane, he glowered out at the entire assembly.

"Lord Palmerston, I presume?" Lincoln said quietly.

Gus nodded. "None other. He looks to be in an angry mood."

"Considering the tenor of his communications with us, I believe he must live in a permanent state of bile."

The Belgian Foreign Minister, Baron Surlet de Chokier, rose and the murmur of voices died away as he addressed the assembly in French.

"He is just reading out a formal and general greeting to all the delegations assembled here," Fox said, leaning over to whisper to the President. "And it is his fond hope that prosperity for all countries will be the fruitful conclusion of these highly significant and most important negotiations."

Lincoln nodded. "You never cease to surprise me, Gus."

Fox smiled and gave a very Gallic shrug of his shoulders.

When the baron had finished, he waved to his clerk, who began to read the protocol of business for the assembly. But Lord Palmerston loudly cleared his throat. He rumbled like a distant volcano as he climbed to his feet.

"Before these proceedings continue, I must protest strongly about the nature and particular membership of this assembly—"

"I beg your lordship to hear the protocol first!" de Chokier said pleadingly—but Palmerston would have none of it.

"A protest, sir, about the very basic nature of these proceedings. We are assembled here in a congress of the great nations of Europe to discuss matters most relevant to countries that are European. I therefore object most strongly to the presence of representatives of the upstart nation from far across the Atlantic. They have no right to be here and have no relevance to the matters at hand. The sight of them is an abomination to all honest men, of whatever nationality. Particularly insulting is the presence in their midst of a military officer who, until recently, was deeply involved in the slaughter of loyal British troops. They give offense, sir, and should be turned out into the street at once."

Abraham Lincoln was no stranger to acrimonious public debate. He rose slowly to his feet, clutching his lapels casually. To those who knew, the mood indicated by the droop in his eyes—hiding their cold gaze—did not bode well for his opponents. The instant Palmerston paused for breath, Lincoln's high, penetrating voice echoed from the chamber's wall.

"I believe that the British representative is laboring under a self-imposed delusion, for which I apologize to all of the other delegates present. He should know that all of the nations gathered here were invited officially by King Leopold of Belgium himself. It is a most solemn and important gathering that we attend, for this is no provincial European occasion, but is instead a congress of countries who meet together to discuss matters of world importance. As Britain represents a world-embracing empire, so do we speak for the New World and its countries across the Atlantic Ocean—"

"Your comparisons are odious, sir!" Palmerston bellowed. "How dare you compare the sweep of the British Empire, the might of our world-spanning union, with your ragtag so-called democracies?"

"How dare you single out General Sherman, a brave soldier, for denigration when I see a plethora of uniforms about this room. And please tell me, is that not a general sitting close behind you?"

Palmerston, livid with rage, would have none of it. "You presume too much to speak to me in this manner—"

"Presume, sir? I presume nothing. In fact, I control my impatience as I address the person who was so presumptuous, so rash, that he dared to send armies to attack our peace-loving country. That was an act of war that did not go unpunished. However, it is my greatest hope that the nations convened here will not think of the past and of war. Instead we should look forward to peace in a peaceful future."

Palmerston was beside himself. He crashed his cane again and again across the tabletop until the shocked voices of protest had died away.

"Her Majesty's representatives did not come here to be insulted," Palmerston bellowed. "It would be our pleasure to join the other representatives in a congress of mutual cooperation at some other time. But not here, not today, while these totally repugnant foreign intruders are present in this hall. I am therefore forced to wish you all a good day."

He stalked from the room, his dramatic exit hampered by a stumbling progress caused by his swollen foot, while most of the other members of the delegation hurried after him. The door slammed shut and Lincoln nodded sagely. He slowly regained his seat. "I think the clerk can continue now," he said.

The clerk began to read in a shaky voice until Baron de Chokier interrupted him. "I believe these proceedings should continue after a brief recess. If you please, gentlemen, in an hour's time."

"Got a mighty fierce temper for an old man," Lincoln observed. "I wonder he didn't explode years ago."

"It must have all been prearranged," Fox said, looking worried. "King Leopold is Queen Victoria's favorite uncle and she looks up to him for advice and counseling. Knowing this, her prime minister could not easily refuse the invitation. But coming here was one thing for Palmerston; staying and talking peace with Yankees something altogether different. But now that they have shown their flag—"

"And retreated after the first engagement," Lincoln said. "Can we proceed without their presence?"

"We can," Pierce responded. "But I doubt if we will get very far. The British royal family is related to half the crowned heads in Europe and exercises a great deal of influence. Palmerston will of course report to the Queen and blame us for everything that has occurred here today. It is inconceivable that this congress can continue after Queen Victoria expresses her displeasure to the other crowned heads. The politicians who can make decisions will be recalled, and all that will be left behind will be delegations of second raters and timeservers . . . who will of course block any real agreements and will only drag their feet. I am afraid that this congress, that looked so promising, is going to be a rehearsed performance, with very little to show as a result."

Lincoln nodded. "Well, we must do our part and not retreat at the first volley. Performance or not, we will sit it out. The British cannot blame us for threatening the peace of Europe—or standing in the way of any trade agreements."

Pierce's predictions proved to be most exact. There were discussions of the agenda, but they were all between minor officials as the leaders of the delegations slipped away one by one. At the end of the first week Lincoln did the same.

"Too much talk, too little action," he said. "Ambassador Pierce, I am putting you in charge of this delegation while I attend to pressing business in Washington."

Pierce nodded gloomily. "I understand, Mr. President. General Sherman—might I count upon your assistance?"

"Regrettably no. I will accompany the President to Ostend, where the battle cruiser USS *Dictator* is still tied up. We know that you will do your best."

Pierce sighed and nodded his head. The conference, which had held out such great hope, was now an empty shell, with only minor officials like himself keeping it going. He looked on gloomily as the presidential party departed.

"And you two, are you sure that you won't tell me what you are up to? What mysterious matters take you with me to Ostend?" Lincoln asked Fox and Sherman, once the three of them were in their closed carriage, his interest still piqued by their prolonged silence.

"We dare not," Fox said. "If even a whisper gets out of what we are doing—well, I am afraid that the international consequences might very well be disastrous."

"Now you really do have me interested." Lincoln raised his hand. "But I shall not ask again. But please reassure me that you will report to me as soon as your mission has been accomplished."

"You shall be the first to know—that I promise."

Back in his room at the hotel, General Sherman took his clothes from the drawers of the dresser and laid them on the bed. Then he unlocked his suitcase. There was a sheet of paper inside that had not been there when he had closed it many days ago. He held it in the light from the window and read:

You are being watched closely by British agents.
Proceed with the President and board the USS Dictator.
Mr. Fox will receive further instructions.

The communication was unsigned.

Arrangements had been made well in advance and an entire railroad car reserved for the presidential party—as well as for the numerous armed officers of a household regiment. King Leopold would be very relieved when the Americans were safely aboard the warship in Ostend—but in the meantime they were to be closely guarded. The journey was a quick one, first by train and then by carriage. Sherman had barely set foot aboard the vessel when he was summoned by a sailor to the officers' wardroom. Gus Fox was waiting there, accompanied by a puzzled-looking naval officer. Fox introduced them.

"General Sherman, this is Commander William Wilson, the second officer of this vessel. The commander was a chartered surveyor before he attended Annapolis and began his naval career."

"A pleasure to meet you, Commander," Sherman said, having a strong inkling of what Fox had in mind. When Fox next spoke his suspicions proved correct.

"I told Commander Wilson only the bare fact that you and I were undertaking a mission of great importance to our country. As well as one that might be highly dangerous. As a serving officer, he could of course be ordered to accompany us. However, considering the secrecy—not to mention the delicacy—of this assignment, I felt that the decision must be left up to him. Therefore I asked him if he would aid us without receiving any more information than that at the present time. I am happy to say that he volunteered."

"I am pleased to hear so, Commander," Sherman said. "It is good to have you on our side."

"It is indeed my pleasure," said Wilson. "I'll be frank, General. I find the whole matter very mysterious, and under different circumstances I might reconsider my decision. However, I do welcome the chance to serve under you. Our country owes its very existence to your valor in battle, so I deem this a great honor indeed."

"Thank you, Commander. And I know that Gus will tell you everything as soon as possible. In the meantime we must take our instructions from him."

"Let's start with this," Fox said, taking a box from under the table and opening it to remove three silk hats. "These are as different from uniform hats as I could manage at short notice. I hope that I bought the right sizes."

They traded the hats around, smiling as they tried them on, until they had each found a reasonable fit.

"These will do fine," Fox said, looking into the mirror and tapping his into place at a rakish angle. "Now—will each of you please pack a small bag with personal necessities? No clothes, please, that will be taken care of later. Meet me here at midnight. And please wear trousers without piping. I will have greatcoats for you, also with their insignia removed. The captain has said that he will provide enough squads of armed sailors to sweep the dockside area as soon as it is dark and remove any intruders. This is most important, since we must not be seen as we leave."

"And just where are we going?" Sherman asked.

Fox just smiled and touched a finger to his lips. "All will soon be revealed."

There was no light on deck when, soon after midnight, they emerged into the darkness. Nor was anyone visible on the dock below. They felt their way down the gangway in the moonless night, with only starlight to guide them. There was a black form barely visible on the dock; a horse's whinny revealed a waiting carriage.

"Entrez, s'il vous plaît," a man whispered, holding the door open for them. The carriage jolted into motion as soon as they were seated. Curtains covered the windows. They could not see out—neither could anyone look in. They sat in silence, jostled about as the carriage bumped over cobbles, then picked up speed on a smoother road.

The trip seemed to last forever as they moved swiftly through the dark city. They stopped just once and there was the murmur of voices outside. Afterward, the horses speeded up to a fast trot—until they stopped once again. This time the door was opened by a man holding a blacked-out lantern. He lifted the covering flap of the lantern just enough to reveal the carriage steps.

"If you will please come with me."

They heard the sounds of lapping water and saw that they were at another dock. Granite steps led down from the ground level to a waiting boat. Six silent sailors manned it, oars rigidly upright. Their guide helped them into the stern, then cast off the painter and joined them. As soon as he was seated, he said something in a foreign, guttural tongue. The sailors lowered their oars smartly and rowed them out into the stream. There were lights on the small ship anchored a little ways out, and a uniformed officer waiting at the foot of the gangway to help them aboard. Their guide was out first.

"Gentlemen, if you would be so kind as to follow me."

He led them belowdecks to a large compartment that spanned the width of the small vessel. It was brightly lit by candles and lamps.

"Welcome aboard the *Aurora*," he said. "I am Count Alexander Korzhenevski." He turned to the puzzled naval commander and put out his hand. "These other gentlemen I know, but you, sir, are also very welcome here. I am pleased to make your acquaintance. And you are . . . ?"

"Wilson, sir. Commander William Wilson."

"Welcome aboard, Commander. Now, gentlemen, please. Remove your outer garments and join me in some champagne."

A white-jacketed sailor instantly appeared with bubbling glasses on a tray. They drank and looked around at the luxuriously appointed compartment. Heavy red curtains covered the shining brass portholes. Oil paintings of naval scenes adorned the walls; the chairs were soft and comfortable. The door opened and a young Russian officer with a curling blond beard joined them, taking a glass of champagne, nodding and smiling.

"Gentleman," the Count said. "May I introduce Lieutenant Simenov, our first engineer."

"Bloody good!" Simenov said, shaking Fox's hand industriously.

"Ah—you speak English, then?"

"Bloody good!"

"I'm afraid that is the be-all and the end-all of his English," Korzhenevski explained. "But he is a bloody great engineer."

"Now, if you please," Commander Wilson said. "Will someone be so kind as to tell me just what is happening? I admit to being completely in the dark."

"Of course," Fox said. "It seems that the Count has been kind enough to put his steam yacht at our disposal. We shall sail aboard her, and it is our intent to visit as many British coastal defenses as we can. That is why I asked you to volunteer. I look to your drafting skills to chart these positions."

"Good God! We're to be spies! They'll arrest us on sight—"

"Not quite," the Count said. "I am well-known in naval quarters and my presence is quite acceptable. While you gentlemen will be my guests as . . . Russian officers."

Wilson's face was a study in blank bewilderment. This morning he had been a naval officer on an American warship. Now, a few short hours later, he was to be a Russian officer poking about the English shores. It all sounded very chancy—and very dangerous. He did not speak his doubts aloud since the others seemed quite happy to go along with the subterfuge. Instead he shrugged, emptied his glass, and held it out to be refilled.

"You must all be tired," Korzhenevski said. "But I am afraid I must ask you to stay up for a short time longer." He issued a command in Russian to one of the sailors, who saluted and left the room. A short time later he returned with two men who were carrying tape measures, chalk, and notebooks; obviously tailors. They quickly measured the three Americans, bowed, and left.

"That will be all for this evening, gentlemen," Korzhenevski said. "Whenever you wish, you will be shown to your quarters. But perhaps, first, you would like to join me in a glass of cognac to seal this day's momentous events."

No one said no.

A VOYAGE FRAUGHT
WITH DANGER

Soon after dawn a light tapping on the compartment door awoke General Sherman. A moment later the door opened and a mess boy brought in a steaming cup of coffee and put it on the table by the bed. Close behind him came a sailor carrying a gleaming white uniform. He smiled and said something in Russian and laid it carefully across a chair. On top of it he placed a large, white uniform cap.

"I'm sure that you are right," Sherman said, sitting up in bed and gratefully sipping the coffee.

"*Da, da!*" the sailor said, and left.

It was a handsome uniform, with ornate, gold-braided shoulder boards and two rows of impressive-looking medals across the chest. And it fit perfectly. When he joined the others in the wardroom, he saw that Fox was wearing an equally imposing uniform, as was the embarrassed-looking Wilson.

The Count entered and clapped his hands with delight. "Excellent! Let me welcome you gentlemen into the Russian navy. Your presence here does us great honor. Later, after we have broken our fast, I will explain some slight differences between our naval service and your own. You will discover that we salute in a different manner and do too much heel clicking, which will not be familiar to you. But first, General Sherman—

might I ask you to remove your jacket. Admirable!" He clapped his hands and a sailor led in two men bearing a large container of water, bowls, and jars. Sherman sat rigid as they draped him with towels, wet his beard and hair, even his eyebrows, then combed in a jet-black dye. With a murmured apology one of them even tinted his eyelashes with mascara. It was all done very quickly, and they were finished even as the stewards carried in the breakfast dishes; then his beard was trimmed into a more Russian shape. He admired himself in a mirror as the barbers bowed deeply and backed from the compartment.

"You look quite rakish," Fox said, "and irresistible to the ladies."

He indeed looked much younger, Sherman realized, for the dye had not only colored his red hair, but eliminated the strands of gray that were beginning to appear.

"Barbers and tailors available on call," he said. "What other surprises do you have for us, Count Korzhenevski?"

"Why, there are farriers, blacksmiths, surgeons, lawyers—whatever you wish," the Count said. "We tend to take the long view in Russia. Preparing today for tomorrow's exigencies. Some would call these people of ours spies—and perhaps they are. But they are also reliable and patriotic Russian people who were paid well to emigrate and settle in this foreign land. They are now part of the community, here and in other countries—but they always stand ready to answer the call from the motherland when needed."

"Do you have your agents in England, too?" Sherman asked.

"But of course. In every country where our homeland has an interest."

"In the United States as well?" Gus asked quietly.

"You don't really want me to answer that, do you? Enough to say that our two great countries are allied and united in this glorious mission."

A sailor entered and saluted, then said something to the Count. He nodded, and the man left.

"All the visitors are now ashore. Let our prosperous voyage begin." Even as he spoke, a steam whistle wailed and the decking vibrated as the engines came up to speed. "Pardon me for requesting that you remain belowdecks until we are out to sea. In the meantime—enjoy your breakfast."

They did. Gus introduced Sherman to the joys of beluga caviar.

Washed down, despite the hour, with chilled vodka. Thus began the first day of their perilous voyage.

When they finally came out on deck, the flat Belgian coastline was only a line behind them on the horizon. "We are steaming north for a bit," the Count said. "When we get closer to the British Isles, it is important that we approach from the northeast, presumably coming from Russia. We shall sight Scotland first, then coast slowly south toward England. Now—if you will permit me, I will show you how to salute and walk in the proper Russian manner."

They laughed a good deal as they paraded around the deck, until they could perform to Korzhenevski's satisfaction. It was warm work and they welcomed the chilled champagne that followed.

"Next we will learn a little Russian," the Count said. "Which you will be able to use when we meet the English. *Da* means 'yes,' *nyet* is 'no,' and *spaseba* means 'thank you.' Master these and very soon I will teach you to say 'I do not speak English.' Which is, *'Prostite, no yane govoriu po-angliyski.'* But we shall save that for a later time. Nevertheless, when you have done that, you will have learned all of the Russian that you will ever need during our visit here. The British are not known for their linguistic ability, so you need have no fear of being found out by any of them."

When the Count left to attend to ship's business, Wilson, for the second time, voiced his reservations.

"This trip, this scouting out of the British coast, is there any specific reason for our going? Are we looking for anything in particular?"

"I do not take your meaning," Fox said, although he had a good idea what was troubling the naval officer.

"I mean no offense—but it must be admitted that at the present time our country is at peace with England. Won't our mission be, well, at the least—provocative? And, if we are caught in the act, why, there will surely be international repercussions."

"Everything you say is true. But in the larger sense, military intelligence must never stand still. We can never know enough about our possible enemies—and even our friends. I thought the Count phrased it very well when he said that they tended to take the long view in Russia about future relationships with other countries. They have the experience of centuries of conflict, of countries who were friends one day—and enemies the next. America has no such experience in international conflicts, so we have much to learn."

Sherman sipped some champagne, then set the half-empty glass on the table. His expression was distant, as though he were looking at a future unseen, a time yet unknown.

"Let me tell you something about the British," he said quietly. "A field officer must know his enemy. In the years that we have been fighting them, I have indeed come to know them. I can assure you that our success in battle has never been easy. Their soldiers are experienced and tenacious, and used to victory. If they have any weakness in the field, it is the fact that promotion of officers is not by ability but by purchase. Those with money can buy commissions of higher rank. Therefore, good, experienced officers are pushed aside and others with no experience—other than having the experience in spending a lot of money—take their places. It is a stupid arrangement and one that has cost the British dearly more than once. Yet, despite this severe handicap, they are used to victory because, although they have lost many battles, they have never lost a war. If this has bred a certain arrogance, it is understandable. They have world maps, I have seen them, where all of the countries that are part of their empire are marked in red. They say that the sun never sets on the British Empire, and that is indeed true. They are used to winning. An island race, war has not touched their shores in a very long time. There have been small incursions—like that of the Dutch, who once temporarily landed and captured a city in Cornwall. As well as our own John Paul Jones, who sacked Whitehaven during the War of 1812. These were the exceptions. Basically, they have not been successfully invaded since 1066. They expect only victory—and history has proved them right. Up until now."

"I could not agree more," Gus said. "Our American victories in the field and at sea have caused them great irritation. At times the outcome of battle has been a close-run thing. Many times it has only been our superiority in modern military machines and weapons that has carried the day. And we must not forget that up until the past conflict, they ruled the world's oceans. That is no longer true. For centuries they also ruled in

Ireland—and that is also no longer true. They bridle at this state of affairs and do not want to accept it."

"That is why we are making this voyage of exploration," Sherman said grimly. "War is hell and I know it. But I do not think those in authority in Britain are aware of it. They rule with a certain arrogance, since they are used to continual success. Remember, this is not a real democracy. The powers that are in control here rule from the top down. The ruling classes and the nobility still do not accept defeat by our upstart republic. We in America must work for peace—but we must also be prepared for war."

"Just think about it, William," Gus said in a quieter tone. "We do not hurt Great Britain by charting her defenses, for we have no plans for war. But we must be prepared for any exigency. That is why this trip to Greenwich was arranged. We have no interest in their naval academy—but it does lie just outside London on the river Thames. The route to the heart of England, Britain—the empire. An invasion route first used by the Romans two thousand years ago. I am not saying that we will ever mount an attack here—but we must know what is to be faced. As long as the British bulldog is quiet, we will sleep better in our beds. But—should it rouse up . . ." He left the sentence unfinished.

Wilson sat quiet, pondering what he had heard, then smiled and signaled for more champagne. "What you say makes strong logic. It is just that what we are doing is so unusual. As a sailor, I am used to a different kind of life, one consisting of discipline and danger . . ."

"You shall find that you will need a good deal of both if we are to finish this voyage successfully," Sherman said.

"You are of course right, General. I shall put all doubts to one side and do my duty. For which I will need drawing and drafting materials."

"If I know our friend the Count," Fox said, "I am sure that he has laid in a stock for you. But you must not be seen making drawings."

"I am fully aware of that. I must look and remember, then draw my plans from memory. I have done this before, when working as a surveyor, and foresee no problems."

The warm June weather continued, even when they left the English Channel and entered the North Sea. Being small and fast, the *Aurora* managed to avoid being seen closely by any of the other ships plying these busy waters. The Americans sat on deck in their shirtsleeves, enjoying the sunshine as though on an ordinary holiday cruise, while Wilson honed his artistic skills making sketches of shipboard life and his fellow officers. The Count had indeed laid in an ample supply of drawing materials.

When they reached fifty-six degrees north latitude, Korzhenevski decided that they had sailed far enough in that direction and set a course due west for Scotland. The Russian flag was raised at the stern and the sailors scrubbed the decks and put a last polish on the brass while the officers enjoyed their luncheon. When they emerged on deck they were all dressed in full uniform and saluted one another smartly, clicking their heels with many a *da, da*.

It was midafternoon when they sighted the Scottish coast near Dundee. They altered course and coasted south easily while Korzhenevski looked at the shore through a brass telescope.

"Over there you will see the mouth of the Firth of Forth, with Edinburgh lying upstream. I have had many jolly times in that city with Scots friends, drinking far too much of their excellent whiskey." He focused on a group of white sails scudding out of the Firth. "It looks like a race—how smashing!" He issued quick orders and the yacht moved closer to shore.

"Not a race at all," he pronounced when the sailing ships were better seen. "Just cheery times in this salubrious weather—who is to blame them?"

As they slowly drew level and passed the smaller craft, there were friendly waves and an occasional distant cheer. *Aurora* answered with little toots of her whistle. One of the small sailing craft was now angled away from the others and heading out to sea in their direction. The Count focused his telescope on it, then lowered the scope and laughed aloud.

"By Jove, we are indeed in luck. She is crewed by an old shipmate from Greenwich, the Honorable Richard MacTavish."

The *Aurora* slowed and stopped, rolling easily in the light seas. The little yacht came close, the man at the tiller waving enthusiastically; then he called out.

"When I saw your flag with the two-headed eagle I couldn't believe it. It is you, isn't it, Count Iggy?"

"In the flesh, my dear Scotty. Do come aboard and have a glass of bubbly—does wonders for the tummy!"

The boarding ladder was thrown over the side as a line from the little yacht was hauled aboard. A moment later MacTavish was scrambling over the rail and pounding the Count on the back.

"You're a sight for sore eyes, Iggy. Where have you got to these last years?"

"Oh, just tootling about . . . you know." Korzhenevski sounded a bit bored and a little simple. "I say—shouldn't you bring your friends aboard as well?"

"Not friends, if truth be spoken," MacTavish said. "Just some locals I let crew."

"Well then, you must meet some fellow Russian officers who joined me for this little cruise."

MacTavish took a glass of champagne as the three Americans clicked their heels and took a brace on the stern deck. The Count smiled and sipped his champagne as well.

"From left to right Lieutenant Chikhachev, Lieutenant Tyrtov, and Commander Makarov, the one with the dark beard. Unhappily, none of them speak English. Just give them a smile, that's right. Look how happy they are."

MacTavish got his hand pumped enthusiastically and there were plenty of *da*s.

"As you see, not a word of English among them," the Count drawled. "But still good chaps. You just say *da* back; well done! Let me top up your glass."

MacTavish was working on his second glass of champagne when a head appeared at deck level. "I say, Dickie," an angry voice called out, "this is a bit much."

"On my way," he called out, draining his glass. With many shouted farewells and protestations of eternal friendship, he climbed back down to the yacht. The Count waved after them and smiled as they darted back toward land.

"A good chap," he said, "but not too bright. Last in the class, as I remember. Gentlemen, you did most excellently."

"*Da!*" Wilson said, and they all laughed.

A puff of smoke rose from the stack as the engine started up again. Their course south along the coast toward England.

Beyond the coast that they were passing—and farther south, well inland, just two and a half miles from Birmingham city center—a tent city had sprung up in what, until recently, had been the green pastures around the noble house of Aston Hall. The camp covered an area of over ten acres of churned-up mud, still soaked from the recent rains, which was now drying slowly in the sun. Duckboards had been laid between the tents, but the mud oozing up between them rendered them almost useless. Women were moving about listlessly, some of them cooking in pots hung over the open fires, others hanging up clothes on lines stretched between the tents; children ran along the duckboards shouting to one another. There were very few men to be seen.

One of them was Thomas McGrath, who now sat on a box in the opened flap of a tent, puffing slowly on his pipe. He was a big man with immense arms and slightly graying hair. He had been a gaffer in a Birmingham tannery up until the time of his arrest. He looked around bitterly at the tents and the mud. Bad enough now—but what would it be like in the autumn when the rains came in earnest? Would they still be here then? No one had told him anything, even when they came to arrest him and seize his family. Orders, the soldiers had said. From whom—or for what reason—had never been explained. Except that they were Irish, like every other person in the concentration camp. That's what the camps were called. They were concentrating the Irish where they could be watched. He looked up at the sound of footsteps to see Patrick McDermott walking toward him.

"How you keeping, Tom?" he asked.

"The same, Paddy, the same," McGrath said. McDermott had worked with him in the tannery; a good man. The newcomer squatted down gingerly on the duckboards.

"I've got a bit of news for you," he said. "It seems that I was over there, standing by the main gate, when the ration wagons drove in just now. Two soldiers, a driver and a guard, in each of them, just like always. But they are wearing totally different uniforms from the guards that are stationed on the gates. Sure, I said to myself, and there must be a new regiment come to look after us."

"Now is that true, you say?" McGrath took the pipe from his mouth and knocked the dottle out on the side of the box and rose to his feet.

"With my own two eyes."

"Well then, there is no time like the present. Let's do it—just like we worked out. Are you ready?"

"Never readier."

"When they come you look to the driver. I'll be having a word with the wife first. She'll talk to your Rose later."

The horse-drawn carts came every day or two to distribute food. Potatoes for the most part, since the British believed that the Irish ate nothing else. The two Irishmen were waiting when the wagon came down between the row of tents, stopping where the small crowd of women waited for the food. McGrath had chosen this spot because the tents blocked any view of the soldiers at the gates. There was only this single wagon in sight, with one of the prisoners in the back passing down the potatoes. McGrath knew the man from the pub, but couldn't remember his name.

"Let me give you a hand with that," he said, clambering up into the wagon.

The guard, with the musket between his legs, sat facing backward next to the driver. Out of the corner of his eye McGrath saw Paddy standing by the horse.

"You, get down from there," the guard called out, waving him off with his gun.

"He's been ill, your honor, he's that weak. I'll just give him a hand."

McGrath seized up a sack of potatoes, saw Paddy stepping forward. He swung the bag and knocked the soldier's rifle from his grasp. The man was gape-jawed, but before he could respond, McGrath bent him over with a punch to the belly. He gasped and fell forward; McGrath's other fist felled him with a mighty blow to the jaw.

At the same moment as McGrath swung the bag, Paddy had reached up and pulled the surprised driver from his seat down to the ground, kicking him in the side of the head as he fell into the mud.

It had taken but an instant. The man who had been unloading the potatoes stood with a bag in his hands, shocked. The women did not move but looked on silently; a child started to cry but went silent, his mother's hand over his mouth.

"Dump most of these potatoes," McGrath told the other man. "See that they get spread around the camp. And you know nothing."

On the ground Paddy had stripped the unconscious soldier of his clothes and was pulling them on. He wiped some of the mud from the uniform with the man's neckcloth. "Get some rope," he said to the watching women. "I want him bound and gagged. The same for the other."

McGrath was struggling into the guard's uniform jacket; not an easy fit and impossible to button. He picked up the man's gun and took his place on the seat, stuffing his and Paddy's wadded-up clothes under the seat beside him. The entire action had taken less than two minutes. The women had carried the bound and unconscious soldiers into an empty tent and tied the open flap shut. The Irishman who had been unloading potatoes was gone. Paddy made a clicking sound and shook the reins. The horse plodded forward. Behind them the women and children dispersed. McDermott let out a pleased sigh.

"That was well done, me old son," he said.

"Jayzus, I thought you had taken his head off, the punch you hit him."

"It did the job. The gate now—and keep your gob shut if they want to talk to you."

"Aye."

The horse, head low, plodded slowly toward the gate. There were four green jackets on guard there, one of them a sergeant with an ample belly. He signaled and two of the soldiers started to open the gate. Paddy pulled up the horse while he waited for it to swing wide.

"You're finished damned fast," the sergeant said, glancing suspiciously into the cart.

"Pushed the bleedin' fings out, that's what," Paddy said in an acceptable Cockney accent, for he had worked for many years in London. "Them last ones is rotten."

"Do up that tunic or you'll be charged," the sergeant snapped. McGrath fumbled with the buttons. The sergeant grunted and jerked his thumb for them to proceed, then turned away, no longer interested.

Paddy drove slowly until a bend in the road and a grove of trees shielded them from sight of the camp; snapped the reins and urged the horse into a trot.

"I thought I would die when that sergeant spoke to you like that."

"Stupid pigs!" McGrath was suddenly angry. Angry at life, the concentration camp, at the people who had seized him and brought him and his family to this desperate place. "There, that stand of trees. Pull in there and we'll get out of these uniforms. See if there is any money in the pockets. We are going to need a few bob for the train if we want to put some miles behind us before the alarm is raised."

INTO THE LION'S LAIR

The low-lying English coast lay directly ahead as *Aurora* made a slow turn to starboard. With her engine thudding quietly she steamed toward Dungeness near the mouth of the river Thames, where the Trinity House cruising cutter was established at the rendezvous for London-bound shipping. Count Korzhenevski had the nautical chart of the coastal waters spread out on the table on the forward deck. The three Americans looked on intently as he tapped it with his finger.

"Here, off Dungeness," he said, "is where we must stop to pick up the pilot. Every morning and every evening a tender from Dover tops up the number of men there, so there are always about fourteen pilots waiting. They will send one of them out to us when we heave to and signal. A pilot is of utmost importance now, because the river estuary here is a maze of shifting sandbanks. However, before the pilot joins us, I will ask you gentlemen to enter the main cabin and remain there as long as he is aboard. But once he is on the bridge, it will be time for Commander Wilson to appear in his role as deck officer to supervise casting off from the buoy. The crew has been directed to act as if they are obeying his instructions. Once we sail, Wilson will remain on deck and act as bow lookout until we approach *this* spot—where the river makes a sharp turn to the right.

Before we reach the turn, he will move to the starboard side of the ship just below the bridge. Once he has taken up his position there, he will be out of sight of the pilot and can direct his attention to the defenses along the riverbanks. It is a matter of public record that a few years ago Prime Minister Palmerston ordered a spate of fort building; this was during the last French invasion scare. There is a new fort here at Slough Point, farther upstream at Cliffe Creek and Shornmead as well. But *here* is the place that you will really examine."

The Count tapped his fingertip on the chart again and they leaned forward to look at the indicated spot on the riverbank. "There is a small defensive position at the water's edge called Coalhouse Fort. The last time I passed this way it was unmanned and the guns were gone. That may have changed. But most important of all is what is around this next bend in the river, where the Thames turns sharply to starboard. The river narrows at this point, and right at the bend, dominating the river, is the most dangerous armed position of Tilbury Fort. There are many gun emplacements in it, as well as extensive walls, moats, and other defenses. On the other bank, just opposite Tilbury Fort, there is a new fort and gun emplacements here in Gravesend. Once past these forts, the Thames becomes very narrow and built up along both shores; consequently, it is of no military interest. Therefore, once we are past the fort, the commander should join his comrades in the cabin and transcribe what he has observed of the river defenses. The curtains will be drawn, because very soon after that we will be tying up at Greenwich. Is this all clear?"

"Very much so," Sherman said. "What is not clear is what will happen after we arrive in Greenwich."

"That is in the hands of the gods, my dear general. My classmate Commander Mark Johnstone is on the teaching staff there, and before we left Ostend, I sent him a cable about our imminent arrival. I hope that our stay will be a brief one, but we will just have to wait and see. On a previous visit I had him aboard for a little banquet and a few bottles of champagne. We will just have to see what happens this time. But the long and the short of it is that we must stop at Greenwich. After all, our presence on the river is predicated upon a visit to the Naval Academy, and that we must do."

As agreed, Sherman and Fox stayed belowdecks and out of sight. Very soon after *Aurora* had tied up to a buoy and had signaled, a boat drew away from the waiting cutter and headed their way. They had a quick glimpse of the pea-jacketed figure sitting in the stern, then saw no more, for the steward closed the curtains as the boat approached. There were voices on deck and the stamp of feet as the Count showed the pilot to the bridge and stayed with him there.

The pilot had gray hair and a scraggly beard; his clothing smelled strongly of fish. Unhappily, the bridge was too small for Korzhenevski to get far from the man. He closed the door and put his back against it. The pilot took a newspaper from his pocket and offered it to the Count. "Just arrived," he said. "Only two bob and it's yours."

Korzhenevski nodded and paid two shillings for the overpriced newspaper; he knew that this was a harmless bit of larceny that the pilots indulged in. Sailors who had been weeks at sea would be curious about recent events. Pocketing the coins, the pilot then peered through the front ports and turned to the helmsman.

"Don't get this ship above five knots," he said. The man ignored him.

"The helmsman, he don't speak English?" the pilot asked suspiciously.

"No more than you do Russian," the Count said, forcing himself to ignore the man's stupidity. "I will translate."

"Slow ahead. Five knots maximum speed. That's the East Margate buoy ahead. Keep it to port for the Princess Channel or we will be onto the Margate Sands."

The Count called down to the deckhands and they let go one end of the line through the eye of the buoy and pulled it aboard. Wilson in his role of deck officer pointed and tried to look as though he were in command. Gathering speed, the *Aurora* puffed slowly away from her mooring and out into the channel toward the mouth of the Thames.

The tide was on the ebb and the downstream current was very strong. The riverbanks moved slowly by; green fields on both sides, with the occasional village beyond them. When Wilson saw the turn in the river appearing ahead, he walked casually around the deck to position himself out of sight of the bridge.

The Count had been wrong; Coalhouse Fort was not deserted, but

AN INCREDIBLE SIGHT

boasted a new battery of big guns. Wilson counted them and made a mental note.

Then they were coming up on Tilbury Fort and he gasped at the size of it. It was built on the spit of land just where the river narrowed, and it dominated the river—and could target any vessel coming upstream. It was star-shaped, with high, grim bastions looming above the water. Gun muzzles studded these defenses; more muzzles were visible behind the gunlines at the water's edge. Wilson stared at the fort until it vanished behind them, then stepped into the main cabin and opened his drawing pad. General Sherman lowered his binoculars and turned from the porthole.

"Impressive," he said.

"Disastrous," Wilson answered, quickly sketching in the lines of the fort. "Any ship, no matter how armored, will never get past her unharmed. I can truthfully say that as long as that fort is there, London is safe from any invasion by sea."

"Perhaps the fort could be taken from the land side."

"Hardly. There is an inner and an outer moat—with gun positions in between them, a redan as well, then the brick bastions of the fort itself. They can probably flood the marshland beyond if they have to. I would say that this fort is next to impregnable—except possibly by a long siege—"

"Which is of course out of the question," Sherman said, watching the outlines of the fort take shape on the paper. He touched the drawing, tapping the west gunline on the riverbank. "Twelve heavy guns here; I counted them. From the size of their muzzles they could be hundred-pounders."

Wilson was still hard at work on his drawings when the engine slowed then stopped. *Aurora* bumped lightly against the fenders of the seawall as they tied up. There were shouted commands and the sound of running feet on deck. The Count came in and went to Wilson to look at his drawings. "Most excellent," he said. "This voyage is starting very auspiciously. But the same is, unhappily, not true of the rest of the world."

He took a newspaper from his jacket pocket and opened it on the table. "The pilot sold me this overpriced copy of *The Times*. This item will be of interest to us all."

AMERICAN TRADE POLICY DENOUNCED IN COMMONS
Threat to British Cotton Trade Taken Under Advisement

"What is it about?" Sherman asked, looking at the lengthy article.

"I read it with great attention while we were coming upriver. It seems that Prime Minister Palmerston has accused your countrymen of dumping American cotton on the European market at ruinous prices, thereby undercutting the British cotton trade."

"There is nothing new in this," Fox said. "The British have been going to the Empire countries for cotton ever since the War Between the States began. Mostly Egypt and India. But their cotton is inferior to the American variety and more expensive to produce. Therefore, Yankee traders have been selling cotton to the French and German mills. The British do not like this. We have been here before."

"I hope you are right. But in his speech Palmerston threatens the American trade if it continues in this fashion."

"Any specific threats?" Sherman asked.

"Not really. But he is a man to be watched."

"He is indeed," Fox said, seating himself with the newspaper and giving it his close attention.

Korzhenevski crossed the room and took a sheet of crested notepaper from the sideboard. He wrote a quick note and closed it with a wax seal.

"Simenov has been here with me before, so he can find his way to the college. He'll deliver this note to Johnstone and wait for an answer. I'm inviting him for dinner tonight. If he accepts, we might very well be out of here tomorrow. We'll decide what to do as soon as Johnstone leaves. I'm also taking the precaution of sending a sailor with Simenov. He will be carrying a bottle of champagne. Harbinger of joys to come! Might I suggest, Commander, that you continue your engineering pursuits in your cabin? Thank you."

Fox seemed more concerned with the newspaper than with his champagne, reading not only the article that had attracted the Count's attention but all the other news as well. A distant look entered into Sherman's eyes, one that Korzhenevski noticed.

"Is something disturbing you, General?"

"Something is, you are right. Is it really necessary for a ship to be guided by a pilot to proceed up the Thames?"

"Not only necessary but essential. The sands here are in constant motion, and it takes a pilot skilled in local knowledge to find the correct channel."

"Does every ship need a pilot?"

"Not necessarily. On a clear day a small group of ships could follow the first one with the pilot in line astern." The Count drank some champagne and easily followed Sherman's thoughts. "You are right, this is a very serious concern. I suggest that you leave that matter to me for the time being. I am sure that something can be done."

There was a knock on Wilson's cabin door; Sherman, standing behind Wilson and Fox, looked up from the drawings when he heard the Count's voice.

"One moment," said Sherman. He went over and unlocked the door.

"Most industrious," Korzhenevski said, looking at the growing sheaf of drawings. "I am pleased that our little voyage has begun so well. Now— I would appreciate it if you would turn over all of the plans, as well as the drawing instruments."

"You have a reason?" Sherman asked, frowning.

"A very good one, my dear general. We are now in the heartland of a country which, while not an enemy country, would still object to the presence of foreign observers inside their military establishments. I am sure that Mr. Fox here will agree that the authorities would not take kindly to the presence of what they would surely see as spies in their midst. Commander Johnstone will be coming aboard soon, and our little ship must be Russian to the core. There are English as well as Russian books in my cabin—but that is to be expected. Mr. Fox, might I ask you to undertake a delicate task for me?"

"And that is?"

"Would you—I do not dare say 'search'—would you see to it that none of you possess any English documents? Or anything else—such as clothing labels—that might identify you as Americans."

"That is a most reasonable request."

His mien was most serious; Sherman nodded grim agreement. If they were discovered, it would be a severe and momentous disaster.

Dinner was a time of great stress. Commander Johnstone was no empty-headed aristocrat like the Honorable Richard MacTavish. He was a professor of navigation, well versed in astronomy and mathematics, and he shrewdly examined the three disguised officers when he was introduced to them. Johnstone only sipped his champagne as he and the Count became involved in a technical discussion of Russian and British naval merits. When the meal was finally finished and the port passed around the table, the Count gave them blessed relief.

"I'm afraid that Chikhachev here must relieve Simenov on the bridge— while Tyrtov and Makarov have their duties to perform."

"A pleasure to meet you gentlemen," Johnstone said; there was much heel clicking in return. As they filed out, Johnstone spoke to the Count. "You must write down their names for me for the invitations. Your arrival at this time was most fortuitous. There will be a formal dinner at the college tomorrow, celebrating the Queen's birthday. You—and they—will be our honored guests."

Sherman closed the door on the English officer's voice and muttered a savage oath. Fox nodded agreement as they went down the passageway.

"Dangerous. Very dangerous indeed," Fox said darkly.

Count Korzhenevski summoned them to the wardroom as soon as his guest had departed.

"This is going to be a situation where we must tread carefully," he said.

"Any way of avoiding it?" Sherman asked.

"I am afraid not. But we can better the odds. Commander Wilson, for a number of reasons, should stay aboard. Lieutenant Simenov will abandon the engine room and go in his place. Mr. Fox is skilled in these matters and will play his role well. So it will be up to you, General Sherman, to be an actor in a game that is far removed from your career in the field."

"I do not understand."

"Let me clarify. If I am correct, when you as an officer are involved in combat, you receive reports, make decisions, and act upon them. It is legend that in the thick of battle you are the most cool, the most courageous of men. Now you must summon up your intelligence to face a different kind of battle. You must do the part of a middle-aged Russian naval officer—who may well have faced some of your fellow diners in battle. You don't like them, perhaps you are suspicious of their true intent in having you there. We Russians can be very gloomy and suspicious—and that is how you must feel. Not displaying these emotions at all times, but feeling them. Do you understand?"

"I think that I do. It is something like being in a play, acting a role."

"Perfectly expressed," Fox said happily. "I think that tomorrow you will do fine, just fine."

The meal, while a strain, went as well as could be expected. They were seated with the junior officers, far from the high table with its admirals and even a marine general. Toasts were drunk to the Queen, something the Americans had mixed feelings about. It was noisy and hot, which made it very easy to drink too much, so caution had to be shown. Sherman was seated across from a veteran naval captain who had many decorations and much gold bullion on his uniform. After his first terse nod of greeting, the captain had ignored the Russians and attended to the eating and drinking. Now, very much in his cups, he began to take a firm dislike to Sherman.

"You speak English, Russki? Do you know what I am saying?"

He raised his voice as though volume would increase comprehension.

"*Nyet, nyet,*" Sherman said, then turned away and sipped from his wineglass.

"I'll bet you do. Sitting there and eavesdropping on your betters."

Fox saw what was happening and tried to defuse the situation. "*Pardonnez-moi, monsieur,*" Fox said. "*Mon compagnon ne parle pas anglais. Parlez-vous français?*"

"And none of that frog talk either. Your lot should not be here. We whipped you like curs in the Crimea, now you come crawling around like spies . . ."

Korzhenevski, farther down the table, stood up quickly and barked what sounded like an order in Russian. Lieutenant Simenov pushed his chair back from the table and jumped to his feet; Fox and Sherman saw what was happening and stood as well.

"I am afraid that our presence here is an embarrassment and that we must leave," the Count said.

"You'll leave when you are damn well told to leave," the captain shouted, climbing unsteadily to his feet.

It was Commander Johnstone who appeared suddenly and tried hard to calm the situation.

"This is not the time nor place for this—"

"I agree, Mark," Korzhenevski said, pointing his thumb toward the door. "It would be wisest, though, if my officers and I just left. Thank you for your kindness."

They beat a quick retreat, anxious to be clear of the situation, relieved when the door closed behind them to cut off the captain's drunken shouts.

"That was not good," Korzhenevski said as soon as they were out of the building. "There is still much bad feeling here about the Crimea, and this sort of thing only stirs up old hatreds. We don't dare sail tonight, much as I would like to. Too suspicious. But we will start back downriver in the morning as soon as I can get a pilot."

No one slept well that night. At dawn, one by one, they assembled in the main cabin, where the steward had set out a steaming pot of fresh coffee.

"I shall return with the pilot as soon as is possible," the Count said. He put down his cup and slapped his side pocket, which clanked heavily. "I am prepared to bribe my way if I must. A continental custom which has not yet caught on in this country. Though people do learn very quickly at the sight of a gold coin. Lieutenant Simenov is watch officer, which means that the rest of you can stay out of sight."

Less than an hour later Fox had just finished shaving and was pulling on his jacket when he heard the shouting at the gangway. He hurried on deck to witness an angry encounter. An English army officer had climbed the gangway to the deck—with five armed soldiers behind him. Simenov was blocking his way and shouting at him angrily in Russian.

"*Da!*" Fox called out, all he could think of at the moment. Simenov turned and called out to him. Fox nodded sagely and turned to the angry officer.

"*Excusez-moi, mais nous ne parlons pas anglais. Est-ce que vous connaissez français?*"

"No bloody frog—nor bloody Russian either. You are in England now, and if you don't speak English you are not welcome. This is my authority!" The officer waved a sheet of paper under Fox's nose. "An English officer has filed a complaint against certain officers of this ship. He says that you are spies. I want you to know that this is a military establishment and charges of this kind are taken very seriously. This is my warrant to search this ship."

Fox accepted the sheet of paper, shook his head with lack of comprehension, and passed the warrant back.

"Follow me," the officer called out, and the armed soldiers clumped up the gangway. Simenov barred their way.

"*Nyet!*" Fox shouted, and waved the Russian officer aside. Simenov started to protest—then realized the futility and danger of what he was doing. Reluctantly, he stepped back.

"Search the ship," the officer said as he led the soldiers below. Fox stayed close behind him. The first door at the foot of the gangway was General Sherman's. It was unlocked. The officer threw it open and marched in. Sherman looked up from the chair where he was seated smoking a cigar.

And reading a book!

"I'll take that," the English officer said, taking it from his hand.

Fox leaned close. Should he attack the man? Would the crew help them to seize the soldiers? Was there anything that could be done?

The officer held the book up and the gold-stamped Cyrillic lettering could be seen on the cover. He flipped through the pages of Russian print, then handed the book back to Sherman, who nodded gravely as he drew heavily on his cigar.

"We found something, Captain," one of the soldiers said, looking in from the gangway. Fox was sure that his pounding heart would burst in his chest. He stumbled after them as the soldier led the way to Korzhenevski's cabin, then pointed at the book rack on the wall. The officer leaned forward and read aloud.

"Bowditch on Navigation. Disraeli—Shakespeare." He turned away. "I was told that the Count speaks English, so he must read it as well. Keep searching."

The search was thorough, but the *Aurora* was not a very big ship and it did not take very long. The army captain was just leading the soldiers back on deck when Korzhenevski came up the gangway, followed by the same pilot who had brought them upriver. His voice was intense with anger as he faced the officer. "What is the meaning of this?" he snapped, so forcefully the man took a step backward as he held out the search warrant.

"I have my orders. A complaint has been filed—"

The Count tore it from his fingers, glanced through it—then hurled it onto the deck.

"Leave my ship at once. I am here at the invitation of officers in the Naval Academy. I have friends in your English court. This matter will be ended to my satisfaction—not yours. Leave!"

The officer beat a hasty retreat, his men coming after him. Korzhenevski shouted a brief command to Simenov, who nodded and called down the companionway. There was a rush of sailors on deck. The *Aurora* was being cast off just as the engine turned over. The Count stayed on the bridge with the pilot as the boat drew away from the shore, helped swiftly downriver by the outgoing tide.

Not until the pilot was safely off the ship at Gravesend did Korzhenevski join the Americans in the wardroom.

"A very close run thing," he said after Fox had briefed him. "Luck was on our side."

"I think it was more your planning than any luck," Sherman said. "If they had found any evidence to confirm their suspicions, we would not be sailing safely away right now."

"Thank you, General, you are most kind."

Korzhenevski crossed to the bulkhead, where the barometer and compass were mounted on a mahogany plaque. He felt under the lower edge and touched something there. The plaque swung wide to reveal a deep storage space. He reached in and took out the bundle of drawings and handed them to Wilson.

"You will want to work on these while we are at sea. But not before you all join me in a medicinal cognac. It is early, I know, but I think it is very much called for."

AN OUTRAGEOUS ACT

It had been a fast passage and Captain James D. Bulloch was quite pleased. Now, with a following west wind and all the sails drawing well, he was passing along the Dutch coast with the Frisian Islands to starboard. They should be in the Deutsche Bucht soon, which meant that the *Parker Cook* would be able to tie up in Wilhelmshaven before dark. Her holds were filled with the best Mississippi cotton and would fetch a good price. Captain Bulloch was indeed a happy man.

This was a busy part of the Atlantic. Farther north the sails of two other ships were visible, while closer to shore there were a number of small fishing boats. Almost due ahead was the smear of smoke from a steamship, growing larger as the ship approached. Soon the black upperworks of a naval vessel could be seen.

"German?" the captain asked.

"Can't rightly tell, sir," First Officer Price said. He was on the bridge wing peering intently through a telescope. "Wait—I had a glimpse of the flag at her stern—not German, yes, I believe that she is British."

"A long way from home. What business does she have in these waters?"

He had his answer soon enough. The warship made a wide turn until she was running close to the *Parker Cook* and matching her course and speed. An officer on her bridge appeared with a megaphone.

"Heave to," he called out. "We wish to examine your papers."

"Damn their eyes!" Captain Bulloch said. "Let me have the megaphone." He stalked over to the rail and shouted his angry reply.

"This is the United States ship *Parker Cook* sailing on the high seas. You have no jurisdiction here . . ."

His answer was not long in coming. Even as he finished speaking the bow cannon on the warship blossomed with fire and a column of water leaped high some yards ahead of the bow.

"Heave to."

The captain had no choice. Once the sails were lowered, the ship lost way, wallowing in the waves. A boat was quickly and efficiently lowered from the warship. The two vessels were close enough for Captain Bulloch to read the ship's name.

"HMS *Devastation*. Stupid name."

The Americans could only look on numbly as the boat approached. A uniformed officer—followed by six armed marines—climbed to the deck to face the angry captain.

"This is piracy! You have no right—"

"The right of force majeure," the officer said disdainfully, waving toward the heavily armed warship. "I will now examine your ship's papers."

"You shall not!"

"What is your cargo?" The officer offhandedly loosened his sword in its scabbard as he spoke; this was not lost on the captain.

"Cotton," he said. "American cotton on its way to Germany, and no concern of yours."

"I beg to differ. If you were aware of world affairs, you would know that due to unfair trading practices, Great Britain has banned the sale of American cotton to Germany and France. Your cargo is therefore declared contraband and will be seized and taken to a British port."

"I must protest!"

"So noted. Now order your crew on deck. A prize crew will man this ship and take her into port."

Captain Bulloch cursed impotently. He was no longer a happy man.

The fine weather petered out as one went north; the Midlands glistened under a steady, drumming rain; Scotland as well. But Thomas McGrath and Paddy McDermott walked out into the teeming Glasgow rain with immense feelings of relief. The train trip from Birmingham had been long, slow, and almost unbearably tense. McGrath, with his Cockney accent, had bought the two third-class tickets and they had boarded the train just as it was leaving. They had sat in silence all the way to Scotland, fearful that their Irish voices would arouse suspicion. The Irish were looked at with distrust in Great Britain these days.

"You say you've been here before, Paddy?" McGrath asked.

"Aye, for a year, after I came over from Belfast."

"Many Irish here?"

"For sure. But not our kind."

"Proddies?"

"To a man."

"Could you pass as one?"

"Jayzus! Why would I want to do a thing like that?"

"Well, you sound like one, right enough."

"To you mebbe. But as soon as they heard my name and where I lived, they would know right enough I'm a Taigh."

"What if you gave them a different name, a different address?"

"Well—might work. But not for long."

"It doesn't have to be for long. We have to find an Irish bar near the fishing ships. They'll be going out to sea, fishing the same grounds as the Irish do. We've got to find a way to use that contact, get you, or a message, across to the other side. Say something about a death in the family, a funeral you have to attend, anything. Offer them money."

"And where would I get the brass? We're that skint. Cosh someone mebbe?"

"If it comes to that, why not?" McGrath said grimly. "Word about the concentration camps has got to reach Ireland."

Through the ceaseless rain the lights of a pub could be seen ahead, beside the Clyde. Heads down, they went toward it. Paddy glanced up at the signboard above the front entrance.

"McCutcheon's," he said. "I've been here. It's about as Irish as you can get."

"I hope so," McGrath said, his voice betraying a native suspicion. "But let me talk until we are absolutely sure."

His suspicion was well founded. They sipped silently at their pints and listened to the voices around them with growing concern. They drank quickly and left the dregs in the their glasses, went back into the rainy night.

"Not an Irishman among them," Paddy said. "Scots to a man."

"It's the English," McGrath said darkly. "Protestant or Catholic—they can't tell them apart. A Paddy is just a Paddy to them."

"What do we do?"

"Get some money and get down to the coast. Fishing's a hard life. We'll just have to find a fisherman in need of a few bob to take a passenger or two. That's what we have to do."

Parliament was in session, and a very boisterous session it was proving to be. It was prime minister's question time and Benjamin Disraeli, the leader of the opposition, was vying with many others for the attention of the speaker. Once recognized, he climbed to his feet, looked ruefully at Lord Palmerston, and shook his head.

"Would the house agree with the incredulity that the Prime Minister's words have stirred in my breast? Are we really to believe that Britain is best served by stopping ships at sea, searching and seizing them? Does not memory of 1812 raise certain uncomfortable memories? A useless war started at a time of great peril to this country. Started, if memory serves me correctly, by British men-of-war stopping American ships at sea and pressing their seamen into our service. America would not abide that practice then, and I doubt if they will do so now. The Prime Minister's reckless policies have led this country into two disastrous wars. Must we now look forward to a third?"

There were shouts of agreement from the floor—mixed with boos and cries of anger. Palmerston rose slowly to his feet, then spoke when the barracking had died down.

"Does the honorable gentleman intend that as a question—or just an exercise in demagoguery? International trade is the heart's blood of the Empire. While it flows we all profit and live in harmony. Cotton is as essential to the fields of India as it is to the mills of Manchester. I would be remiss if I did not take action against those who threaten that trade—and the Americans are doing just that. The coins in your pocket and the clothes on your back are the profits of international trade. Threaten that and you threaten the Empire, you threaten our very existence as a world power. Britain will rule the seas today and in the foreseeable future—just as she has ruled in the past. The sea-lanes of the world shall not be the pathway of American expansionism. The enemy is at the door, and I for one shall not let them in. Perilous times need positive policies."

"Like the policy of seizing and imprisoning certain sections of our society?" Disraeli said.

Palmerston was furious. "I have said it before, and repeat it here again—matters of military policy will not be discussed in this house, in public, in the presence of the press. If the honorable leader of the opposition has a legitimate question about matters of government policy—why, the door at Number Ten is always open to him. What I cannot, will not, abide is any mention of these matters in public. Do I make myself clear?"

Disraeli dismissed the matter with a wave of his hand. Palmerston would not be drawn out on the matter of the Irish. What was happening was known even to the press, who dared not print it and risk the Prime Minister's wrath. But Disraeli would keep picking away at the opposition's dangerous policies. Make them known to the voters, give them something to worry about. An early election might easily see a change of government.

Benjamin Disraeli was looking forward to that day.

TEMPTING FATE

General Sherman came up on deck of the *Aurora* soon after they had dropped the pilot off at the cutter off Dungeness, when the little yacht had steamed well clear of the shoal waters at the mouth of the Thames. It had been warm and close below, and he now savored the fresh sea air with pleasure. A short while later Fox and Korzhenevski joined him.

"That was too closely run for me," Fox said. "I thought I was no stranger to fear, yet I am forced to admit that I am still quaking inside. I think that it was something about being so defenseless while being surrounded by one's enemies. I realize all too clearly now that it is one thing to issue orders to field agents—and another thing altogether to do the job yourself. A most humbling experience. I respected my agents before, but now I have nothing but outright admiration for those who face this kind of danger on a daily basis."

The Count nodded in agreement; Sherman merely shrugged. "What is past is done. Battles cannot be refought."

Korzhenevski smiled. "I envy you your calm, General. To a man of war the affair at Greenwich must have been no more than an amusing incident."

"Quite the opposite. I found it most disconcerting to feel so helpless while surrounded by the enemy. I think I prefer the battlefield."

"I sincerely regret putting you in such danger," the Count said. "I will plan better in the future and work hard to avoid such encounters."

"Then what do you think we should do next?" Sherman asked.

"That is for you to tell me. But you should know that at this moment we are approaching a very sensitive part of Britain. Not too far from here, on the south coast of England, are the main naval ports of Southampton and Plymouth. Almost all of the British fleet is based at one or the other of them. I am sure there will be matters of great interest at those two ports."

"Must we risk detection by sailing into military ports?" Fox asked, worried. "I am afraid that last night's disturbing proximity to the enemy was more than enough for me for the time being."

"I am tempted to agree with Gus," Sherman said. "I see no reason to put our heads into the lion's jaws yet again."

The Count bowed and clicked his heels. "I acknowledge your superior wisdom and withdraw any suggestion of a visit to either of these seaports. The fact is that I have other agents in England, people who are above suspicion, who can look in on them and chart their ship movements if they are so ordered. Please put the entire matter from your minds."

Sherman nodded agreement. "Being naval officers, you gentlemen naturally look to the sea and matters maritime. For me it is the land and the terrain that is most important. I would be pleased if we could take that into consideration. I would like to know a good bit more about the English fortresses, countryside, and railroads—"

"But of course!" the Count called out, clapping his hands with pleasure. "I have Russian charts below, but they begin at the coastline and reveal little or nothing of the country's interior. My general—we must get you a copy of a *Bradshaw*."

"I'm afraid that I don't understand . . ."

"But I do," Fox said. "I have one in my library in Washington City— which of course will be of no help to us here. A *Bradshaw* is an English publication that contains timetables of all the trains that run in the British Isles."

"I would certainly be pleased to have one."

"And that you shall," the Count said. "I had planned a stop at Dover for fresh supplies from the ship's chandlers there. While that is being done I shall visit a local bookshop. Since Dover is the main port of entry from the continent, they will certainly have this invaluable guide for sale there."

The good weather still held, so Korzhenevski ordered luncheon to be served on deck. They did not wait for Wilson, who was still deeply involved in his charts and drawings. They had cold beetroot soup that the Count referred to as *borscht*, which they greatly enjoyed. Along with the ever-flowing champagne. By the time they had finished, they were already anchored outside Dover Harbor. The Count excused himself and took the boat ashore to arrange for the provisions. Sherman and Fox enjoyed a cheroot on deck while awaiting his return.

"I want no more meetings with the British military," Sherman said. "The risk is too great."

"I could not agree more."

"But that does not mean we cannot go ashore. As long as we keep our mouths shut, the danger should be minimal. There are many things I would like to see before this visit is terminated."

Fox nodded agreement. "I agree completely. We will not have this opportunity for exploration a second time."

When the boat returned and the Count climbed on deck, he was brandishing a thick, red-bound volume. *"Bradshaw!"* he said triumphantly. He carried a thick envelope as well. "And detailed maps of Britain."

"My thanks," Sherman said, weighing the book in his hands. "If I could also have your British charts, I will retire to my cabin."

The *Aurora* was coasting down the English Channel as evening fell. This was the time of day when the Russians, like the British, enjoyed their tea. The Americans were happy to conform to this pleasant custom.

"I'm just about done with the drawings," Commander Wilson said as he stirred sugar into his cup.

"Good news indeed," Fox said. "We must get some more work for you to do."

"See if you can't avoid another search of the ship. I'm still shuddering from the last little adventure. I would rather face an enemy broadside at sea than go through that again."

They turned to greet General Sherman when he came in; he had been closeted in his cabin for most of the day. He nodded abstractedly, then took a cup from the servant who stood by the samovar. He remained standing and sipped at it in silence, his gaze miles away. When he finished the tea and put the cup down, he turned to face the others. The abstracted look was gone and a smile of satisfaction had taken its place.

"Gentlemen. If war should come to this part of the world, I would like you to know that I have a plan. Not complete in detail yet, but in overall design it is completely clear to me."

"Do tell us!" Fox said excitedly.

"In due time, Mr. Fox, in due time."

It was his anger at the unfairness, the imprisonment of the women and the wee ones, that kept Thomas McGrath seething. He had asked nothing from the world except the chance to earn an honest living. He had done that, worked hard, earned enough to raise a family. For what purpose? For all of them to be bunged up in a foul camp. To what end? He had done nothing to anyone to have caused him to suffer this disgusting fate. Be honest and hardworking—and look where you ended up. He had never before been tempted by violence or crime, for these were alien to his nature. Now he was actively considering both. The end was worth it—whatever the means. Ireland must be told about the concentration camps.

Sauchiehall Street was well lit, with lamps outside the elegant shops and restaurants. What was to be done? He had seen two peelers already—seen them first before they had spotted him. The rain had died down to a light drizzle, but he was still soaked through. He drew back into a doorway as a light suddenly lit up the pavement. A man in evening dress came down the steps from a restaurant—stepped to the curb and signaled to one of the passing cabs. An opportunity? McGrath could not tell. He walked past the cab as the man entered it, saying something to the driver. Who clicked at his horse and flicked the reins. The cab pulled away slowly.

There were other cabs about, and pedestrians crossing the street. Without walking too fast, McGrath was able to keep pace with the cab, seeing it turn into a darkened street ahead. When he rounded the corner he began to run.

The horse was old and in no hurry; the driver did not use his whip. The cab stopped not too far ahead. McGrath was only feet away when the man finished paying off the driver and turned toward the steps of a finely built house.

"Money," McGrath said, seizing the man by the arm. "Give me all the money that you have."

"I'll give you this!" the man cried out, laying his stick across the side of the Irishman's head. He was young and fit, and the blow drew blood. It also drew savage reprisals. A hard fist struck him in the chest, driving the air from his lungs, dropping him to the wet pavement.

McGrath went quickly through the fallen man's pockets, found his billfold inside his jacket pocket. It had taken but moments; he had not been seen. The cab was just turning the corner and vanishing out of sight. McGrath went swiftly away in the opposite direction.

He was late for their meeting, and Paddy McDermott was already there waiting in the darkened doorway. He stepped out when he heard McGrath approaching.

"I thought you weren't coming . . ."

"I'm here all right. How did it go?"

"Not quite like you said. There were no Irish in any of the bars I visited, none at all. The Brits have swupt them all up—Prods and Taighs both."

"By Jayzus—don't they know what loyalists are?"

"It doesn't look like it. But I went down to the harbor, like you said, and the Scottish fishermen are that angry about it all. They wonder if they'll be next. When they heard my accent they asked if I was on the run. I told them aye and they believed me. It seems that the fishermen here and those from Ulster, they both fish the same banks. I think they do a bit of smuggling for each other, but I didn't want to ask too many questions. They'll take me over in the morning, in time for the funeral I told them about. But it will cost us dear. A tenner to get there, then another ten pounds for the others to get me ashore. We don't have that kind of money."

"Well, let us say that there are those that do," McGrath said, taking the roll of banknotes from his pocket. "Get there, Paddy. Get to Ireland and tell them what is happening here. Dublin must know."

IRELAND ENRAGED

President Abraham Lincoln looked up from the papers he was signing when his secretary, John Nicolay, came in.

"Let me finish these, John, then you will have my full attention. There seem to be more of them every day."

After blotting his signature, he put the sheaf of papers into a pigeon-hole of his desk, leaned back in his chair, and sighed with relief. "Now—what can I do for you?"

"It's Secretary of War Stanton. He would like to speak with you on a matter of some urgency. And he has General Meagher with him."

"Ireland," Lincoln said as he shook his head wearily. "That poor country still continues to suffer after all her tribulations." He stood and stretched. "I've had enough of the office for now. Will you be so kind as to tell them to meet me in the Cabinet Room?"

The President wiped the nib of his pen, then closed the inkwell. He had done enough paperwork for the day. He went down the hall and let himself into the Cabinet Room. The two men standing by the window turned to face him when he came in.

"Gentlemen, please seat yourselves."

"Thank you for seeing us," Meagher said.

"Is it Ireland again?"

"Unhappily it is, sir. I've had the most worrying report."

"As have I," Stanton said in equally gloomy tones. "Another vessel seized on the high seas. A cotton ship on her way to Germany with her cargo. She was taken to England, where her master and officers were released. But her unhappy crew was pressed into the British navy. The officers had to return by way of France, which is why we have just heard about the incident now."

"Then it is 1812 all over again?"

"It is indeed."

Would it be war again—for the same reason? Without realizing, the President sighed heavily and pressed his hand to his sore forehead.

"I have reports as well," Meagher said. "We know that the English have been rounding up and taking away people of Irish descent for some months now, but we had no idea what was happening to them. No one hears from them—it is as though they have vanished. But now a message has reached us and its authenticity has been vouched for. The authorities have set up camps, that they have; concentration camps they call them. Two men escaped from the camp near Birmingham and one of them made his way to Belfast. They say that not only men, but also women and children, are locked up in these vile places. The conditions in the camps are appalling. No one has been charged with any crime—they are just held against their will. This is more than a crime against individuals—it is a crime against a race!"

Lincoln listened in silence, staring out of the window at the growing darkness, felt the darkness growing in himself as well. "We must do something about this—though for the life of me I cannot think what. I must call a cabinet meeting. Tomorrow morning. Perhaps cooler and wiser heads will have some answers. I suppose a government protest is in order . . ."

Stanton shook his head. "They'll ignore it just the way they have ignored all the other ones." Then, the thoughts obviously linked, he asked, "Is there any word from General Sherman yet?"

"None. And how I wish that there were. During the past years of war I have come to depend upon him. This country owes him an immense debt.

Without any doubt he is the man to rely on in a national emergency. I am concerned with his safety because I am sure he is involved with some desperate matter. I just wonder where he is now."

Across the ocean, on the shores of the country that so tried the President and his men, Sherman was staring through a spyglass at a peninsula jutting out from the rapidly approaching coast.

"It's called the Lizard," Count Korzhenevski said. "A strange name—and a very old one. No one knows why the peninsula is so named. But on the modern charts it does look like a lizard—which I doubt the people who named her could have known. Bit of a mystery. The very tip is called Land's End—which it indeed is. The most westernmost place in Britain. That is where Penzance is."

Sherman turned his telescope to focus on the town. "The Great Western Railway line terminates there."

"It does indeed."

"I would like to go ashore and visit the place. Or would that be too risky?"

"It would be a piece of cake, old boy, as Count Iggy might say. This will not be entering a military establishment, visiting the lion in its lair, so to speak. This is a quiet, sleepy little town. With a passable basin where we can tie up among the other yachts. A stroll ashore would be very much in order, drink some warm British beer, that sort of thing. As long as I am the only one who speaks to the natives, there should be no danger."

"Then let us do it," Sherman said strongly.

The sun shone warmly on the slate roofs of Penzance. A steam ferry was just emerging from the harbor as they approached, bound for the Scilly Isles. Clad in yachting outfits, the Count and the three American officers were rowed ashore. Korzhenevski had been right: No attention was paid to their arrival. A fisherman, mending nets on the shore, looked up as they passed. He touched a worn knuckle to his forehead and went back to his work. It was a Sunday, and others in their best clothes strolled along the shore. It was a pleasant day's outing.

There, just ahead of them, was the bulk of the train station. Sherman looked around to be sure he could not be overheard, then spoke softly to the Count.

"Is there any reason we can't go in there?"

"None. I will make some inquiries in the booking office while you gentlemen stand and wait for me."

"And look around," Commander Wilson said, smiling. Since they had come ashore, he had been examining everything with a keen surveyor's eye.

They went up the few steps and entered the station. A train was just leaving, and like many others, they watched as the carriage doors were slammed shut and the guard blew his whistle. The stationmaster, proudly uniformed and sporting a gold watch chain across his waistcoat, waved his flag to the driver. Blasting out a burst of steam, the engine's whistle blew, and puffing out clouds of smoke, the train drew out of the station.

"Gentlemen," the Count said loudly, "I do believe there is a refreshment bar over there. It is a warm day and I think that we would all enjoy a glass of ale."

They sat around a table in silence as the glasses were brought to them. They drank slowly, eyes glancing about at the busy scene, finished their drinks, and proceeded at the same lazy pace back to the waiting boat.

"I must make some drawings," Wilson said as soon as they were back on board. "Just quick sketches while memory is still fresh."

"By all means," Korzhenevski said. "There will be ample time to put the papers back into the safe if any other vessels approach us. That was a most satisfactory visit, was it not, gentlemen?"

"It was indeed," Sherman said. "But I would like to see more."

"And what would that be?"

"A little train trip, Count. I would like you to accompany me on a visit to Plymouth."

Korzhenevski found his mouth gaping and closed it sharply. It was Fox who protested.

"General Sherman—are you being realistic? Plymouth is a large naval base, patrolled and well guarded. It would be folly to attempt to enter it."

"I am well aware of that—but I have no intention of going anywhere near the military. Let me show you what I have in mind. Count, if you would be so kind as to get the charts from your safe, I will be happy to explain my thoughts to you."

Sherman spread the charts and maps out on the table and the others leaned close. Even Wilson left his drawing to see what was happening. The general ran his finger along the Cornish coast, where he penciled in a line just inland.

"This is the route of the Great Western Railway, a masterpiece of construction built by the great engineer Isambard Kingdom Brunel. Before the railroad was constructed, there were no roads the length of this mountainous county. Which means that all communication had to be by sea. Not only did Brunel build a railroad through this difficult terrain, but he also constructed, here at Saltash, a great bridge spanning the river Tamar. Just six years ago—I recall reading about it with great interest at the time. It was held as a truism by many people that the river was too wide to bridge. By ordinary means of construction, it surely was. But this great engineer pioneered a completely new method of construction that replaced the ferry, and linked Cornwall by rail to the rest of Britain for the first time. And here, on the other side of the river, is the city of Plymouth. It is my plan to take the train to Plymouth and return on the next train back to Penzance. I have no intention of going anywhere near the naval station."

Fox looked at him shrewdly. "Does this trip have anything to do with the plans that you mentioned a few days ago?"

"Perhaps. Let us just say that I need much information about this country before I can think about finalizing my intentions. But I will need your aid, Count."

"You have it, surely you have it." He paced the cabin, deep in thought. "But we must make careful preparations if this rather—should I say adventurous?—plan can succeed. Your hair and beard will need redyeing if they are not to arouse suspicion. I will take a trip ashore in the morning to buy us suitable clothes, though God knows what gentlemen's attire I will find here. Then I must buy tickets—first-class tickets—and I assume you have looked closely at your *Bradshaw* and have worked out a schedule?"

"I have." Sherman took a slip of paper from his jacket pocket and passed it over. "These are the trains we will take. With proper preparations I feel that this trip will be a successful one."

"Well then!" the Count said, clapping his hands happily. "We must have some champagne and drink to a prosperous journey."

A SECRET REVEALED

General Ramsey, head of the United States Army Ordnance Department, had traveled down from Washington City to Newport News, Virginia, on the previous afternoon. He had enjoyed a good meal and a pipe in the bar afterward, then passed a pleasant night in the hotel. He was happy to be away from the endless labors of his position in the War Department for at least a few hours. Now, well relaxed, he was having a coffee in the station café when he saw a plump man pause at the entrance and look around. Ramsey stood so that the newcomer could see his uniform. The man hurried over.

"You are General Ramsey, sir? I received your message and I am most sorry to be tardy."

"Not at all, Mr. Davis." Ramsey took his watch from his pocket and glanced at it. "I have been informed that the train is running late, so we have plenty of time. Please join me. The coffee here is, if not wonderful, at least drinkable. You are, as I understand it, John Ericsson's works manager?"

"I have that pleasure."

"Then perhaps you can enlighten me about your employer's message. He simply asked that I appear here today with at least one general officer, an officer who has had field experience. That is why I contacted General

Grant, who will be arriving on the next train. But I am most curious as to the meaning of this invitation. Could you enlighten me?"

Davis mopped his sweating forehead with a red bandanna. "I wish that I could, General. But none of us are permitted to speak a word about our work when we are outside of the foundry. I hope that you understand . . ."

Ramsey frowned, then reluctantly nodded his head. "I am afraid that I do. A great deal of my work is secret as well. Listen—is that a train whistle?"

"I believe that it is."

"Well then—let us meet General Grant on the platform."

Grant was the first person off the train. The conductor reached to help him, but he waved the man away. He went slowly, holding on to the exit rail with his left hand, his right arm in a black silk sling. Ramsey stepped forward to greet him.

"I hope I did the right thing by asking you to be here, Ulysses. I was assured that you were on the road to recovery."

"Very much so—and damn bored with all the sitting around. This little trip will do me worlds of good. If you want to know, your telegram was a gift from the gods. But did I detect an air of mystery in your request?"

"You did, General, you certainly did. But it is all a mystery to me as well. This is Garret Davis, Mr. Ericsson's works manager. He is also very secretive in the matter."

"I am most sorry, gentlemen," Davis said with a weak smile. "But I have specific orders. If you would please come this way—there is a carriage waiting."

It was a short drive from the station to Ericsson's shipyard. A high wall surrounded the yard itself and there was an armed soldier guarding the gate. He recognized Davis, saluted the officers, then called out for the gate to be opened. They climbed down from the carriage in front of the main building. Davis moderated his pace to accommodate Grant as they entered the building.

Ericsson himself came out to greet them. "General Ramsey, we have met before. And it is my pleasure now to meet with the very famous General Grant."

"Excuse me if I don't shake hands, sir," said Grant, nodding at his immobilized right arm. "Now permit me to be blunt; I wish to know why we have been summoned here."

"It will be with great satisfaction that I tell you—indeed show you. If you will follow Mr. Davis." The Swedish engineer explained as they walked. "I assume that both you gentlemen are acquainted with the steam engine? Of course, you will have traveled on trains, been many times on steamships. So then you will know just how large steam engines must be. This immense size has worried me in the construction of the new iron-clads. These new ships are far bigger than my first *Monitor*, which means that to supply steam to engines that rotate the gun turrets, I must run steam lines about the ship. The lines are very hot and dangerous and therefore require thick insulation. Not only that, but they can be easily broken, and they are unsatisfactory in general. But if I generate steam for each turret engine, I will have created a mechanical monstrosity, with engines and boilers throughout my ship. I am sure that you see my problem. No, I thought, there must be a better solution."

"Smaller, more self-contained engines to move the turrets?" Ramsey said.

"The very truth! I see that you are an engineer as well as a military man, General. That is indeed what I needed. Since an engine of this type does not exist, I, of necessity, had to invent one myself. This way, please."

Davis showed them into a large workshop that was well lit by an immense skylight. Ericsson pointed to the squat metal bulk of a black machine. It was about the size of a large steamer trunk.

"My Carnot engine," he said proudly. "I am sure that you gentlemen know the Carnot cycle. No? Pity. The world should understand this cycle because it is the explanation behind all the forces of energy and propulsion. An ideal cycle consists of four reversible changes in the physical condition of a substance, most useful in thermodynamic theory. We must start with specified values of the variable temperature, specific volume, and pressure the substance undergoes in succession—"

"Excuse me Mr. Ericsson," General Grant interrupted. "Is that Swedish you are talking?"

"*Svensk? Nej.* I am speaking English."

"Well, it could be Swedish as far as I am concerned. I can't understand a word that you said."

"Perhaps—if you were less technical," Ramsey said. "In layman's language."

Ericsson drew himself up, anger in his eyes, muttering to himself. With an effort he spoke again.

"All right, then, at its most simple. A quantity of heat is taken from a hot source and some of it is transferred to a colder location—while the balance is transformed into mechanical work. This is how a steam engine works. But the Carnot cycle can be applied to a different machine. That machine is what you see here. My Carnot engine has two cylinders, and is much more compact than any steam engine which must rely on an exterior source of steam to run. Here, using a very volatile liquid I have refined from kerosene, I have succeeded in causing combustion within the cylinders themselves."

Grant hadn't the slightest idea what the man was talking about, but Ramsey was nodding agreement. Ericsson signaled to a mechanic who was oiling the engine with a long-spouted can. The man put the can down and seized the handle of a crank that was fixed to the front of the machine. He turned it, faster and faster, then reached over and pulled a lever. The engine burst into life with a thunderous roar, then it poured out a cloud of noxious smoke. Ericsson ignored the smoke, fanning it away from his face, as he pointed to the rear end of the machine at a rapidly rotating fitting. "Power, gentlemen," he shouted above the din. "Power to rotate the heaviest turret in the biggest ship. And the end of the deadly steam lines." He reached to pull the control lever back and the roar died away.

"Very convincing," Ramsey said. Grant was less than impressed, but kept his silence. Davis, who left the workshop before the demonstration had begun, had returned with another man, well dressed, small, and rotund.

"Why, Mr. Parrott," General Ramsey said, smiling broadly, "how very good it is to see you again. General Grant, this is William Parker Parrott, the eminent gunsmith."

This General Grant could understand. "Mr. Parrott, this is indeed a

A WONDER TO BEHOLD!

pleasure. I believe that your weapons are the best in the world. God knows that I have fought and won many a battle with them."

Parrott beamed with delight. "I shall treasure those words, General. Now let me show you why I asked Mr. Ericsson to invite you and General Ramsey here. Or rather why Mr. Ericsson and I have collaborated on an invention. It all began when Mr. Ericsson was visiting my office some time ago and saw on my wall a British patent application for a totally impossible invention."

"As it was then designed," Ericsson said. "But improving on the original is not impossible to men of genius—which is a distinction that Parrott and I share." The inventor was never the one to hide his light under a bushel. "When I had finished my Carnot engine, I thought at once of the patent for the impractical steam wagon. Now, I said to myself, now it can be built. And between us we have done just that."

He led them across the room to a bulky form draped with canvas. With a dramatic gesture he pulled away the cover. "There, gentlemen, a practical engine wagon."

It was such a novel machine, so strange to the eye, that they could not take it in all at once. It appeared to be a triangular platform of sorts with spiked wheels on its two front corners, a single wheel at the back. The stocky black engine sat sideways across the device. A cogged wheel was fixed to the engine's shaft. This, in turn, transmitted power to a heavy chainlike device, which, in turn, rotated another cogwheel on the shaft connecting the two front wheels. Behind the engine was a small seat facing some gauges and a tiller that was connected to the steerable rear wheel. The mechanic started the engine and stepped back. Parrott climbed proudly into the seat, worked some levers—and the machine rolled slowly forward. Using the tiller to move the rear wheel, he trundled slowly about the workshop, making a complete circle before he returned to the starting place and turned off the engine. Even Grant was impressed with the demonstration.

"Remarkable!" Ramsey said. "Strong enough to tow a heavy gun over rough terrain."

"Yes, it can do that," Ericsson said with a smile. "But it can do even more." He signaled to the door, where two men were waiting. They went out and returned with a wheeled Gatling gun. With practiced movements they placed a ramp before the machine and rolled the gun up onto the platform between the front wheels.

"So you see, gentlemen, with a single addition the powered wagon becomes a mobile battery."

Grant was still puzzling out the precise meaning of this new machine when Ramsey, who dealt with ordnance on a daily basis, gasped with sudden comprehension.

"A mobile battery—no, not one—but a squadron of them! They could take the battle to the enemy, decimate him.

"Your engine will bring the guns swiftly into battle. Firepower that no army can stand against. Why—I think that this invention will change the face of warfare forever."

IN THE ENEMY'S HEARTLAND

"**A**ll aboard. All aboard, if you please," the guard said, nodding at the two well-dressed gentlemen. They had dark silk hats, expensive suits, gold cuff links; he knew the gentry when he saw them.

"And where is first class?" the Count asked.

"This entire carriage, sir, thanking you."

Korzhenevski led the way down the corridor and slid open the door of an empty compartment. They sat at the window facing each other. General Sherman patted the upholstered seats.

"Cut-glass mirrors and brass fittings," he said. "The English sure know how to take care of themselves."

Korzhenevski nodded in agreement. "They do enjoy their luxuries and little indulgences. But only at the top, I am afraid. If you looked into a third-class carriage on this train, you would not be that impressed. In all truth, I do believe that this country, at many times, reminds me of Mother Russia. The nobility and the very rich at the summit, then below them a modicum of the middle classes to keep things running. Then the serfs—they would be the working classes here—at the very bottom. Poverty-stricken, deprived, ill."

"Why, Count—you almost sound like a republican."

Korzhenevski smiled wryly. "Perhaps I am. If there will be any changes to my country, they will certainly have to come from the top. The bourgeoisie and the *mushiks* don't want to change their lot, while the serfs are powerless."

Sherman looked out of the window, lost in thought, as the train got under way. It rattled along the shore for a few miles, until the tracks turned inland. The train was not fast, but still it was a pleasant journey through the green countryside, past the farms and forests, with the occasional stop at a town along the way. Sherman had a small leatherbound notebook in which he made careful notes, his eyes never leaving the window. They stopped at a larger station, on the hill above a pretty city that was set against the ocean.

"Falmouth," the Count said. "There is a very good harbor here—you can see a bit of it there, above the rooftops."

Sherman looked out through the glass of the compartment's door, then through the corridor window beyond. An officer in naval uniform appeared there, taking hold of the door handle and sliding it open. Sherman looked away as he put the notebook into his inside jacket pocket. The Count stared straight ahead, just glimpsing the newcomer out of the corner of his eye. They of course did not speak to one another since they had not been introduced. After the train had pulled out of the station, Korzhenevski pointed at some buildings outside the window, then said something to Sherman in Russian.

"Da," Sherman said, and continued looking out of the window. Long minutes passed in silence after that, until the newcomer put his fist before his face and coughed lightly. Neither man by the window turned to look at him. Then he coughed again and leaned forward.

"I say, I hope I'm not making a fool of myself, but I would swear, that is, I think that I heard you speak Russian . . ."

The Count turned a cold face toward the man, who had the good grace to blush deeply.

"If I am wrong, sir, I do apologize. But I think that I know you from Greenwich; you were years ahead of me, quite famous. A count; your name, I am afraid I do not remember. I am sorry that I spoke out—"

"Count Korzhenevski. You do have a good memory. But I'm afraid that I don't recall—"

THE AMAZING BRIDGE ACROSS THE TAMAR RIVER

"I say—no need to apologize. I don't believe we ever formally met. Lieutenant Archibald Fowler at your service."

"What a pleasant surprise, Archie. And I see that you are still in the service."

"Rather. Stationed aboard the old *Defender* in Plymouth. Just popped down to see some cousins in Falmouth for a few days."

"How pleasant. This is my friend Boris Makarov. I'm afraid he speaks no English."

"My pleasure."

"Do svedanya," Sherman answered with a bow of his head.

"I shall dine out on this for years," Fowler said enthusiastically. "How we envied you and your friends, the parties, the champagne—yet you were always there, hard at work, on Monday mornings."

"We were young and enthusiastic and, I must say, quite strong, to carry on as we did."

"We did have some smashing times, didn't we? So what brings you to Cornwall now?"

An innocent enough question—or was it? Korzhenevski racked his brain for an answer, bought some time. "For me it is always a pleasure to visit your lovely country, to see old friends."

"Indeed."

"But not this time," the Count said with sudden inspiration. "Makarov here is a professor of engineering at the Moscow Institute. Since we were passing this way, he begged me to accompany him. Otherwise he could not make this trip."

"Trip?" Fowler asked, puzzled.

"Yes. To see the world-famous Tamar Bridge, built by your Mr. Brunel."

"A wonder! I can easily understand his enthusiasm. We used to go out in carriages and picnic on the cliffs above while we watched it go up. Laid bets it couldn't be done. Made a few quid myself, you know. Unspannable, they said. But old Brunel built these ruddy great piers, solid stone. Then the bridge sections, built on land and brought out on barges, then lifted up to the top of the piers. You'll see for yourself, we should be crossing it soon—right after Saltash."

At slow speed the train moved out onto the bridge, under the immense tubular arches. "There, look at that!" Archie said with great enthusiasm. "Arches, strong under pressure. And next to them the suspension cables, equally strong under tension. So the way they are built, the forces cancel out at the ends of the sections; therefore, all of the weight is directed straight down onto the piers. Built in this manner, they could each be lifted as a single unit. A wonder of the world."

"It is indeed."

"*Da, da,*" Sherman added, much taken in by the sight.

The train pulled into Plymouth a few minutes later and they alighted.

"Can I show you around our ship? It would be a great pleasure," Archie said. The Count shook his head. "If we but could. However we must return on the next train; we only had these few hours."

"Next time, then. Well, you know where I am. And I want you to know that an old friend from Greenwich is always welcome."

They shook hands and parted, the lieutenant leaving the station.

"What a bourgeois bore," the Count said, looking distastefully at the naval officer's retreating back. "Old friend indeed! Oh, how that jumped-up creature must have envied his elders and betters."

Sherman and the Count had to find their train. As they climbed the stairs to cross over to the down track, the Count patted his forehead with his kerchief.

"I'm afraid I can't keep as cool as you under fire, General. I hope this little trip was worth the effort."

"Far more than you can realize. After we return to your ship, I would like to ask you to do me one last favor, if you will."

"I am completely at your service."

"Then—could we possibly make a visit to the river Mersey?"

"We could. To Liverpool?"

"To Liverpool indeed. After that, I am sure that you will be happy to hear our little adventure will be at an end."

"*Boshe moi!*" the Count sighed loudly. "Which means something like 'God bless.' It is what Russians say at moments of great stress—or stress relieved. Come, let us not miss our train."

President Abraham Lincoln was not happy. The cabinet meeting was not only not producing an answer to the country's problems—but it was fast becoming a chaos of contrasting opinions.

"There is a limit beyond which we cannot and will not go," Salmon P. Chase, Secretary of the Treasury, said in a firm and unyielding voice. "During the war, yes, people would put up with high levels of taxation, as well as a certain amount of physical discomfort and sacrifice. But the war is long over and they have come to expect some return for their efforts, some creature comforts. I cannot and will not agree to raising taxes once again."

"I don't think that you have heard me clearly, Mr. Chase," Gideon Welles said with cold fury. "As Secretary of the Navy, it is my assignment to follow the dictates of Congress. In their wisdom, the Congress has ordered an expansion of the navy to follow the world trend. When other countries arm we must follow suit to ensure this country's first line of defense. Naval strength today means ironclads. Now they are bigger, faster, stronger, better armed, and better armored. And all of that costs money. Have I made myself clear?"

Before the infuriated Chase could speak again, Edwin M. Stanton, the Secretary of War, broke in.

"At this point I must remind you all that it costs a million and a half dollars a day to keep two hundred thousand well-trained troops in the field. Like the navy, I have been instructed by Congress to build and maintain that army—"

"Gentlemen, gentlemen," Lincoln said, raising his voice to silence the squabbling, "I feel that we are arguing at cross purposes here. That you all have valid points to make, I do not doubt. But I called this meeting today to seek your advice and joint wisdom in facing up to our current and major problem: The intransigence of the British and their flouting of international relationships on a massive scale against our country. That is the intelligence I now desperately need. I beg of you, abandon your differences and speak only to this point, if you please."

The men seated around the long table fell silent. So silent, in fact, that the hum of a bumblebee could be clearly heard as it flew in through an open window. It thudded angrily against the glass pane before it could find the way to exit. In this silence the low voice of William H. Seward could be plainly heard.

"As Secretary of State, it is my duty to answer the President's request. My department has not been idle. Abroad, ambassadors and civil servants have been attempting to get other countries to join us in protest against the British. In this I am forced to admit failure. Many of the European countries, large enough and strong enough to impress the British with their views, are linked to the British royal family, while smaller countries are left unheard. Regretfully, there is frankly little more that we can do."

"I can but advise your representatives to try harder," Judah P. Benjamin said. After being defeated in the presidential election, he had graciously agreed to return to his cabinet post as Secretary for the South. "Every day I receive more and more complaints from the cotton planters. They cannot depend on the domestic market alone, but must look overseas to ensure their profits. The British seizure of so many cotton ships is driving them to bankruptcy."

There were nods of understanding at this unhappy state. Then, before anyone else could speak, the door opened and John Hay, Secretary to the President, slipped in. He spoke softly to Lincoln, who nodded.

"I understand," he said. "Tarry a moment, John, while I put this to the cabinet. Gentlemen, it has been brought to my attention that the President of Ireland is waiting below with the Irish ambassador. He contacted me last night, soon after his arrival, and requested a meeting. I informed him about this cabinet session and asked him to join us. I hope you will agree that what he has to say is of the utmost importance to you all assembled here."

"It is indeed," Seward said. "We must have him in."

Hay went out and the cabinet waited in silence until he returned. When he came back he ushered in two men in dark morning suits. Their mien echoed the color of their garb, for their faces expressed nothing but unhappiness—bordering on despair.

"President Rossa," John Hay said, and the President nodded. "With him is Ambassador O'Brin."

"This is a great pleasure," Lincoln said. "John, do bring over those chairs. Jeremiah, when I saw you last it was during a time of great difficulty."

"Unhappily, Abraham, the difficulties are still there—and if anything, they have grown, until I fear that my poor country is at the mercy of some biblical plague."

"And I can put a name to that plague," the Irish ambassador said. "I beg you, excuse me for speaking out like that, but the words are forced from my soul. The British—they are the plague that is destroying our poor country."

"They are indeed," Rossa said, nodding agreement. "How fondly I remember those halcyon days when President Lincoln attended my inauguration. What hope was in the air! We had just suffered the agonies of war, but none of us regretted the sacrifice. Ireland was free, free after all those centuries of oppression. You could taste the freedom in the air, hear it in the sound of the church bells. We were at last a single country, from Belfast in the north to Cork in the south. United and free to shape our own destiny."

Rossa looked around at the listening cabinet members, his eyes deep-set and smeared dark with despair.

"How quickly it was all to end. Instead of rebuilding and reuniting Ireland, we are being forced once more to defend her. Our fishermen see their boats burned. Our seaside towns and cities are attacked and pillaged. While Irish men and women—and children!—are seized from their homes in England and imprisoned in the vileness of the concentration camps. What can be done? What can be done?"

"President Rossa—we have been asking ourselves the same question," Seward said. "I feel that my department of state is failing the American people. Despite our efforts at finding a peaceful conclusion, our cotton ships are still being seized at sea."

"Perhaps there is only one answer," Rossa said in a voice laden with despair. "Perhaps there is indeed no peaceful solution. Perhaps we must do again the terrible and the threatening. I see no other possible conclusion, given the facts as we know them." He drew himself up and looked around at the assembled cabinet.

"Perhaps we must do as we did—as you did—before. Call on the British one last time to cease and desist their maraudings. Put the weight of history upon them. Tell them they must stop at once. For if they do not, we will come to but one conclusion. That they have declared war upon us. If that is what they decide—so be it. We are a smaller country and a weaker one. But there is not a single person in our land who will not agree that if we are forced to the decision, the Republic of Ireland will declare war upon Great Britain.

"If we do that, will you, the country of democracy and freedom, join us in this noble endeavor?

"Will you join us in a just war against Great Britain?"

TRAPPED!

The *Aurora* sighted the bar light vessel first as they entered Liverpool Bay. In the early afternoon they continued on through the jumble of tide-ripped water that marked the entrance to the Mersey estuary. A summer storm had been building up all day. Blowing in from the Atlantic, it had grown in strength while it was crossing Ireland, and was now churning up the Irish Sea. Count Korzhenevski and General Sherman were on deck, wearing oilskins to give them some protection from the driving rain. The low-lying shore on both sides of the river was barely visible through the mist and rain.

"Should we drop anchor and wait for the storm to clear?" the Count asked.

"Only if you feel it necessary. I don't want to stay in this area very long. I just want to see the approaches to Liverpool and its relation to the river."

"That will be easy enough to do, rain or no. We have come this far and we are reaching the end of our mission. Yes, let us do it—then leave these waters. I am sure that we will all be immensely relieved once we are done with all this."

"I am in complete agreement. We shall press on."

IN THE ENEMY'S HEARTLAND

The wind abated somewhat when they left the open sea for the shallower waters of the landlocked estuary, but the rain continued to fall relentlessly. Despite this they could easily find their way. The channel was well marked by buoys, and with the incoming tide behind them, the little steam yacht made very good time. They passed smaller fishing boats under full sail, then an immense side-wheel freighter thrashing its way downriver to the sea. By late afternoon the church towers of Liverpool were visible ahead. The *Aurora* swung closer to the riverbank as the first docks loomed up out of the rain. In the lounge belowdecks, driven there by the rain, Commander Wilson sketched the shoreline as best he could, looking out through a porthole and muttering imprecations at the filthy weather.

The river was narrowing and the little ship stayed in the channel in the center, letting the incoming tide carry them upstream.

"I think that dock we passed back there appears to be the final one," Sherman said.

"I am sure of it. Any vessel with a draft deeper than ours would be grounding itself about now."

"Good. I think that we have seen enough—and I don't want to place our faithful vessel in any more danger. We can go back if you wish to."

"Wish to! I yearn to." The Count shouted orders up to the bridge and the bow began to swing about. Despite having to breast the incoming tide, they went downriver at a steady pace. They were making good progress when Sherman and the Count went below. As they shook themselves out of their oilskins, the Count called out to the steward, who, moments later, came in with glasses and a bottle of cognac on a tray. The Count poured, then handed one brimming glass to the general.

"Shall we drink to a mission successfully accomplished?"

"A noble idea. Then we can change into some dry clothing."

The deck door opened to admit a spray of rain, and the deck officer, Lieutenant Chikhachev, pushed in. He said something in rapid Russian and the Count cursed out loud and began to pull his oilskins on.

"There is a large ship ahead, coming upstream toward us," he said.

"We've seen others," Sherman said.

"But none like this. It has guns. It is a ship of war."

Sherman dressed hurriedly and joined him on deck. The rain was ceasing and the ironclad could be clearly seen coming upstream toward Liverpool. The two-gun turret in the bow was pointed ominously in their direction.

The Count called out a command in Russian. "I ordered us closer to the shore," he said, translating. "I want to give them as much room as possible."

"I'm sure it is just a chance meeting," Sherman said.

As he finished speaking, the gun turret slowly swung in their direction, and for the first time they could see the ship's name clearly.

"*Defender!*" Sherman said. "Wasn't that the name of the ship in Plymouth—the one that the officer in the train said he was stationed on?"

The Count had no time to answer him—but his shouted commands were answer enough. Clouds of smoke poured from the yacht's funnel as the engine raced up to full speed. At the same time they heeled sharply as they came about in the tightest turn possible. Then their stern was to the battleship and they were at full steam back up the river.

"It was that damnable little swine, Archie Fowler," Korzhenevski growled out angrily. "We should have killed him when we were alone with him on the train."

"I am afraid I do not understand why."

"In hindsight it is all too transparently clear. After leaving us, he returned to his ship—where he bragged about meeting me. You could tell that he is a great snob. Someone there was at the dinner in Greenwich—or had heard about it. Whatever it was, we know that the British have no love for the Russians and would certainly resent our snooping around their shores. Once their suspicions were aroused, the *Aurora* would certainly have been easy enough to follow, since we have made no secret of our presence in these waters—"

He broke off as one of the guns in the forward turret of the ironclad fired. An instant later a great tower of water sprang up off their starboard bow. Then the second gun fired and a shell hit the water to port.

"Bracketed!" Sherman called out. "I'm glad they have no third gun."

The distance between the two ships grew larger, since the smaller vessel had reached its top speed more quickly. But *Defender*'s engines were soon turning over at their maximum, and while she did not gain on them, she did not fall farther astern.

"They've stopped firing," Sherman said.

"They don't have to shoot. There is no way we can escape them. We are in a bottle and they are the cork."

"What can we do?"

"Very little for the moment other than stay ahead of them." The Count looked up at the darkening sky and the driving rain. "The tide will turn in about an hour; that will be high water."

"And then . . ."

"We will be in the hands of the gods," the Count said with dark Russian fatalism.

They plowed upriver, with their black iron nemesis steaming up steadily behind them. Liverpool swam out of the rain to port and moved swiftly by. Then they passed the last dock and the river narrowed.

"They're slowing, dropping back!" Sherman called out.

"They must—they can't risk running aground. And they know well enough that they have us in a trap."

HMS *Defender* surged to a stop in the river. They watched her grow smaller until a bend in the Mersey cut her off from sight.

"Do we stop, too?" Sherman asked.

"No. We keep going. They might send boats after us. They could also contact the shore, have the army come trap us. And this *is* a trap." The Count looked up at the sky, then at his watch. "It won't be dark for hours yet. Damn these long summer nights." He hammered his fist angrily on the rail. "We must do something, not just stand and shiver like a rabbit in a snare." He looked down at the muddy river water, then at his watch again. "We'll wait until the tide turns, no longer than that. It won't be too long now. Then we will act."

"What can we do?"

The Count smiled widely, almost baring his teeth. "Why then, my dear general, we head downstream at top speed. That, and the outgoing tide, will mean that we will be exposed to their gunfire for the smallest amount of time. Hopefully we can get by the enemy ship and show her our tail. After that we must trust only to chance and, hopefully, we will have an inordinate amount of luck! If you are a religious man, you might pray for divine intercession. God knows we could use it."

The *Aurora* continued slowly upriver until the Count became concerned about the Mersey's depth; they dropped anchor.

By this time Fox and Wilson were on deck as well, ignoring the rain, and Sherman explained what was happening. Little was said—little could be said. They were safe for the moment. The Count went to the bow and stood, staring down at the river, looking at the debris floating by.

"It will be some time before the tide changes. Let us get out of the rain and into some dry clothes."

In his cabin General Sherman pulled off his clothing and toweled himself dry. He dressed again, scarcely aware of what he was doing because he was deep in thought. This was a dangerous situation. When he rejoined the others in the main cabin, the Count was just doling out what appeared to be water tumblers of brandy. Sherman accepted one and sipped at it.

"I suppose that there is nothing we can do, other than wait for the tide to turn."

"Nothing," the Count said grimly, draining half of his glass. "If anyone, other than myself, could pass as an Englishman, I would put him ashore with all the maps and charts and have him take them to a neutral country. But there is no one—and I cannot bring myself to desert my ship."

"Should we destroy the charts?" Sherman asked.

The Count shook his head. "I think not. If the ship goes down—they go down with her. And if we do succeed in escaping—why, they will make all of our trials worth the while." He finished his glass and put it down; the strong spirits did not seem to affect him in any way.

"Is the game worth the candle?" Wilson asked, depressed.

"It is!" Fox said, most firmly. "When this information is brought home, it will be beyond price—that I can assure you. Modern warfare has come to depend on military intelligence. Modern armies don't just move forward until they meet the enemy, then do battle. Such tactics went out with Napoleon. General Sherman will tell you. The telegraph brings swift information to the general in the field. Trains bring the munitions and materials for support. Without informed intelligence the warring army is blind."

"Mr. Fox is correct," the Count said. "The game, my dear Wilson, *is* worth the candle." He glanced up at the clock mounted on the bulkhead. "The tide should be turning soon."

Unhappy at staying below, the Americans followed him up on deck. The rain had settled down to a steady drizzle. The Count walked to the rail and looked down at the river. Most of the drifting debris was just bobbing about now. Then, ever so slowly, a change began to take place. Instead of staying still, the leaves and branches began to drift downstream, faster and faster. The Count nodded with satisfaction and called an order out to the bridge. The anchor was raised and the engine came to life; the propeller began to turn.

"Gentleman, the die is cast. Only fate knows what will happen to us now."

Smoke poured out the funnel as they worked up speed, moving so fast that the ship heeled over when they went around the first bend in the river. Faster and faster *Aurora* raced downstream toward her destiny.

Around the next bend they surged . . .

And there was *Defender* blocking the reach before them.

A CONVOY IN DANGER

"**I**'m sorry, Captain, but they are not answering my signals."

A number of abrasive answers sprang to mind, but Captain Raphael Semmes controlled his tongue and just nodded. This shambles of a convoy could not be blamed on the signalman. Ever since they had left Mobile Bay, it had been one damned thing after another. Signaling was probably the worst part of the difficulty; the cotton ships misread his signals or ignored them. Or they asked them to be repeated over and over again. Not that their assignments were that complex. He simply wanted them to stay together, and not stray or fall behind.

And every dawn it was the same—they were all over the Atlantic, some even hull down on the horizon. So he had to round them up yet once again, signaling with angry hoots on USS *Virginia*'s steam whistle to get their attention. Herding them back into their stations, like a shepherd with wayward, stupid sheep.

And there was *Dixie Belle* again, the eternal miscreant. Fallen behind and ignoring all of his attempts at communication. The worst part was that she was a steamship, the only one in the five-ship convoy. A powered vessel that should be relied upon to keep position. While the white-sailed cotton clippers rode easily before the westerly wind, day after day the steamship kept falling behind. His biggest concern was always *Dixie Belle*.

"Hard aport, slow ahead," he ordered the helmsman. "We're going after her."

Virginia's wake cut a wide swath in the sea as she turned in her tracks and headed back toward the errant ship. This was a bad place for the convoy to start coming apart. The French coast was less than a hundred miles ahead—making this the hunting ground of the British war craft. They had seized too many American cotton ships here, which had necessitated the need for guarded convoys. Which were only as strong as their weakest link. His ironclad warship could offer protection only if the convoy stayed together.

Virginia turned again, this time to match the other ship's course, slowed to stay abreast of her. Semmes raised the megaphone as they closed to within hailing distance—and strongly resisted the temptation to execrate the captain for ignoring his signals; this would be but wasted energy.

"Why have you slowed down?" he called out instead. He had to repeat his words when the other captain finally appeared on deck.

"A shaft bearing running hot. I'm going to have to stop the engine to replace it."

Why was it running hot? Because of the lazy incompetence of an oiler, that was why. It took all Semmes's strength of will not to curse the captain out for his crew's slackness; this would avail nothing.

"How long will repairs take?"

He could see a consultation on deck, then the other man raised his megaphone again. "Two, mebbe three hours."

"Get on with it then."

Captain Semmes hurled the megaphone down on the deck, cursing like a trooper. The helmsman and the signalman exchanged wary nods of agreement behind the captain's back. They all felt as he did—nothing but contempt for the merchantmen they convoyed. Better a swift passage—or even a battle at sea; anything but this.

Semmes was in a quandary. Should he take his other four charges into port and leave the miserable *Dixie Belle* to her fate? It was very tempting. The thought of her being snapped up by a British man-of-war was indeed attractive. But that was not his role. His assignment was to protect them all. But if the other ships stopped to wait for the errant vessel, there would be endless complaints over lost time at sea, late arrival at port, possibly an investigation.

Yet he had no other recourse. As they caught up with his charges again, he spoke to the signalman.

"Send the signal to heave to."

Of course it did not happen at once. There were some angry queries; others completely ignored him. He sent the signal again, then swept down on them at full speed, cutting under their bows; that got their attention. One of them still hadn't stopped, the *Biloxi*; her captain was the most recalcitrant of the lot. *Virginia* went in pursuit, the whistle screeching. Semmes had only a quick glimpse back at the *Dixie Belle*, now some miles away.

The captain of the *Biloxi* did not want to heave to and was eager to go on by himself. Semmes, who quickly tired of the shouted exchange between their ships, sent an order to the bow turret to put an explosive shell into the sea ahead of the cotton ship. As always, this worked wonders and he saw her sails flap loosely as she went about.

"Captain," the lookout called down. "Smoke on the horizon, off the port bow."

"Damnation!" Semmes swore, raising his glasses. Yes, there it was, moving in the direction of the stranded *Dixie Belle*. "Full ahead," he ordered as they started back toward the stopped ship.

The two steamships were on closing courses and rapidly approaching each other, their towering plumes of smoke marking their speed. The other was hull up now, a black hull—and yes, those were gun turrets. British surely, no warship of any other country would be prowling about out here.

It was a closely run thing. *Virginia* curved between *Dixie Belle* and the other ship, stopped engines.

"She's flying the white ensign, sir," the lookout called down.

"She is indeed," Semmes said, smiling happily. Ships at sea, antagonists at sea. This was the life he relished—that he really enjoyed. During the war, when he had carried cotton from the South to England, he was happy for every moment of every voyage. He had been much pursued when running the blockade with cotton cargoes but never caught.

"Now let us see what you are going to do, my fine English friend. This is not another chance to bully an unarmed merchantman. You are up against the pride of the American navy. Go ahead. Get off a shell. Give me some excuse to blast you out of the water."

The turrets on the other warship were turning his way. Semmes was still smiling. But it was the cold grimace of a man ready for anything.

North of the antagonistic ironclads, close to where the river Mersey joined the Irish Sea, a confrontation of a totally different kind was taking place. This was no battle of the giants, but it might appear to an onlooker that the smaller ship was attacking the larger. *Aurora* came around the bend in the river with her engine turning at top revolutions. The sweating, soot-smeared stokers sent shovelful after shovelful of coal into the furnace. Lieutenant Simenov in the engine room looked at the pressure gauge—then quickly away. It was moving steadily toward the red; he had never had the pressure this high before. Yet the Count had asked for maximum speed—and that is what he would get.

On the bridge Korzhenevski was just as cool as a naval officer should be. "Look," he said. "Her bow is still pointing upstream. She will have to turn to follow us."

"If we get by her," Sherman said grimly. "Won't her guns bear on us as we go past?"

"They will if I make a mistake," the Count said. Then he spoke into the communication tube to the engine room in Russian. "Half speed," he said.

Sherman's eyes widened at this, but he said nothing. He depended on the Russian's professionalism now. Korzhenevski took a quick glance at him and smiled.

"I'm not mad, General, not quite yet. I'm watching her bows, waiting for them to turn—yes, there they go. Hold the speed. She's turning to starboard, so we'll pass her on that flank." He snapped a command in Russian to the helmsman. "We'll stay as close to her bow as we can. That way she won't be able to depress her forward guns to reach us—and the rest of them will not bear until we are past."

It was a difficult maneuver, and had to be conducted with extreme precision. Too slow, or too fast, and the guns would be able to fire on them.

"Now—full speed!"

HMS *Defender*'s length was almost the same as the width of the river at this point. Her bow was in danger of striking the bank. *Aurora* had to get through the rapidly closing gap. The foam roiled from *Defender*'s propeller as she went hard astern. The Count laughed happily.

"Her captain is not thinking fast enough for this emergency. He should have let her touch the bank, plugged up our escape hole. If he had done that, his ship would suffer no grave injury—but we certainly would if we had hit her ironclad bow—there!—we are through. Top speed now."

The little yacht surged downstream. The British battleship was now almost halted across the river. She was starting to turn again, but very slowly. *Aurora* hurtled on—and into sight of the warship's guns.

One after another, as they came to bear, they fired. Columns of water rose up before her and well beyond her.

"They can't depress the guns low enough to hit us yet. They should have waited. Now they must reload."

The Count was jubilant; Sherman cold as ever under fire. Smoke roiled up from *Aurora*'s stack as they tore down the river at top speed. The guns began to fire again, but their aim was wildly erratic with the opening distance and the ship turning at the same time.

There was a sudden tremendous explosion in the rear of the cabin deck, fire and smoke. Someone screamed over and over. Luck could take them just so far.

"I'll take care of that," Sherman said, moving swiftly toward the stairway.

The shell had hit the rear of the main cabin, tearing a great hole in the wall. One of the stewards was lying on the floor, soaked in blood, still screaming. Fox was bent over him with the tablecloth he had torn from the endboard, trying to bind up the man's wounds. A crewman appeared with a bucket of water and threw it on the smoldering fire. Through the opening in the wall more explosions were visible in the river.

Then the shelling stopped.

The Count appeared, took in the scene with a single glance. "There has been no major damage to the hull. Poor Dimitri is our only casualty. And we are past a bend in the river. *Defender* will be after us soon, and it will then be a stern chase. I think that we are faster than her. *Aurora* was built for speed, while our pursuer was built for battle. It is for fate to decide now."

Fox stood, shaking his head unhappily. "I'm afraid that he is dead."

The Count crossed himself in the Russian Orthodox way. "A tragedy to die so far from Russia. He was a good man—and he died in a good cause." He called out orders in Russian. "I'll be on deck while this is cleaned up. Then we must wait. In the end we shall drink cognac to a successful voyage—or we will be prisoners of the British."

"What are the odds?" Sherman asked.

"Very good—if we can outrun our pursuer. If we can do that, why, then it is straight across the sea to Ireland."

They stood, side by side on the bridge, looking back at their mighty pursuer through the sheets of driving rain. Ahead of them the sky was getting darker.

"Are we faster than she is?" Sherman asked.

"I do believe that we are."

As sunset approached and the distance between them grew, the captain of HMS *Defender* reluctantly took a gamble. The ship's silhouette suddenly lengthened as she turned her bows so her length faced them. The guns fired as soon as they could bear. Once again *Aurora* suffered a bombardment, but none of the shells fell close.

The ship was a small target and constantly moving, changing course, elusive. The rain was heavy, night was falling, and soon after this last broadside *Aurora* was invisible to their pursuer.

"And now the cognac!" Korzhenevski shouted aloud, laughing and slapping Sherman on the back, then seizing his hand and pumping it enthusiastically. Sherman only smiled, understanding the Russian's happiness.

They had gotten away with it.

A DISASTROUS ENCOUNTER

The approaching British ironclad slowed her engines and her bow wave died away. Captain Semmes looked at her coldly as she drew closer to the USS *Virginia*. There was her name, spelled out in large white letters, DEVASTATION. Maybe, just maybe, the British captain would decide on aggression. Would that he did. Semmes knew that his ship was the match for any in the world, with three steam-powered turrets, each of them mounting two breech-loading guns. While the enemy outgunned him, he doubted very much that she outclassed him. Her muzzle loaders had a much slower rate of fire than his own guns.

He recognized her type; one of the newly built *Warrior*-class ironclads. She had all the strengths of the original—twenty-six sixty-eight-pounders and ten hundred-pounders—and could unleash a terrible broadside. Also, according to the intelligence reports that he had seen, the builders had overcome *Warrior*'s weaknesses by armoring her stern, then eliminating the masts and sails. Semmes was not impressed, even by these changes. The greatest naval engineer in the world, John Ericsson, had designed every inch of his ship, and she was the most advanced ever known to man.

A signalman appeared on the other ship's bridge.

"They're sending a message, Captain," his signalman said. "It reads—"

"Belay that," Semmes snapped. "I have no desire to communicate with that ship. We will remain here on station until she leaves."

Devastation's captain was infuriated.

"Doesn't she read our signals? Send the message again. We are well within our rights to inspect the manifests of a vessel suspected of breaking international law. Damme, still no response—yet I can see them on the bridge there, brazenly staring at us. Bos'un, fire off the saluting cannon. That should draw their attention."

The little gun was quickly loaded, powder and no shot, and went off with a cracking bang.

Aboard *Virginia*, Captain Semmes was just sending a signal to *Dixie Belle* inquiring as to her repairs when he heard the explosion. He spun about and saw the puff of white smoke just below the other ship's bridge.

"Was that a shot?"

"Yes, sir. Sounded like a saluting cannon."

Semmes stood, frozen for a long moment, while the smoke thinned and dispersed. He had a decision to make, a decision that might end these frustrating months of convoy duty.

"Bos'un—was there a cannon fired aboard the British ship?"

"Aye, sir. But I think—"

"Do not think. Answer me. You saw the smoke, heard the sound of a cannon being fired aboard that British ship?"

"Aye, aye, sir."

"Good. We will return fire. I want the gunners to aim for her upper works."

The six guns fired almost as one. The hail of steel fragments swept the other ship's decks clear, wrecked both her funnels, blew away her bridge and officers, steersman, everyone. The surprise was complete, the destruction total. No order was given to fire aboard the battered ship, and the guncrews, trained to obey orders and not to think, did nothing.

Semmes knew all about the ship he had just engaged. He knew that all of her guns were in a heavily armored citadel, an iron box that was separate from the rest of the ship. They pointed to port and starboard—and only a single hundred-pound pivot gun that was on her stern deck pointed aft.

A DISASTROUS ENCOUNTER

Virginia crossed *Devastation*'s stern, and all of her guns, firing over and over, pounded this single target.

No ship, no matter how well built and heavily armored, could survive this kind of punishment. The pivot gun got off one shot, which bounced from *Virginia*'s armor before being dismounted and destroyed. Shell after shell exploded inside the ironclad's hull, gutting her, blowing gaping holes in the outer armor. Igniting a store of powder.

The ripping explosion blew most of the ship's stern away, and the ocean rushed in. With the ship deprived of her buoyancy, the bow rose in the air. There were more explosions deep in the hull and immense clouds of vapor as the boilers were flooded. The bow was higher now, pointing to the zenith. Then, with immense burbling and retching, the ironclad sank down into the ocean and vanished from sight. Nothing but wreckage remained to mark the spot.

"Lower the boat," Semmes ordered. "Pick up any survivors." He had to repeat the order, shouting it this time, before the stunned sailors sprang into action.

Out of a crew of over six hundred, there were three survivors. One of them was so badly wounded he died even before they could bring him aboard. It was a resounding victory for American sea power.

And HMS *Devastation* had fired the gun that started the conflict. Captain Semmes had many witnesses to that fact. Not that there would be any real questions asked; the affair was a fait accompli. The act was finished.

There was no going back now. The deed was done.

Once the *Aurora* was out of Liverpool Bay, safe in the darkness and the open and rainswept Irish Sea, she slowed to a less strenuous pace and eased the reckless pressure in her boilers. There were extra lookouts posted, on the off chance that their pursuer might still be after them, while the sailors cleared away the wreckage and covered with a tarpaulin the hole that had been blasted into the cabin. Once this was done, they settled down for a late dinner with, as always, copious quantities of the Count's vintage champagne. Because the galley fires were still out, it was a cold meal of caviar and pickled herring; there were no complaints.

"How did they find us?" Wilson said, sipping gratefully at the champagne. "That is what I don't understand."

"My fault completely," Korzhenevski admitted. "After that little contretemps in Greenwich, I should have been more on my guard. Once suspicion was aroused, they would have easily traced us to Penzance. Plenty of people there saw us cruise north from there. I was equally foolish when we stopped for fresh supplies in Anglesey. I bought maps of the estuary here, and of the bay, in the chandler's. Once they knew that, they knew where to find us. The rest, as they say, is history."

"Which is written by the victors," General Sherman said, holding up his glass. "And a toast to the Count, the victor. Whatever crimes of omission you think you have committed in leading the British to us, you have well vindicated yourself by what to me, a mere landsman, appeared to be an incredibly skilled bit of boat handling."

"Hear, hear," Fox said, raising his glass as well.

"Gentlemen, I thank you." The Count smiled and settled back in the chair with a sigh.

"What is next?" Sherman asked.

"Ireland. We are now on a northwest heading to stay clear of Anglesey and the Welsh coast. In a few hours we head due west for Ireland and

Dublin Harbor. We will arrive around daybreak. And then—what happens next is up to you, General. My part of our interesting tour of exploration is finished. I will have *Aurora* repaired in Ireland, then will sail north to Russia, since these waters are no longer as friendly as they once were."

"I'm sorry about that," Sherman said. "About the end of your friendship with the English—"

"Please don't be! Ever since the Crimean War, my friendship has been nothing but a sham. In a way I am glad that the playacting is over. They are now as much my enemy as they are yours." His face grew grim. "Will there be war?"

"That I do not know," Sherman said. "All I know is that if war does come, we will be prepared for it. With all thanks due to you."

"It was all worth doing if you obtained the military intelligence that you needed."

"I did indeed."

"Good. Then—a single favor. If there are hostilities, would you recommend me for a post in your navy?"

"With all my heart—"

"And I as well!" Commander Wilson cried loudly. "I know that if you were my commander I would be proud to serve under you, anytime, sir."

"I am most grateful . . ."

Only Fox demurred. "I'll be sorry to lose you."

"I understand. But I have had enough of stealth, of creeping about in the darkness. I will see that you will still have all of the assistance that we can possibly supply. When next I go to war I hope that it will be aboard one of your magnificent fighting ships. That is what I want very much to do."

"You must tell us how to contact you," Sherman said. "With a little luck we'll be out of Ireland without setting a foot on dry land. After the British raids there is always an American navy ship or two stationed in Dublin. That will be our transportation."

"A cable to the Russian Navy Department will quickly reach me. Now—I wish you Godspeed."

The rain had cleared away during the night and the wet rooftops of Dublin glinted golden in the rising sun as they passed the Pigeon Coop lighthouse and entered the Liffey.

"There is an ironclad tied up by the customs house," Korzhenevski said, peering through his binoculars.

"May I look, sir, I beg of you!" Wilson said with obvious excitement. He raised the glasses and took only the briefest of glances. "Yes, indeed, I thought so. It is my ship, the *Dictator*. A good omen indeed."

Sherman nodded. "You are indeed right, Commander. The best of omens. President Lincoln, when we parted, insisted that I report to him as soon as our mission had been accomplished. I think that your commanding officer will go along with a command from his commander in chief and provide me the needed transportation."

They bade their farewells to the Count and boarded the ship's boat; their luggage had already been stowed aboard. They waved good-bye to the Count and the little ship. At a shouted command all of the sailors aboard her snapped to attention and saluted.

"I shall miss her," Wilson said. "She's a grand, stouthearted little vessel."

"With a fine captain," Sherman said. "We owe a great debt to the Count."

When they boarded the *Dictator*, they discovered that she was preparing to go to sea. In the wardroom Captain Toliver himself told them why.

"Of course you would not have heard—I've just been informed myself. *Virginia* stopped at Cork on the way home. Telegraphed me here. She has been in battle. Apparently she was attacked by a British ironclad."

"What happened?" Sherman asked, his words loud in the shocked silence.

"Sunk her, of course. Only proper thing to do."

"Then it means . . ."

"It means the President and the government must decide what must be done next," Sherman said.

Captain Toliver nodded agreement. "There will be new orders for all of us. I hope that you will sail with us, General; you as well, Mr. Fox. I am sure that Washington will have assignments for us all."

To say that the British were perturbed by the sinking would be the most masterful of understatements. The ha'penny newspapers frothed; the *Thunderer* thundered. Parliament was all for declaring war on the spot. The Prime Minister, Lord Palmerston, was summoned by the Queen. It was an exhausting two hours that he passed in her presence. Lord John Russell waited patiently at Number 10 for his return. Looked up from his papers when there was first a rattling at the door, and then it was pushed wide. One of the porters stepped in, then opened the door as far as it would go. A bandage-wrapped foot came through first, gingerly followed by the rest of Lord Palmerston, seated in a bath chair that was pushed by a second porter. A moment's inattention caused a wheel of the chair to brush against the man who was holding the door open. Palmerston gasped out loud and lashed out with his gold-headed stick. But it was a feeble blow and the porter merely cringed away. Russell put down the sheaf of papers that he had been studying and rose to his feet.

"I have read through all of the armament proposals," he said. "They all seem most sensible and very much in order."

"They should be. I drew them up myself."

Palmerston grunted with the effort as he pulled himself out of the bath chair and dropped into the armchair behind his massive desk, then waved a dismissing hand at the porters. He took a kerchief from his sleeve and mopped his face and did not speak again until the door had closed and they were alone.

"Her Majesty was unconscionably unreasonable today. Thinks we should go to war by tomorrow morning at the very latest. Silly woman. I talked of preparations, organization, mustering of troops until I was blue in the face. In the end I just outlasted her. She summoned her ladies-in-waiting and swept out."

Palmerston spoke in a thin voice, very different from his normal assertive self. Lord Russell was worried, but knew enough not to speak his reservations aloud. After all, Palmerston was in his eighties, tormented by gout—in addition to all the usual ailments of old age.

"She has been like that very much of late," Russell said.

"The German strain has always had its weaknesses—not to say madness. But of late I despair of obtaining any cooperation or reasonable response from her. Yes, she despises the Yankees and wishes to exact a high price from them for their perfidy. As do we all. But when I urge upon her approval of one action or another, she simply flies into one of her tempers."

"We must take her wishes as our command and act accordingly," Russell said with the utmost diplomacy. He did not add that the irascible Prime Minister was no stranger himself to bullheadedness and irrational fits of temper. "The yeomanry are being assembled for active duty, as is required in any national emergency. Orders have gone out to India and the antipodes for regiments to be transferred here as soon as is possible. For almost two years now the shipyards on the Clyde and the Tyne have been building the finest ironclad vessels ever conceived by the genius of our engineers. There is little else that can be done to prepare for any emergency. While on the diplomatic front our ambassadors press on indefatigably to wrest every advantage from the Americans—"

"All this I know," Palmerston said testily, dismissing any argument with a wave of his hand. "Preparations, yes, we have enough of that. But preparation for what? Is there any overall strategy to unite all this and the nation into a cohesive whole? If there is, I see it not. Certainly the Queen cannot provide us with any aid or succor in this matter."

"But the Duke of Cambridge, commander of the armies, can certainly be relied upon to—"

"To do what? Vacillate? Get drunk? Spend his time with one of his ladies? No salvation there. He has some good men on his staff, but he overrides them more often than not."

"Then, unhappily, the burden is still yours."

"It is indeed." Palmerston nodded weary agreement. "But the years begin to show. I should have put myself out to pasture long before this. But there is always one more crisis, one more decision to make—with no end in sight."

He had slumped deeper in his chair as he spoke. His face, despite the fullness of his jowls, was slack and pendulous, his skin an unsightly gray. Russell had never seen him look this ill in all their years of association, was about to remark upon it but held his comment for now. He temporized instead.

"You have worked too hard of late, taken too much upon yourself. Perhaps a spell in the country, a good rest—"

"Cannot be considered," Lord Palmerston said fiercely. "The country is going to hell in a handbasket, and I shall not be one to hurry it on its way. There is too much to be done, too much . . ."

Yet even as he spoke these words, his voice died away, ending in a wordless mumble. Russell looked on horrified as his eyes rolled up in his head and he fell forward in a slump, his head dropping onto the desk with a resounding thud. Russell jumped to his feet, his chair crashing to the floor, but even as he hurried forward, Palmerston dropped heavily onto the carpet and slid from sight.

COMMAND DECISION

General Sherman had met President Lincoln at the White House. From there they strolled over to the War Office together. They talked a little about the hot weather that had seized the city in a relentless grip for almost two weeks now. Then Sherman inquired about Mrs. Lincoln's health, which was improving. Lincoln reported that everyone was pleased that General Grant's wounded arm had healed so well. They talked about everything except the matter that was of the greatest concern to them. But Gus Fox had been adamant about this; no discussions about the details of the trip aboard *Aurora* unless it was in Room 313. Which was where they were headed now.

The two guards snapped to attention when they came down the corridor.

Sherman returned the salute, then rapped on the door. Fox unlocked it from the inside and stepped aside so they could enter. He locked the door behind them, then crossed over the small anteroom and unlocked the other, inner room. Once inside, they discovered that the windows were all closed and sealed and it was stifling hot.

"Just a moment," Fox said, quickly throwing wide the curtains and opening both of the windows. Thick bars prevented any access from outside, but at least the air could circulate now. Lincoln took out his kerchief and patted his face and neck dry, then dropped into an armchair, letting his long legs dangle over one arm.

"Am I at last to discover the facts about your mysterious mission?"

"You are," Sherman said. "It was dangerous, perhaps foolhardy, but since it was very successful, I imagine that the risks were justified. I suggest that you tell the President about our Russian friend, Gus."

"I will do just that. It all began while we were all still in Brussels; that was when we met a Count Korzhenevski, someone very high up their navy—and in their military intelligence as well. I can vouch for his authenticity because I have had contacts with his organization in the past. He speaks perfect English and was educated in England, and actually attended Greenwich Naval College. However, since the Crimean War, he has grown to detest the British who invaded his country. Knowing about our difficulties with Britain, he saw our two countries as natural allies. That was when he made a very generous offer, when he told us that he would like to put his yacht at our disposal. To take us wherever we wished to go."

"Very nice of the Count." Lincoln smiled. "You should have asked him to take you to England."

"That is just where we went."

The President was rarely caught out—but he was this time. He looked from one to the other of them with bewilderment.

"Do you mean that? You—went *there*?"

"Indeed we did," Fox said. "In the guise of Russian officers."

"I've heard some tall stories in my time, but this beats the pants off any of them. Pray tell me, in greatest detail, about where you went and just what you did."

Sherman sat back and listened in silence while Gus outlined the various aspects of their precarious journey. For the moment the President did not appear to be interested in what they had discovered, but rather in all the surprises and close escapes in their exploration of the English mainland.

Gus finished, ". . . we sailed all that night and reached Dublin in the morning. That is when we heard about the naval engagement between the two ironclads. Of course we had to return here, so that was the end of our little voyage of exploration."

Lincoln leaned back with a heavy sigh—then slapped his knee with enthusiasm. "If I had heard this story from anyone else, Gus, anyone other than you, why, I would say he got the liar of the year—no, of the century!—award. You were right not to have informed me of your plans before you left. I would have vetoed them instantly. But now that you have returned, about all I can say is—well done!"

"Thank you, Mr. President," Sherman said. "In hindsight our little voyage of exploration does appear a mite foolhardy. But we got away with it. We have studied the English ports, cities, and countryside. And we have taken the measure of their defensive ability. It was intelligence hard gained—unhappily at the price of a man's life. One of the Russian sailors was killed when the ironclad fired on us. But the trip was well worth doing, I assure you."

"And your conclusions?"

"Militarily we know a great deal more about the British defenses than ever we did before. What is to be done with that knowledge of course depends upon the state of international affairs. The newspapers are all in a frazzle and contain more rumor than news. Before I go on, I would like to hear about the official reactions of the British to the loss of their ship."

The lines of worry were deep cut between Lincoln's eyes again. He had forgotten his troubles while listening to the tale of their daring adventures. Now memory flooded back.

"They are livid, intransigent, calling their men to arms, preparing their country for war. They demand immediate payment of ten million pounds' compensation for the loss of their ironclad."

"Can war be avoided?" Sherman asked.

"If we pay them the millions that they ask for, and stop shipping our cotton to world markets, also permit their men-of-war to arrest and search all of our ships at sea, and more. They have endless demands and bristle with threats. The situation is very tense."

"How did the naval engagement come about?"

"I doubt if we will ever know. Captain Semmes says that his ship was fired upon. His officers and men all agree with him. That is what they say, and I sincerely doubt that they are lying to us. It still remains a mystery why the British vessel opened fire. The two English survivors knew nothing, other than the fact that there was gunfire and explosions and they were blown into the water. Neither of them appeared to be too bright, according to their interrogators. Apparently they worked in the ship's galley and were on deck dumping rubbish—which is what saved them. Of course, after they were sent back home, they changed their stories—or they were changed for them—and *Virginia* is now supposed to have fired in an unprovoked attack. But this matters little. The original cause has been forgotten in the cloud of political invective."

"Will it be war?" Gus asked, almost in a whisper.

Lincoln sagged back deep into the chair and shook his head with a most woeful expression upon his face.

"I do not know, I cannot tell you . . . I just have no idea where all this will end."

"If war comes," Sherman said with icy resolution, "we will be prepared for it. And I also know now how it can be won."

They both looked at him, waiting for him to continue. His face was set and he was looking out of the window, not seeing the hot and brassy sky—rather, another land far across the ocean.

"There are many ways to attack a country like that and I am completely sure that I know how it can be successfully done. But first, *what* we must do is far more important than how we do it. To begin with, unless we want to be immersed in a long, protracted, and murderous war, we must be prepared to fight the new kind of lightning warfare, just as we did in the battle for Ireland. In order to succeed we must first assess the enemy's strengths—and weaknesses—in every detail. This, along with war preparations, will take some months at least. So I would say that we will be prepared for any venture by spring at the earliest. Can we buy that time?"

Lincoln nodded slowly. "A politician can always buy time; that is the one thing we are good at—that, and wasting time. The negotiations will plow ahead. We will make some concessions, then let them think that there are more are on the way. King Leopold of Belgium has offered us neutral ground on which to discus our differences. We shall avail ourselves of his offer and set in motion the ponderous machinery of international negotiations yet another time."

"Is there any possibility that they may strike before we are prepared?" Gus said worriedly. Sherman considered the question.

"It is not that easy to launch an attack across an ocean. Surely your intelligence sources will keep you informed of all preparations?"

Gus shook his head. "Our informants in Great Britain were all Irish—and are all now seized or in hiding. But I had many discussions with Count Korzhenevski, and he will be happy to supply us with intelligence from his network there. We are now in the process of arranging a working relationship."

"I must be informed of all developments," Sherman said.

"You will be. You as well, Mr. President."

Sherman returned to the War Department and wrote a number of telegraph orders. It took only a day to make the necessary arrangements. When they were done he sent for Ulysses S. Grant.

"General Grant, sir," the captain said, opening the door and standing aside.

"Why, you are sure a sight for sore eyes," General Sherman said, standing and coming around his desk, smiling with obvious pleasure. He started to raise his hand—then dropped it. "How is the arm?"

"Well healed, thank you, Cumph." Grant proved this by seizing Sherman's hand and shaking it strongly. Then he looked down at the drawings spread over the desktop and nodded. "I sent these over because I was sure that they would interest you as much as they did me."

"More than just interest; this mobile gun position is the answer to an unspoken prayer. Of late, my thoughts have been turned to the possibilities of lightning attacks and expeditious victories. This invention of Parrott and Ericsson fits in with all that I plan to do."

"Do we plan to go to war?" Grant asked, his face suddenly hard and grim.

"A soldier must always be ready for war. If not now, I think that we will be facing the prospect of battle by spring. But please, do sit down." Sherman seated himself and tapped the drawings. "I need this infernal machine. The British talk of war and are at their most bellicose. It is a possibility that we must consider strongly. That is why I have invited engineer Ericsson to join us this morning." He took out his watch and looked at it.

"He will be here at any time now. Before he comes, I must tell you about a little scouting trip I have just finished to the English shore."

"You didn't!" Grant sat back in his chair and laughed out loud. "I swear—you have more brass than an entire band."

"It was indeed an interesting time. But other than the men who went with me, only you and the President know of the visit—and we must keep it that way. It was a most fruitful exploration, for what I did discover was just how that country could be successfully invaded."

"Now you do have my complete attention."

Sherman outlined roughly what he planned to do, including what would be Grant's vital contribution to a successful invasion. When Ericsson was announced they put away the papers and maps that they had worked on and turned their attention back to the plans for the mobile battery.

"I have many things to do and do not enjoy wasting time on trips to the city of Washington," Ericsson said testily as he was shown in.

"A pleasure to see you again," Sherman said, ignoring the engineer's outburst. "You of course know General Grant."

Ericsson nodded curtly. Then, "Why was I summoned here?"

"Well, for one thing," Sherman said, opening a drawer in the desk, "I understand that the navy has been slow in paying you for the new ironclads that are now under construction."

"Always late! I have a large workforce, and there is iron and steel must be purchased—"

"Perfectly understandable." Sherman slid an envelope across the table. "I think that you will find dealing with the army much more satisfactory. This is a check for the first payment for the development of the mobile battery."

Ericsson smiled—for the first time that they had ever seen. Tore open the envelope and squinted down at the check. "Most satisfactory."

"Good. Then we can get down to work." Sherman pointed to the drawings on his desk. "I have been examining these in great detail ever since General Grant gave them to me. I have some suggestions."

Ericsson's face grew hard. "You are not an engineer . . ."

"No—but I am the officer in charge of the armies that must use this device. I want you to consider this. The driver and the gunner will be

ARMED FOR COMBAT

under intense fire from the enemy. Is there any way we can protect them with some armor?"

"That will not be a problem. I have already had this under consideration." He took a pencil from his jacket pocket and pulled over the drawings. With quick, precise strokes he sketched in an iron shield.

"If we attempt to armor the vehicle on all sides, it would be too heavy to move. But since it will be attacking the enemy, then a shield on the front should provide all the protection that it will need as it rides into battle. The muzzles of the Gatling will fire through this opening in the armor."

"Sounds most promising," Sherman said, smiling with pleasure. "How long will it take to build the prototype?"

"One week," Ericsson said without the slightest hesitation. "If you will be at my works one week from today, you will see the new machine in action."

"That will indeed be satisfactory." Sherman tugged at his beard, deep in thought. "But we must have a name for this new invention."

"I have thought about that. It must be a heroic name. So I suggest Fafnir—the dragon of Norse legend, breathing out fire and destruction on all who oppose it."

"I think not. We want a name that if it is overheard, or mentioned in correspondence, will be most innocuous and bear no relation to the war vehicle. The secret of its existence must be kept at all costs."

"Innocuous!" Ericsson's temper had snapped again. "That is ridiculous. If you want innocuous, then why not call it a bale of hay—or—or a water tank!"

Sherman nodded. "A capital suggestion. A water tank, an iron tank—or just plain tank. So that is settled. But there is another matter that I want to consult you about. A military matter."

"Yes?"

Sherman took a key from his waistcoat pocket, unlocked the top drawer of his desk, and took out a sheaf of drawings. He slid them across the desktop to Ericsson.

"These are different elevations and details of a fort defending a river bend."

Ericsson took them and nodded agreement. "Obviously. A typical construction that you will see right across all of Europe. It is roughly a triangular redan. These spurs flank the approaches to the fort, and see, opposite the salients here, the walls take the form of a star, a development of a tenaille trace. This ravelin has an important defense role in defending the main entrance. A well-worn design—but also well past its time. It cannot stand up to modern artillery. I assume you want to reduce this fortress?"

"I do."

"Easily enough done. Get a siege train within range, and in three or four days you will have reduced the walls to rubble."

"That will be impossible. It is surrounded by water and swamps. Also—that would take too long."

"Too long! You want a miracle, then."

"I don't want a miracle—but I do want the guns destroyed in hours, not days. I am not interested in the fabric of the fort itself; it will be bypassed in any case."

"Interesting," the engineer said, picking up the aerial view of the fort. "The river here, of course. With the guns silenced, the ships of war may pass. You come to me because I am a nautical engineer and this will require a nautical solution. May I take these drawings with me?"

"You may not. Study them as long as you like—but they must not leave this room."

Ericsson scowled at this prohibition and rubbed his jaw in thought. "All right, I can do that. But one more question: The fleet that sails up this river, will they be riverine ships?"

"No, they won't be. They will have crossed an ocean before they reach the river mouth."

"Very good, then." Ericsson climbed to his feet. "I will show you how it can be done when I see you in a week's time to demonstrate my new hay bale."

"Tank."

"Bale, tank—it is all nonsense." He started for the door, then turned back. "At that time I will be able to show you how to reduce those guns. An idea I already have been working on." He went out, slamming the door behind him.

"Do you think he can do it?" Grant asked.

"If he can't, why, there is no one else in the world who can. He is an original thinker. Never forget that it was his *Monitor* that changed naval warfare forever."

On the other side of the Atlantic a far more commonplace event was taking place. In the port of Dover, the morning steam packet from Calais had just arrived after an uneventful crossing of the English Channel from France. Albert Noireau was just one of the many passengers who came down the gangway and stepped onto the English soil.

Most of the other passengers hurried on to board the London train. But a few, like Monsieur Noireau, had business here in the seaport. His visit could not have been intended to be an extensive one, for he carried no baggage. He also appeared to be in no hurry as he strolled along the seafront. Sometimes stopping to gaze at the ships gathered there, at other times he looked at the shops and buildings that faced the docks. One in particular attracted his attention. He peered at the chiseled nameplate outside the door, then went on. At the next turning he paused and looked about. As far as he could tell, he was unobserved. He took a moment to glance at the slip of paper in his pocket and nodded slightly. It was indeed the same name he had been told to look for. *Trinity House.* He walked back toward it, then entered the public house in the adjoining building. The Cask and Telescope. *Très naval.*

The newcomer ordered a pint of beer in good English—although he had a thick French accent. His French was perfect, he had lived in France for many years, and had long since submerged Mikhail Shevchuk under his new persona. But he never forgot who his masters were.

It was easy to strike up conversations at the bar. Particularly when he was most generous when his time came for buying rounds. By late afternoon he had talked to a number of pilots from Trinity House and had discovered what he needed to know. To them he was an affable agent for French ship's chandlers, with well-filled pockets.

They called after him cheerfully when he hurried to get the afternoon packet back to France.

BOOK TWO
THE WINDS OF WAR

★

SEAGOING THUNDER

The year 1865 ended with a winter of discontent. It proved to be the coldest December in many years, with endless snowstorms and hard ice. Even the Potomac froze over. The British government's continuing legal and diplomatic assaults on the Americans had eased somewhat when Lord Palmerston, who had never recovered his strength after his stroke and was now in his eighty-first year, caught a chill and, after a short illness, died in October. Lord John Russell relinquished his office of Foreign Minister and became Prime Minister in his place. Government policies continued unchanged, and although there was a brief hiatus when his new government was formed, the pressure on the United States continued into the spring of 1866.

A second delay had occurred in December when King Leopold of Belgium died. His intercession had aided the difficult negotiations between the two countries. His son ascended to the throne as Leopold II, but he was never the diplomat that his father was. Difficulties and confrontations continued unabated, but outright war was still avoided.

Lincoln had kept his promise and bought the time that General Sherman had said that he needed. Sherman was a perfectionist and a very hard man to please, but by March 1866 he felt that he had done everything possible to prepare the country for war. Not just to fight a war—but to win it. It was a raw and blustery day when he met General Grant and Admiral David Glasgow Farragut at Ericsson's foundry and ship works in Newport News.

"Have you seen the new sea batteries yet?" Admiral Farragut asked, then took a sip from his sherry glass. They were waiting for Ericsson in his office, but as usual, he was busy somewhere else in the giant factory.

"I haven't," Sherman said. "And I look forward to them with great anticipation. Our victory or defeat depends on these batteries. But I did inspect the new transports in the harbor here and am more than pleased with them."

Farragut frowned deeply. "I am concerned with those ramps inside the ship that exit at various levels. They violate the integrity of the hull."

"They are vital to our success, Admiral. Accurate measurements were made at high and low tide at our intended port, enabling the ramp doors to be precisely engineered to the correct height." He did not mention how these measurements had been obtained; Fox and the Russians were working closely together.

"The pressure of heavy seas should not be discounted," Farragut said.

"Presumably not. But Ericsson assures me that the watertight seals on the doors will be satisfactory even in the most inclement weather."

"I sincerely hope that he is right."

General Grant looked at the inch of sherry in his glass and decided against adding any more. "I have every faith in our Swedish engineer. He has been proven correct in everything that he has done so far. Have you inspected the gun-carrying tanks, Admiral?"

"I have—and they are indeed impressive. An innovation that I can appreciate, but only abstractly, for I cannot imagine how they will be used in battle. I am more at home at sea than on land."

"Believe me," Sherman said, with grim certitude. "They are not only important but are vital to my strategy. They will change the face of the battlefield forever."

"Better you than me going to war with those contraptions." Farragut was still skeptical. "The new armored warships with their rotating turrets

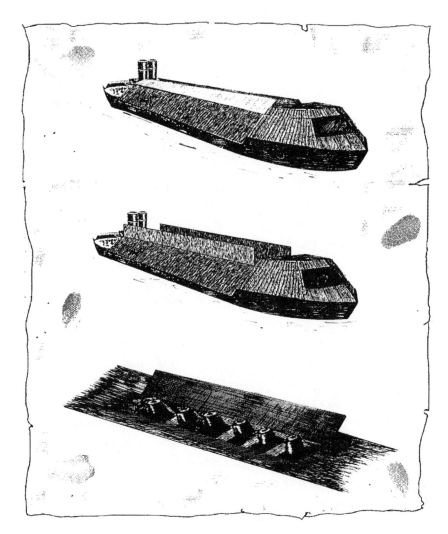

SEAGOING THUNDER

and breech-loading guns are more in the line of work that I am interested in."

"The British have new warships as well," Grant said.

"They do—and I have examined reports on them. I am sure that in battle they will be outgunned and outfought by our own ships."

"Good," Sherman said, and turned as the door opened. "And here is the man himself."

Ericsson muttered something incomprehensible as he hurried to his workbench and rifled through a sheaf of drawings there. His hands were smeared with grease, but he did not notice the dark marks that he made on the drawings. "Here," he said, extracting a drawing and holding it up for inspection. "This can explain how the sea batteries are constructed. Far better than words can. See?"

His finger traced along the bottom of the drawing, pointing out a thick iron structure. "You will note the mortars are aligned along the centerline of the vessel, directly over this iron keel. When they fire, in turn I must insist, the recoil is absorbed by the keel. Mortars of this size have never been mounted in a ship before. It is my fear that if they were all fired at once, it would blow out the bottom of the hull. Is this clear, Admiral; do you understand precisely what I am saying?"

"I understand clearly," Farragut said, making no attempt to conceal his anger at the engineer's overbearing attitude. "All of the ship's officers have been well briefed. They will fire only when your electric telegraph is activated."

"The telegraph is just a machine—and it could easily fail in combat. The central gunnery officer sends an electric signal that activates a solenoid at a gun position—which raises the red tag instructing the position to fire. But if the machine is broken, signals must be passed along manually. That is when there should be no confusion. One gun at a time, that is most important."

"The instructions have been given. All of the officers are aware of the situation and have been trained to act accordingly."

"Hmmph," Ericsson muttered, then sniffed loudly. Obviously believing in the perfection of machines—but not of men. His bad temper faded only when he looked at the drawing again.

"You will have noted the resemblance of this design to the Roman military 'turtle' defensive maneuver. Where the outer ranks of an attacking party held their shields on all sides to protect them from enemy missiles. While the center ranks held their shields over their heads in a defense similar to a turtle's shell. So do our sea batteries. There is six inches of iron armor, backed by oak, in the hull, rising higher than the guns. Sections of iron shielding are positioned above to cover the decks for protection. These are hinged on the sides and are opened by steam pistons, but only when the mortars are ready to fire."

While his description of the shielding was confusing, it was clearly indicated in the drawing.

"Come," Ericsson said, "we will inspect USS *Thor*, the first ship completed. The god of thunder—and the one who wields the hammer which will smite the enemy."

After years of pressure from the inventor to put a Viking name to one of his ships, the Navy Department had relented begrudgingly. However, in addition to *Thor*, there were the USS *Thunderer*, *Attacker*, and *Destructor*. Apt names for these mighty vessels.

When they left the office building and walked to the dock, they appreciated for the first time the raw strength of the mortar vessels. The guns themselves were siege weapons, never designed to be seaborne. A man could have easily fit into the wide muzzle of one of the barrels; the explosive shell that it fired would wreak hideous destruction on any gun batteries, no matter how well protected.

"Admirable," Sherman said, nodding as he looked at the grim strength of the sea battery. "Admirable. This is the key that will unlock our victory. Or rather one of two keys to that victory. In the attack the gun-carrying tanks will be in the fore."

"I will show you now their new protections."

"I am afraid you must excuse me, then," Admiral Farragut said. "They are your responsibility, General Sherman, not mine. I have no wish to see them again."

Not so Sherman and Grant. When they looked at the deadly machines, they saw victory in battle, not black iron and harsh angles.

"This is the latest improvement," Ericsson said, patting the curved steel shield that protected the gunner. Only the projecting barrels of the Gatling gun could be seen. "The shield, of course you can see that, obvious to anyone, but inside the device itself you will find the works of mechanical genius." He lifted a door and pointed into the entrails of the machine. "There, to the rear of the engine, you see that casing?"

The two generals nodded that they did, but did not speak aloud the knowledge that it meant nothing to them.

"Consider the transmission of energy," Ericsson said, and Sherman groaned inwardly at what he knew would be another incomprehensible lecture. "The engine rotates a driveshaft. It must then turn the second shaft on which the wheels are mounted. But they are unmoving. How can the energy of rotation be transmitted to them?"

Ericsson, carried away by his passion for his invention, was blissfully unaware of the looks of bafflement on their faces. "Thus my invention of a transfer case. A roughened steel plate is fastened to the end of the rotating shaft. Facing it is a second steel plate affixed by splines to the wheel shaft. A lever, this one, forces the second plate forward so the two plates meet and the power is transmitted, the wheels turn, the vehicle moves forward."

"Indeed a work of genius," Sherman said. If there was any irony in his words, it was lost on the Swedish engineer, who smiled and nodded agreement.

"Your machines are ready for battle, General—whenever you are."

SHADOWS OF WAR

The battle plans were now as final as they could possibly be. Countless folders and drawers of detailed documents rested in the files of Room 313 in the War Department. General Sherman knew exactly what he wanted done. Knew to a man the sizes of the military units that he would command, the number and the strengths of the ships that he would employ. Army officers, not clerks, were now working in the greatly expanded Room 313; they fleshed out these orders with exact details of manpower, officers, material, and support. They were not as efficient, or as fast, as trained clerks were, but they knew very well how to keep secrets. The near disaster at the Navy Department after the theft of orders was too recent to be ignored. Lieutenants and captains, muttering to themselves about doing school lessons, nevertheless transcribed the hundreds of copies needed by modern warfare. Since sea power was essential to the coming operation, Admiral Farragut was Sherman's constant companion. His advice was vital, and between them, the two commanders decided what forces would be required, then shaped the fleet of varied ships that would be needed to support the landing forces and assure victory. With a passion for detail that exhausted his officers, Sherman went over and over the organizational plans until they were precisely what he desired.

"It is a new kind of war," he told General Grant. It was the first day of April and an early spring held Washington in a warm embrace. "I have given it much thought and have reached the reluctant conclusion that it is machines not men that make the difference now."

"You cannot fight a war without soldiers."

"Indeed you cannot. They must man the machines. First think about the repeating, breech-loading rifle and how it changed the battlefield. Realize how one man can now fire as many shots as a squad used to. Then go on to the Gatling gun. Now the single man has the firing power of almost an entire company. Put a number of Gatling guns together behind defensive shielding and you have an impregnable position that cannot be taken by enemy soldiers—no matter how brave they be. Now put the Gatling guns onto their powered carriers and you have a new kind of deadly cavalrymen who can sweep away any enemy that they face."

"There is more slaughter than valor in this new kind of war," Grant said, uneasy.

"How right you are. If this new kind of army attacks in force, it can destroy all who stand before it. The faster the attack, the quicker the end of the conflict. That is why I call it lightning war. Take the war to the enemy and destroy him. As you said—slaughter instead of valor. And certain victory. That is the way our future battles must be fought. The tiger of machine warfare has been loosed and we must ride it. Or perish. The old ways are gone, replaced by the new. My hope is that before the enemy discovers that fact, it will too late, and they will be destroyed. In the past it was passion and bravery that won battles. North and South were so evenly matched at Shiloh that the battle might have gone either way."

"It didn't," Grant said. "You would not let it. You led from the front that day and your soldiers took inspiration from you. It was your courage that won the victory."

"Perhaps. Please believe me, I am not putting down the will and bravery of our men. They are the best. But I want to give them the weapons and the organization that win battles. I want them to live through the coming conflict. Never again do I want to see twenty thousand dead in a day on the field of battle, as we did at Shiloh. If there are to be dead, let them be from the ranks of the enemy. In the end I want my avenging army to march home victorious to their families."

"That is a tall order, Cumph."

"But it can be done. It will be done. There are only a few remaining details to be ironed out, and I know that I can leave them safely up to you."

"Don't you fear, they'll get done well before you get back."

"Particularly since I am not going away."

"That is true. Officially you will be joining Admiral Farragut in an inspection of the fleet. That's what it says in the newspapers—and we know that they never lie. When are you off?"

"Tonight, just after dark. General Robert E. Lee will meet me on the ship."

"Despite the fact he is taking some leave at his home?"

"You must always believe what you read in the papers. I know it may be considered presumptuous of me to take a mighty ship like the *Dictator* all the way to Ireland and back for my personal needs—but this trip is vital. I must be present when Lee and Meagher meet. We must all be of a single mind as to what is to be done."

"I agree completely and I know that it is only the truth. Give my respects to General Meagher. He is a fine officer."

"That he is. And I know that he won't let us down, he and his Irish troops. But I must impress on him how vital his role is—and how even more important is exact timing. I know that he will understand when I explain the entire operation to him. It is amazing the organizational work he has done with the limited facts of the coming operation that have been supplied to him."

"That is because he has faith in you, Cumph. We all have. This new kind of warfare is yours and yours alone. Yes, most of the weapons and machines were all there for anyone to see. But you saw more than we did. You had the foresight and, I dare say it, the genius to put everything together into a new kind of battle order. We will win, we *must* win a decisive victory. To settle the British question once and for all. Then maybe the politicians will take notice and decide that wars are too awful now to keep on fighting them."

Sherman smiled wryly. "I wouldn't hold my breath waiting for that to happen. As you know I personally think that war is hell—but most people don't. I firmly believe that the politicians will always find reasons to fight just one more war."

"I'm afraid that you are right. Have a good and fast voyage—and I will see you upon your return."

It was a wet day in April in Ireland—it almost always was—but General Thomas Francis Meagher scarcely noticed the rain-lashed fields and the sodden tents of the Burren. His men were fresh troops, green and untested troops—but men with the hearts of lions. They had rallied to the tricolor flag when the call had gone out for volunteers, coming from all parts of the country. Theirs was the newest nation in the world and was now under threat by one of the oldest. Ireland had been a republic just long enough to taste the benefits of freedom. Now that this newfound independence was under attack, her people rallied to its defense.

A year ago, when Meagher had inspected his first volunteers, his heart had sunk. They were willing enough, God knows, but generations of ill nourishment had exacted its toll. Their arms were pipe-thin, their skins gray and pallid. Some of them had legs that bowed out, the classical sign of bad diet and rickets. All of the noncommissioned officers in the new army were from the Irish Brigade, all of them Irish-American immigrants just one or two generations away from the old country. But what a difference those few generations had made. Through industry and hard work they had improved their lot—but a decent diet had improved their physiques as well. Most of them were a head taller than their Irish cousins, some weighing half as much again.

General Meagher had called upon the American military doctors for advice. They had years of experience in caring for large groups of men, caring for their health and well-being as well as their combat wounds.

"Feed them up," the surgeon general had said. He had made an emergency visit to Ireland at the behest of the doctors of the Irish Brigade. He had been shocked by what he had seen. As soon as he could, he arranged a meeting with General Meagher and his staff.

"I am surprised that any of them lived long enough to reach young manhood. Do you know what the diet in the country consists of? Potatoes—almost completely potatoes. A valuable source of nutrients indeed, but not to be eaten on their own. And if the potatoes are peeled before they are cooked, this removes many of the nutrients. They are eaten dipped in salt water for flavor, washed down by black and unsweetened tea. That is not a healthy diet—it is a death sentence."

"But they are used to it," Meagher said. "They strongly resist eating made dishes, and what they call folderols . . ."

"This is the army," the surgeon general growled. "They will obey orders. Porridge in the morning; if they don't like it salted, they can sweeten it with sugar to make it palatable. I know that they say that oats are only for horses—but they can emulate their Scotch cousins and eat their oatmeal every day. And no tea until the evening meal! If they are thirsty, why then, provide them with jugs of milk. Then make sure that they have meat, at least once a day, and vegetables like turnips and cabbage. Leeks as well. There is a most tasty Irish dish called colcannon, made of cabbage and potatoes. See that they have some of that. Then exercise, not too strenuous at first, but keep building it. They will put on muscle and body weight and be the better for it."

The doctors had been so right; in less than a year the changes had been remarkable. And as the men's health had improved, so had their military prowess. The trained soldiers of the American Irish Brigade had been spread evenly through the new Irish army. Those with the needed skills and intelligence were made noncommissioned officers; the remaining ones acted as a trained central corps, an example to the boys from the farms and the cities' slums. They were eager to learn, anxious to do their part in the defense of their country.

Meagher was immensely cheered by all this. Though at times progress had been heartbreakingly slow. But these mostly illiterate young men had the unshakable will to succeed—and win. They were told what needed to be done and they did it with enthusiasm. Now there was an army that could wheel and march on parade, that also showed a growing skill at the rifle butts. They could put down a volley of withering fire from their breech-loading Spencer repeating rifles. If they had the spunk to stand up to the enemy, they would be a formidable force in the field.

Training artillerymen had not been as easy. But there were farm boys who knew about horse handling and harnessing, and they had fleshed out the ranks. A hard core of Irish-American gunners provided the skill and knowledge to create an efficient gunnery corps.

This had been done. Before going out to attend parade, General Meagher stood in the doorway of his tent and watched the men drilling in the endless rain. They persevered. Nearby a company was erecting new tents; one of the tents, sodden with water, collapsed on the soldiers working below it. They emerged dripping—and laughing at their misfortune. Morale was fine. Soon these men would be tested in battle. General Sherman, the General of the Armies, had sent word by the weekly packet to Galway that he and General Robert E. Lee would be arriving in Ireland very soon, directly by warship to Dublin. Sherman would explain what was needed. Meagher remembered clearly what he had said at their last meeting in the War Department in Washington City, some months ago.

"You must build me an army, Francis, one that will fight and follow where you lead. If war does come, why, yours will be the most vital role in guaranteeing our victory. You will be joined by American forces, but your men must be ready to fight as well. You will have losses, that cannot be avoided, but I want every man in your ranks to know, before they face battle, that it is for the freedom of Ireland that they fight. Victory in the field will mean independence forever at home."

They will be ready, Meagher thought, nodding his head. *They will be ready.*

The storm was clearing, dark clouds racing by overhead. The sun broke through to the south, sending a sudden shaft of gold to illuminate the landscape. *An omen,* he thought. *A good omen indeed.*

Blown across England by the prevailing westerly wind, the storm that had lashed Ireland had now reached the English Channel. The passengers who emerged from the Calais packet lowered their heads and held on to their hats in the driving rain. The big man with long hair and a flowing beard ignored the rain, walking slowly and stolidly along the shore. He paused when he came to the public house, slowly spelled out the words THE CASK AND TELESCOPE, nodded, and pushed the door open.

There were a few sideways glances from some of the men drinking there, but no real interest. Strangers were common here at the dockside.

"Beer," he said to the landlord when he walked over to serve him.

"Pint? Half-pint?"

"Big vun."

"A pint it is, then."

Foreign sailors were no novelty here. The landlord put the glass down and pulled some pennies from the handful of change the man had laid on the bar. The newcomer drank half of the glass in a single mighty swig, belched loudly, and thudded the glass back onto the bar.

"I look for pilot," he said in a guttural voice, in thickly accented English.

"You've come to the right place, my old son," the landlord said, putting a polish onto a glass. "That's Trinity House just a few yards away. All the pilots you want in there."

"Pilots here?"

"My best customers. That table against the wall, pilots to the man."

Without another word, the newcomer took up his glass and clumped across to the indicated table. The men there looked up, startled, when he pulled up a chair and dropped into it.

"Pilots?" he said.

"None of your bleeding business," Fred Sweet said. He had been drinking since early morning and was very much the worse for wear. He started to rise, but the man seated next to him pulled him back down.

"Try next door. Trinity House. All you want there," he said quietly. The newcomer turned to him.

"Want pilot name of Lars Nielsen. He my *brodersøn*, what you say . . . nephew."

"By george—it looks like our friend here is related to old Lars. Always thought he was too mean to have any family."

"Took a collier to London yesterday," one of the other drinkers said. "Depending on what he gets coming back, he could be here at any time now."

"Lars—he here?" the big stranger asked.

After many repetitions he finally understood what was happening. "I vait," he said, pushing back from the table and returning to the bar. He was not particularly missed by the pilots.

The handful of change on the bar was much smaller by many pints by late afternoon. Lars's uncle drank slowly and steadily, and patiently, only looking up when a newcomer entered the bar. It was growing dark when a gray-bearded man stumped in, his wooden leg thudding on the floorboards. A ragged cheer went up from the pilots in the room.

"You got company, Lars," someone shouted.

"Your family wants the money back you stole when you left Denmark!"

"He is as ugly as you are—you must be related."

Lars cursed them out loudly and savagely and stomped his way to the bar. The bearded man turned to look at him.

"What you staring at?" Lars shouted at him.

"Jeg er deres onkel, Lars," the man said quietly.

"I never saw you before in my life," Lars shouted in Danish, looking the other man up and down. "And you sound like you're from København— not Jylland. My family are all Jysk."

"I want to talk to you, Lars—about money. Lots of money that could be yours."

"Who are you?" Lars said suspiciously. "How do you know me?"

"I know about you. You're a Danish sailor who has been a pilot here for ten years. Is that correct?"

"Ja," Lars muttered. He looked around the barroom, but no one was paying them any attention now that they were speaking Danish.

"Good. Now I will buy you a beer and we will *snakker* like old friends. Lots of money, Lars, and a trip back to Aarhus as well."

They talked quietly after that, their heads close together over the beer-stained table. Whatever was said pleased Lars so much that his face cracked into an unaccustomed smile. They ordered some food, a large quantity of meat, potatoes, and bread, which they consumed completely. When they had finished, they left together.

The next day Lars Nielsen did not report for duty at Trinity House. Then the word got out that he had told the landlord at the pub that he had come into an inheritance and was going back to Denmark.

No one missed him in the slightest.

LET BATTLE BEGIN

In ones and twos the big ships had come from America, convoyed the entire way by United States armorclads. The transports were many and varied, a few of them even wooden sailing ships that had been fitted out with steam engines. Some of these converted ships had limited bunker space, so all of the convoys made a stop at St. John's, Newfoundland. The seaport there was empty now of any British ships; the locals gave the Americans a warm welcome. After this landfall, the convoys had sailed far to the north in the hope of avoiding British patrols; this plan had succeeded. Only a single British warship had been encountered, which fled the field at the sight of the bigger warships. Their route took them north, almost to Iceland, before they turned south to the rendezvous in Galway. When the arriving ships had unloaded their cargo, mostly munitions, to go by train to Dublin, the now empty ships had moved out to anchorage in Galway Bay. By late spring the bay was dark with ships, more than had ever been seen there before. They stayed peacefully at anchor, awaiting their orders.

These were not long in coming. USS *Avenger* herself, the victor of the Battle of the Potomac, brought the final commands. One morning she steamed majestically up the bay to dock at Galway City. *Avenger* was now commanded by the veteran Captain Schofield, since the aging Commodore Goldsborough had taken his long-deserved retirement. She also had a new first lieutenant, a Russian of all things, a Count Korzhenevski, who had actually gone to the British Naval Academy. Schofield's first suspicions of this unusual arrangement soon gave way to appreciation, for the Count was a willing and able officer.

The orders that *Avenger* had brought went out swiftly to the waiting ships, while an army colonel, with an armed guard, took the fast train to Dublin with orders for General Meagher and General Robert E. Lee.

There was nothing precipitous or hurried about the preparations. They moved with stately finality so that, at dawn on the fifteenth of May, 1866, the ships, one by one, hauled up their anchors and steamed out to sea. Past the Aran Islands they sailed, coasting northwest off the coast of Connemara, then turned north, their course set for the North Channel between Ireland and Scotland. Long before they reached the channel, off Donegal Bay, clouds of smoke on the horizon revealed the presence of the waiting American ironclads.

A war fleet this size had never been seen before, not even during the earlier invasion of Ireland. No British fleet, no matter how strong, would dare face up to this mighty armada.

But there was no enemy in sight; the American fleet movement had caught the British by surprise. South the ships moved, through the North Channel, where they could easily be seen from Scotland. They were indeed observed as they passed the Mull of Kintyre, and the telegraph from Campbeltown quickly spread the news south. But by the time that there could be any reaction, the cargo vessels were safe in Dublin Harbor and Dun Laoghaire.

The ironclads were stationed out to sea to intercept any vessels rash enough to approach the Irish shore. The few that did come close were seen off quite quickly. Ashore, the troops filed aboard the waiting ships while the gun batteries approached the novel transports built specially for the coming invasion. Iron-hulled ships that, after they docked, opened up great ports in their sides from which, propelled by steam cylinders, slid out metal ramps. They were ridged with wooden crosspieces so that horses

LET BATTLE BEGIN

could easily pull the guns and limbers into the ships. Cavalry boarded the same way, as well as grooms with the officers' mounts. Embarkation was completed just after dusk on the night of May 19.

Soon after midnight, on May 20, the ships took in their lines and went to sea. It was a straight run of less than a hundred and forty miles across the Irish Sea to the British shore. Dawn found them in Liverpool Bay, with the first warships already steaming up the Mersey.

The attack was a complete surprise to the shocked Liverpudlians, the crashing of heavy guns the first intimation that their country was again at war. Every fort, gun battery, and military installation had been carefully marked on the American charts. Years of spying had not been in vain. Each of the ironclads had its own specific targets. The sun was still low in the eastern horizon when the first guns fired.

High explosives smashed into the defenses, sending guns, masonry, and pieces of men hurtling out from the maelstrom of death that was spread by the heavy shells. A cavalryman, clutching his wounded arm, galloped his horse through the empty streets to the central telegraph office. He hammered on the sealed door with the pommel end of his saber until he finally broke it open. A terrified operator soon appeared, sat down at his machine still wearing his nightclothes, and sent word of the invasion to London.

For the first time in over eight hundred years, Britain was being invaded. Shock—and then horror—spread through the island.

The barbarians were at the gate.

General Sherman had set up his headquarters in the customhouse in Cork City. This was a handsome white stone building that stood at the very end of the island on which the center of the city had been built. From the tall windows he had a fine view of the river Lee. The North Channel and the South Channel of the river joined together just before his windows, blue and placid, flowing out into Cork Lough. Filled now with the varied ships of the southern invasion fleet. The transports were close in, many of them tied up at the city's wharves. Farther down the river, in Cork Harbor, were the ironclad ships of war, with others on patrol farther east where the river met the sea. Enemy warships had probed in this direction, but were driven off long before they could observe a thing. As much as possible all ship movements had been kept secret—other than the few chance observations that could be expected. The Americans had proclaimed publicly that they were protecting Irish shipping from the incursions of foreign powers. The British protestations about entry into their coastal waters were pointedly ignored.

General Grant entered the room and looked at the large MAY 20 displayed on the calendar before he sat down across the desk from General Sherman. He ran his fingers thoughtfully through his thick beard.

"May the twentieth," he said. "Dublin telegraphed as soon as the last ships sailed. Barring breakdowns at sea, the city of Liverpool will have come under attack this morning."

"A percentage of ship losses was allowed for in the operating orders," General Sherman said. "So the attack will have gone ahead as planned."

"When will we know anything?"

"It will be hours yet. Only after all strongpoints have been taken and the first trains seized will word be carried back to Dublin by the fastest vessel. They'll know first, then will telegraph the news on to us."

Sherman nodded his head toward the open door and telegraphists working in the room across the hall. Wires were festooned from the ceiling and ran out of the window, connecting them to the central post office and the fleet.

"The waiting is not easy," Grant said. He took a black cheroot from his breast pocket, struck a sulfur match, and lit it.

"It never is," Sherman said. "But patience must be our watchword. One thing we can be sure of is that word of the attack will be telegraphed to London by now. Undoubtedly they will want to order instant mobilization. We must allow them at least one day to find out what has happened, then to come to a decision as to what must be done."

"That will be tomorrow, the twenty-first."

"It will indeed. And I am also allowing that one day for confusion. The government must sit, plan, seek advice, run to the Queen, and back."

"You estimate that an entire day will pass like that before any firm actions are taken by them?"

"I do."

Grant puffed out a cloud of smoke, looked unseeingly out of the window. "You are a man of decision, Cumph. I would not like to be in your position and be responsible for the progress of this war. I would have continued the invasion at once."

"Then again perhaps you would not, if you were in my shoes. It is a command decision—and once made it cannot be altered. In London, evaluations will have to be made as well, orders written and transmitted. Their thinking will have to change completely, which is never an easy thing to do, because they have never been in this position before. For the first time their armies will not be attacking—but defending. Of course, there is always the possibility that plans have been made for such an eventuality. But even if they have plans, they will have to be unearthed, examined, modified. If anything, I think that I am being overly conservative in allowing only a single day for confusion. But it is too late to change all that. I am sure that tomorrow will be a quiet day for all the enemy forces in the country. I am positive that meaningful movement of troops will not happen until the twenty-second."

"And then they will all be marching toward the Midlands to counter the invasion."

"They will indeed," Sherman said; there was no warmth in his smile. "So it will be on the twenty-third that you will sail with your men."

"I look forward to that moment, as do all the troops. By which time we will surely have been informed how the first invasion, at Liverpool, is proceeding."

"I am counting upon you to drive your attack home."

"I will not fail you," Grant said in an even voice that was firm, even gruff. He would get the job done all right. Sherman knew that if any general in the entire world could succeed, it was Ulysses S. Grant.

As soon as the Liverpool fortifications had been leveled and the guns silenced by the naval fire, the transports of the invading army tied up one by one at the city's central docks. The ships that were already berthed there had their hawsers unceremoniously cut and were towed to the Birkenhead side of the river, where they were run aground. Even while this was happening the gangways on the Irish ships were dropped. The first men ashore were Irish riflemen, who fanned out in defensive positions and took shelter from any counterattack. They were scarcely under cover before the loading ramps of the special transports were extended and the American cavalry galloped out into the morning light.

Within an hour the waterfront was secured while the attackers fanned out through the city. There were pockets of resistance, which were swiftly reduced because after the cavalrymen left the transports and charged forward into battle, the cannon were unloaded. As they emerged they were prevented from too fast progress down the ramps by restraining ropes that were wrapped around deck winches. Slowly and carefully they were rolled down onto the dock. The horses were in their traces within minutes. The Gatling guns, being much lighter, were manhandled down the ramps to the dockside, where their horses were hitched up. The cannon, with caissons and limbers attached, were soon ready to go into battle as well. The advance continued into the city, slowly and inexorably.

General Robert E. Lee had set up his headquarters close by the Mersey. Runners, and an occasional cavalryman, brought their reports to him.

"There is a strong defense at the barracks, here," Colonel Kiley said, touching his finger to the map of the city spread out on the table.

Lee nodded. "That was to be expected. Were they bypassed?"

"They were indeed, General, just as you ordered. A company left behind to keep up fire, along with two of the Gatling guns."

"Fine. Get a battery of guns down there to clear them out."

While the attack into Liverpool was slow and precise, the spearhead of troops launched against Lime Street Station was not. The cavalry had galloped ahead, cutting through any determined defenses, charging on. Pockets of resistance were bypassed, leaving the infantry to mop them up. The mobile Gatling guns sent torrents of bullets into any troops bold enough to stand in their way. It was the station, the trains, the marshaling yards that had to be seized intact at any cost. Lee only relaxed, ever so slightly, when the reports reached him that the primary targets had been taken.

"I am moving my headquarters to the station as was planned. Send runners, see that all units are informed." He stepped aside as officers hurried to roll up the maps.

"This operation will now move into the second and final phase. General Meagher and the Irish troops will begin leaving as soon as possible." He waved over a cavalryman and passed him the message he had just written.

"Take this to the commander of the *Darter*. He is to get under way for Dublin at once."

The officer saluted, then vaulted into his saddle and galloped to the ship. Lee nodded after him.

Everything was going just as they had planned.

THE SWORD IS DRAWN

It was like using a steam hammer to crack a nut: the forces employed were well out of proportion to the chosen target. Yet the success or failure of the entire invasion depended upon the simple act of getting one man ashore at the right place in Cornwall—armed with a single vital tool. USS *Mississippi* and USS *Pennsylvania* were chosen for the task. They were newly built and improved ironclads of the two-turret *Monitor* class. Like their predecessor, *Virginia*, they were named after states of the Union. The politically aware Navy Department made sure that they were named alternately after a Northern and a Southern state.

The two ironclads had raced ahead of the rest of the armada when it left Cork harbor. Steaming due south, they did not turn east until they had crossed fifty degrees north latitude and were at the mouth of the English Channel. After this they kept a course well south of the Scilly Isles; the islands were seen just as small blurs on the horizon to port. It was late in the afternoon by this time, and they slowed their progress until dark. Now was the time of greatest peril: they were less than forty miles away from Plymouth, the second-largest naval base in the British Isles. The lookout posts were double-manned and the men swept the horizon continuously. There were fishing boats close inshore, but these could be ignored. It was

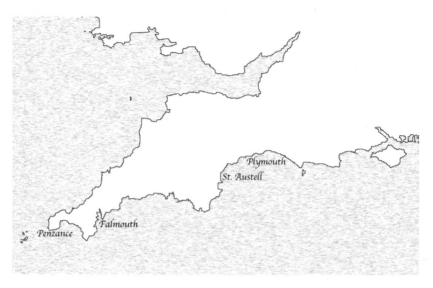

the British navy that they were concerned with; for good reason. Surprise was of the essence.

It was growing dark when *Mississippi* sent a signal to *Pennsylvania*. She was sailing well ahead of her sister ship, as well as standing farther out to sea. This positioning was deliberate—and vital—as her brief message reported.

Unidentified naval vessel sighted ahead. Am intercepting.

Even as she was sending the report, *Mississippi* was belching out clouds of smoke as she gained speed. On a southeast course. When she was seen, if chase were given, the action would take place well out of sight of the *Pennsylvania*.

The plan succeeded. Night fell. Now, unseen in the darkness, with her engine barely turning over, the American warship crept in toward the Cornish shore.

"That must be the light at Zone Point," the first officer said as they neared the coast. "It's at the mouth of Falmouth Bay—and those will be the lights of Falmouth beyond."

"Steady on your course," the captain ordered.

It was just after midnight when they slipped past St. Austell and into

St. Austell Bay. When the gaslights of the town were behind them, the engines were stopped and the ship drifted forward, the light waves slapping against her iron sides.

"Landing party away."

There was the hammer of running feet on deck. Moments later there was the slight creak of the well-greased davits as the two boats were slung over the side and lowered down into the sea. The sailors went down the rope ladders first, ready to help the clumsier soldiers into the waiting boats. The telegraph men were next, followed by the rest of the party. Their rifles were unloaded and their ammunition secured in closed pouches. It would have to be silent gun butts and bayonets if they encountered any resistance.

Hopefully they would not. This part of the coast had been selected for two very important reasons. Most of the land adjoining the coast here was forest, private land, where deer roamed freely. It should be deserted at night, for there were no farms or other habitations nearby, here where the rail line ran between the shoreline and the steep hills. And this train track was the reason they were here.

Cornwall has a rocky spine of hills running the entire length of the peninsula. When the Great Western Railway left its westernmost terminus in Penzance, the tracks turned inland, away from the sea. Through Redruth and Truro they went, then on to St. Austell, where the tracks came in sight of the sea again, well over halfway from Penzance to Plymouth. Skirting the bogs of Blackmoor, the rail line ran along the shore for some miles before turning inland a final time. This stretch of line was their target.

The boats grated on the gravelly shore. There were whispered commands as the sailors jumped into the knee-high surf and dragged the boats farther up onto the beach. A waning moon provided enough light for the disembarking soldiers. One of them fell with a clatter as his gun crashed onto the pebbles. There was a quick yelp of pain as someone trod on his hand. He was pulled to his feet and all movement stopped at the officer's hissed command. The night was so silent that an owl could be heard hooting in the trees on the far side of the single railroad track. Its rails gleamed silver in the moonlight.

Next to the tracks was a row of poles that carried the telegraph wires.

"Sergeant, I want men posted left and right, twenty yards out. And quietly this time. Telegraph squad, you know what to do."

When they reached the rails the telegraph men divided in two, with one squad walking down the ties to the east. Even before they had vanished into the darkness, the man delegated for this task was belting on his climbing irons. Up the poles he went, swiftly and surely, the pointed ends of his irons thokking into the wood as he climbed. The sharp click of wire cutters sounded and there was a rustle as the telegraph wires fell to the ground.

"Gather up the wire," the sergeant said quietly. "Cut it free and throw it into the ocean."

A hundred, two hundred yards of wire were cut out and dumped into the water. The soldiers had finished their appointed task and returned to the boats long before the second party. The men fidgeted about until the sergeants hushed them into silence. The lieutenant paced back and forth, tapping his fingers restlessly on his pistol holster, but did not speak aloud. The wire-cutting party had been told to proceed down the track for fifteen minutes, or as near as they could judge the time. They were to cut down another section of wire there and return. It seemed well past the allotted time now; it probably was not, he realized.

Private O'Reilly, one of the sentries stationed by the track, saw the dark figure approaching. He was about to call out when he discerned that the man was coming from the west—while the second wire company had gone east. O'Reilly leaned over and pulled the corporal by the sleeve, touching his forefinger to his lips at the same time. Then he pointed down the track. The two soldiers crouched down, trying to blend into the ground.

The figure came on, strangely wide across the shoulders, whistling softly.

Then he stopped, suddenly aware of the dark forms ahead of him beside the rails. In an instant the stranger turned and began to run heavily back down the track.

"Get him!" the corporal said, and led the way at a run.

The fleeing man slowed for an instant. A dark form fell from his shoulders to the tracks. Freed from his burden, he began to run again. Not fast enough. The corporal stabbed forward with his rifle, got it between the man's legs, sent him crashing to the ground. Before the man could rise, O'Reilly was on him, pinning him by the wrists.

"Don't kill me, please don't kill me!" the man begged in a reedy voice. This close they could see that his long hair was matted and gray.

"Now, why would you go thinking a cruel thing like that, Granddad?"

"It weren't me. I didn't set the snare. I just sort of stumbled over it, just by chance."

O'Reilly picked up the deer's corpse by the antlers. "A poacher, by God!"

"Never!" the man squealed, and the corporal shook him until he was quiet.

"That's a good man. Just be quiet and nothing will happen to you. Bring the stag," he whispered to O'Reilly. "Someone will enjoy the fresh meat."

"What's happening here?" the lieutenant asked when they dragged the frightened old man up the beach. The corporal explained.

"Fine. Tie his wrists and put him into the boat. We'll take him back— our first prisoner." Then, coldly, "If he makes any noise, shut him up."

"Yes, sir."

"O'Reilly, go with him. And bring the deer. The general will fancy a bit of venison, I shouldn't wonder."

"Party approaching." A hushed voice sounded through the darkness.

There was more than one sigh of relief when boots could be heard crunching on the gravel.

"Push the boats out! Board as soon as they float free!"

The wire was cut. They had not been seen.

At first light the landings would begin.

For the poacher the war was over even before it began. When he finally realized what had happened to him, he was most relieved. These weren't Sir Percy's gamekeepers after all; he would not be appearing at the Falmouth assizes, as he had feared. Being a prisoner of war of the Americans was far better than transportation to the other end of the world.

★

The lights in Buckingham Palace had been blazing past midnight and well into the early hours. There was a constant coming and going of cavalrymen as well as the occasional carriage. All of this activity centered on the conference room, where a most important meeting was taking place. There was a colonel stationed outside the door to intercept messages; a second colonel inside passed on any that were deemed important enough to be grounds for an interruption.

"We will not have the sanctity of *our* country violated. Are *we* clear?"

"You are, ma'am, very clear. But you must understand that the violation has already occurred; the landings are a thing of the past now. Enemy forces are well ashore in Liverpool, the city has been captured, all fighting ended according to the last reports."

"My dear soldiers would never surrender!" Victoria almost screeched the words, her voice roughened by hours, if not days, of deep emotion. Her complexion was so florid that it alarmed all those present.

"Indeed they would not, ma'am," Lord John Russell said patiently. "But they might very well be dead. The defenders were few in number, the attackers many and ruthless. And it appears that Liverpool is not the only goal. Reports from Birmingham report intense fighting there."

"Birmingham—but how?" Victoria's jaw dropped as, confusedly, she tried to master this new and frightful information.

"By train, ma'am. Our own trains were seized and forced to carry enemy troops south. The Americans are great devotees of trains, and have made wide use of them in their various wars."

"Americans? I was told that the invaders were Irish . . ."

"Yankees or Paddies—it makes little difference!" the Duke of Cambridge snapped. The hours of wrangling had worn down his nerves; he wished that he were in the field taking this battle to the enemy. Slaughtering the bastards.

"Why would the Irish want to invade?" Victoria asked with dumb sincerity. To her the Irish would always be wayward children, who must be corrected and returned to the blessing of British rule.

"Why?" the Duke of Cambridge growled. "Because they may have taken umbrage at their relatives being bunged up in those concentration camps. Not that we had any choice. Nursing serpents in our bosom. It seems that Sefton Park, the camp east of Liverpool, has been seized. Undoubtedly Aston Hall outside of Birmingham is next."

While he was speaking he had been aware of a light tapping on the door. This was now opened a crack and there was a quick whispered exchange before it was closed again. The group around the conference table looked up as the colonel approached with a slip of paper.

"Telegram from Whitehall—"

The Duke tore it from the officer's fingers even as Lord Russell was reaching for it.

"Goddamn their eyes." He was seething with fury. He threw down the message and stamped across the room to the large map of the British Isles that had been hung on the wall.

"Report from *Defender*, telegraphed from Milford Haven—here." He stabbed his finger on the map of western Wales where a spit of land projected into St. George's Channel. "It seems that some hours earlier they caught sight of a large convoy passing in the channel. They were proceeding south."

"South? Why south?" Lord Russell asked, struggling to take in this new development.

"Well, it is not to invade France, I can assure you of that," the Duke raged. He swept his hand along the English Channel, along the southern coast of Britain. "This is where they are going—the warm and soft underbelly of England!"

At first light the attacking armada approached the Cornish shore. The stone-girt harbor at Penzance was very small, suitable only for pleasure craft and fishing boats. The Scilly Isles ferry took up the most space inside where she tied up for the night. This had been allowed for in the landings, and the steam pinnace from *Virginia* was the only American boat that attempted to enter the harbor. She was jammed tight with soldiers, so many of them that her bulwarks were only inches above the sea. The men poured out onto the harbor wall in a dark wave, running to the attack and quickly securing the customhouse and the lifeguard station.

While all along the Penzance coast the small boats were coming ashore. Landing on the curving strand between the harbor and the train station, and the long empty beaches that ran in an arc to the west of the harbor. The first soldiers to land went at a trot down the road to the station, then on into the train yards beyond. General Grant was at the head of the troops; the trains were the key to the entire campaign. He stamped through the station and into the telegraph office, where two soldiers held the terrified night operator by the arms.

"He was sleeping over his key, General," a sergeant said. "We grabbed him before he could send any warning."

"I couldn't have done that, your honor," the man protested. "Couldn't have, because the wire to Plymouth is down."

"I've asked him about any down trains," Major Sandison said. He had been a railway director before he raised a company of volunteers in St. Louis and led them off to war. His soldiers, many of them former railway men, had taken the station and the adjoining yards.

"Just a goods train from St. Austell to Truro, that's all that's on the line."

Sandison spread the map across the table and pointed to the station. "They should be on a siding before we get there."

"*Should* is not good enough," Grant said.

"I agree, General. I'm sending an engine, pushing some freight cars, ahead of our first train. Plus a car with troops. Sledgehammers and spikes in case there is any damage to the rails. They'll make sure that the track is clear—and open."

"General—first Gatlings coming ashore now," a soldier reported.

"Good. Get the rest of them unloaded—and down here at once."

Sherman and Grant had spent many hours organizing the forces for this attack on Cornwall.

"The harbor is impossibly small," Sherman had said. "I've seen it with my own eyes, since our yacht was tied up inside. But there is deep water beyond the outer wall of the harbor. I had *Aurora*'s crew make soundings there when we left. The navy agrees that cargo ships of shallow enough draft can tie up on the seaward side and winch heavy equipment ashore."

"Cannon?"

Sherman shook his head. "Too heavy—and too slow to unload. And we have no draft animals to move them. They would also be too clumsy to load onto the trains even if we managed to get them to the yards. No cannon. We must move fast."

"The Gatling guns, then."

"Exactly. Light enough to be towed by the men."

"What about their ammunition? They consume an astonishing amount in battle."

"Soldiers again. You'll pick out the biggest and the strongest of your men. Form special gun companies. Arm them with revolvers rather than rifles. They will be lighter to carry, and just as effective in close conflict. Assign special squads to each Gatling gun. Some to pull the guns, others to carry the ammunition. That way each Gatling will be self-sufficient at all times."

"It has never been done before," Grant said, running his fingers through his beard, deep in thought.

Sherman smiled. "And lightning warfare like this has never been fought before."

"By God—you are right, Cumph!" Grant laughed aloud. "We'll come down on them like the wolf on the sheepfold. Before they even know what has hit them, they will be prisoners—or dead!"

And so it came to pass. The first black-hulled freighter threw out fenders and tied up to the seaward side of Penzance Harbor. The fenders creaked ominously as the hull moved up and down in the swell, but nothing gave way. The steam winches clanked and the long cargo booms lifted the deck-loaded Gatling guns into the air, swung them onto the wide top of the harbor wall. As the sailors untied the slings, waiting soldiers ran them ashore, where the gun companies were being assembled on the road. As soon as a gun company was complete with ammunition and bearers, it went at a trot down the harbor road to the station, where the first train was already assembled. General Grant himself rode the footplate beside the driver when it puffed its way out of the station and headed east along the coast.

The second American invasion of the British mainland was well under way.

A CLASH IN PARLIAMENT

"**T**his country, today, is faced with the greatest danger that it has ever encountered in its entire history." The members of Parliament listened in hushed silence as Lord John Russell spoke. "From across the ocean, from the distant Americas, a mighty force has been unleashed on our sovereign shores. Some among you will say that various enterprises undertaken by the previous government went a long way toward igniting the American fury. I will not deny that. I was a member of Lord Palmerston's government, and as a member I feel a certain responsibility about those events. But that is in the past and one cannot alter the past. I might also say that certain mistakes were made in the governance of Ireland. But the relationship between Britain and Ireland has never been an easy one. However, I am not here to address history. What has been done has been done. I address the present, and the disastrous and cowardly attacks that now beset our country. Contrary to international law, and even common decency, we have been stabbed in the back, dealt one cowardly blow after another. Irish and American troops have landed on our shores. Our lands have been ravaged, our citizens killed. So it is that now I call for you to stand with me in a unified government that will unite this troubled land and hurl the invaders back into the sea."

Russell was not a prepossessing man. Diminutive and rickety, he wriggled round while he spoke and seemed unable to control his hands and feet. His voice was small and thin; but a house of five hundred members was hushed to catch his every word. He spoke as a man of mind and thought, and of moral elevation. Yet not all were impressed. When Russell paused to look at his notes, Benjamin Disraeli was on his feet in the instant.

"Will the Prime Minister have the kindness to inform of us the extent of the depredations of the Yankee invader? The newspapers froth and grunt and do little else—so that hard facts are impossible to separate from the dross of their invective."

"The right honorable gentleman's interest is understandable. Therefore it is my sad duty to impart to you all of the details that the Conservative leader of the House has requested." He looked at his papers and sighed. "A few days ago, on the twenty-first of May, there were landings in Liverpool by foreign troops, apparently Irish for the most part—but we know who the puppet master is here. That city was taken. Our gallant men fought bravely, although greatly outnumbered. The attackers then proceeded to Birmingham, and after a surprise and savage attack secured that city and its environs."

Disraeli was standing again, imperious in his anger. "Is it not true that the attacking troops went straight to Sefton Park in Liverpool, where they engaged our soldiers and defeated them? As you undoubtedly know, there is a camp there for Irish traitors to the crown. Is it not also true that while this was happening other invaders seized trains and proceeded to Birmingham? It appears that because the telegraph wires had been cut, the troops there had no warning and were attacked and butchered at Aston Hall. Is this also true?"

"Regrettably, it is true. At least the newspapers got these facts right."

"Then tell us—is it also not true that there were camps at these sites where citizens of Irish extraction were concentrated—women and children as well as men? People who had been seized and imprisoned without being charged with any crime?"

"Your queries will be answered in a short while. If I am permitted to continue I will answer any questions later in great detail."

There was a murmur of agreement from the members. Disraeli bowed to their decision and seated himself again.

"As soon as we learned of these cowardly attacks, this country's military sprang to its defense. Under the Duke of Cambridge's instruction, Scots troops from Glasgow and Edinburgh are now on their way to the Midlands. Cavalry and yeomanry as well as the other troops are now in the field, and we expect imminent news of victory. The following regiments have been ordered to . . ."

His words died away as a rustle of voices swept the chamber. He looked up to see that one of the parliamentary clerks had let himself into the hall and was hurrying toward the front seats, a single sheet of paper in his hand. He thrust it forward and Russell took it.

Gasped and staggered as though he had been struck a blow.

"Attacked," he said. "Another attack—this time on the naval base at Plymouth!"

It was the moment of decision. The engine of the first troop train had stopped in Saltash station. A wisp of smoke drifted up from the stack and the metal of the hot boiler clicked quietly. General Grant swung down from the engine and went forward to the advance engine that had halted just before the Albert Bridge across the Tamar River. Troops looked out of the windows of the two cars as he approached; a young captain swung down from the engine and saluted.

"You took care of the telegraph wires?" Grant asked.

"Just as you ordered, General. We dropped off a squad at every station to grab the telegraph operator, if there was one. After we left each station we used the train to pull down a half-dozen poles, then took up the wire. Got a passel of it in the freight car."

"Good. To the best of your knowledge, then, no warning was sent ahead?"

"Absolutely none, sir. We moved too fast. None of the operators were at their keys when we busted in."

"Well done." Grant looked across the bridge for a long moment; he could see no activity at the other end. The railway authorities would know by now that the telegraph was out of service the length of Cornwall. Had they thought it necessary to inform the military of this? There was only one way to find out.

"You will proceed across the bridge. Go slowly until you reach the other side. Then open the throttle and don't slow down until you go through Plymouth station. Stop there—but leave room for the troop trains behind you. Keep your weapons loaded—but return fire only if you are fired on first. Good luck."

"To us all, General!"

The officer sprinted back to the engine, which started to move even as he was climbing aboard. It pulled slowly out onto the long span of the incredible bridge. The troop train followed a hundred yards behind. Once safely off the bridge, they sped up, faster and faster through the local stations: St. Budeaux, Manadon, and Crownhill. The three following trains would stop at these stations, dispensing troops to seize and envelop the cities from the hills above. Shocked passengers on the platforms fell back as the train plunged through the stations, braking to a stop only after entering Plymouth station itself. The troops jumped down from the cars and fanned out, ignoring the civilians. There was a brief struggle as a policeman was overwhelmed, bound, and locked into the telegraph room with the operator, who had been trying to send a message down the line to London when they seized him. He did not succeed because the advance party had done their job and torn down the wires beyond the station.

The troops from the train formed up and marched out of the station. General Grant was with them. There was a row of waiting cabs just outside the station.

"Seize those horses," General Grant ordered an aide. "They can pull some of the Gatlings."

"What is happening here? I demand to know!" A well-dressed and irate gentleman stood before Grant, shaking his gold-headed walking stick in his direction.

"War, sir. You are at war." The man was seized by two troopers and bustled away even as Grant spoke.

The advance down through the streets of Plymouth was almost unopposed. There appeared to be no military units in the city itself; the few sailors they encountered were unarmed and fled before the menacing soldiers. But the alarm had been raised and the Americans came under fire when they approached the naval station.

"Bring up the Gatlings," Grant ordered. "The lead squads will bypass any strong points and let the Gatling guns come after and subdue them."

The Royal Marines put up a spirited defense of their barracks, but the machine guns chewed them up, tearing through the thin wooden walls. Roaring with victory, the American troops charged into the buildings; the few survivors quickly surrendered. The small number of sailors who took up arms were cut down by the Gatlings—and the marksmanship of the veteran American soldiers.

No cannon from any of the shore batteries were fired at the attackers because they were all trained out to sea. An attack from the land side of the port had never been expected.

The Americans were unstoppable. In Devonport they overran and occupied the navy vessels tied up there. The Plymouth docks were larger and more confusing and it took time to work through them. The American attack slowed—but still pushed forward.

As chance would have it, HMS *Defender*, which had arrived that morning, was tied up at a buoy in the stream. Her captain was on deck, summoned by the watch officer when they had heard the sound of firing from the city.

"What is it, Number One?" he asked when he had climbed to the bridge.

"Gunfire, sir, that is all that I know."

"What have you done about it?"

"Sent the gig ashore with Lieutenant Osborne. I thought that a gunnery officer might make sense of what is happening."

"Well done. Sounds like a bloody revolution . . ."

"Here they come, sir, rowing flat out."

"I don't like this at all. Signal the engine room. Get up steam."

"Aye, aye, sir."

Lieutenant Osborne was panting with exertion as he climbed to the bridge. Yet his face was pale under his tropical tan.

"Gone all to hell, sir," he said, saluting vaguely. "Troops everywhere, shooting, I saw bodies . . ."

"Pull yourself together, man. Report."

"Aye, aye, sir." Osborne straightened his shoulders and came to attention. "I had the gig wait at the dockside in case we had to get out in a hurry. I went on alone. Almost ran into a group of soldiers. They were pushing three matelots along that they had taken prisoner. They were shouting and laughing, didn't see me."

"What kind of troops?" the captain snapped. "Be specific."

"Blue uniforms with the sergeants' stripes wrong side up. They sounded like—Americans."

"Americans? Here? But how . . . ?"

The hapless gunnery officer could only shrug. "I saw other parties of them, sir. In the buildings, even boarding the ships. All kinds of gunfire. It was coming closer to me, even flanking me. That's when I decided that I had better get back and report what I had seen."

The captain quickly marshaled his thoughts. He had a grave decision to make. Should he take his ship closer to the dock to fire upon the invaders? But how could he find them? If they had seized any of the British warships, would he fire on his own sailors? If the attack had been as successful as the gunnery officer had said, why, the entire port could well be in enemy hands. If the telegraph lines were down, then no one would even know what had happened here. It was his duty now to inform Whitehall of this debacle.

It took long seconds to reach this conclusion, and he realized that the bridge was silent while they awaited his orders.

"Signal slow ahead. Have that line to the buoy cut. There is nothing that we can do here. But we can contact London and tell them what has happened. As soon as we are clear of the harbor, set a course for Dartmouth. Full revolutions. There will be a telegraph station there. I must report what we have seen."

Smoke pouring from her stack, the ironclad headed out to sea.

STRIKING A MIGHTY BLOW

As soon as the landings at Penzance were complete, USS *Pennsylvania* raised steam. When the message reached the ship that General Grant and his forces had left for Plymouth with the trains, she upped anchor and headed out to sea. The two other ironclads that remained anchored offshore would be more than force enough to secure the city should any enemy ships be so unwise as to attack. Captain Sanborn had received specific instructions from General Grant. He was to proceed to the part of the coast he was familiar with from the previous night's action. *Pennsylvania* steamed slowly east until they reached St. Austell, where they anchored in the deep water offshore. The previous night's landings had been good experience for the junior officers. But now Sanborn wanted to see the enemy country for himself.

"I'll command the landing party," he told the watch officer. "Bank the boilers and see that the watch below gets some sleep; some of them have been awake for two days now. I want two lookouts at the masthead with glasses. They are to report to you anything larger than a fishing boat. If they do sight any ships, you must then sound three long blasts on the whistle, and get up steam. Understood?"

"Aye, aye, sir."

The ship's four boats were hung on davits outside her armor. If they were destroyed in battle they could easily be replaced; the *Pennsylvania* could not be. Now they were lowered into the water, then swiftly boarded by the landing party and rowed ashore. The ship's marines landed first and ran across the beach to the street. Sanborn followed after them with his sailors, at a more leisurely pace, smiling at the shocked expressions of the pedestrians. He followed the train tracks to the tiny station, then returned the salute of the sergeant who came out to meet him.

"Station secured, sir, telegraph wires cut. I've got some prisoners locked in there, including two local policemen."

"Any trouble?"

"Nothing to speak of, sir. General Grant said that I was to expect you."

It was a long wait, most of the afternoon. Captain Sanborn shared some rations with the soldiers and heard about the capture of Penzance and the victorious train ride through Cornwall. Occupying each station as they came to it, then silencing all the telegraph communication as they went.

Around them the little town was silent, pacified—stunned, in fact—with most people staying off the streets. There was obviously no need for a large occupying force here, so the sailors were ordered back to the ship and only the marines remained. Sanborn was almost dozing off when he heard the sound of a train whistle up the line toward Plymouth. He joined the soldiers on the platform as the engine pulled in, pushing a single car ahead of it. The army officer swung down before they stopped and saluted the ship's commander.

"You will be Captain Sanborn?"

"I am."

He took an envelope from his locket and passed it over. "From General Grant, sir."

"How did it go in Plymouth?"

"I would say perfectly, sir. Before I left it was clear that all of the harbor defenses and docks had been captured. Most of the enemy ships had already being boarded and occupied. There was some resistance—but they couldn't stand before the Gatlings."

"It sounds like a job well done." Then the question that was foremost in his mind: "Did any of the enemy ships get away?"

"At least one, sir. An ironclad. I saw her standing out to sea when I was in the railroad station. Just the one, though."

"One is enough. My congratulations to the general."

The envelope was unsealed, so it was obviously meant for Sanborn to read. But that could wait until he was back aboard his ship; he had been away long enough now. And General Sherman would be waiting for this report. He knew its importance. The fate of the entire campaign depended on what was in this envelope.

Waiting was the hardest part.

General Sherman sat in his office in Cork, staring unseeingly out of the window. The now-familiar river Lee did not attract his attention. Instead he was looking past it toward England, trying to visualize the evolving situation in that country, fleshing out the bare reports that were spread out on the desk before him. The landings at Liverpool had been a brilliant success. The concentration camp there, and the other one near Birmingham, had been seized. The latest communication from each of them said that counterattacks had been reported. But they had been sporadic and disorganized; the well-armed defenders had successfully held their positions. This could easily change. Once the mighty British war machine began to roll, it would be unstoppable on its own soil. Heavy guns would batter the Irish and American troops; when their ammunition ran out they would be overwhelmed. That had been the risk from the very beginning of the operation. They were expendable and they knew it. But they would die fighting.

But that need not be. The British commanders surely would be rattled by the seizure of their naval base at Plymouth. It had been over twenty-four hours since that attack, and the authorities in London would have heard about it long since. Troops would be on the way there—might easily have arrived by now.

But it had been almost four days since the camps had been attacked and taken. The fighting would be desperate. Would his gamble succeed? Would the attack on Plymouth cause the British forces to be diverted from the two Midland cities? Would the British generals realize that they were wasting time and troops on tactically unimportant targets? Or was the British military mind too thick to reach that conclusion? If it was, why then, only the troops occupying the concentration camps would suffer. This would have no effect on the invasion, which would still go ahead as planned.

The worst part was that Generals Lee and Meagher knew about the dangers—as did their men who had captured the camps. They had still insisted on going. They would all be volunteers for what might be considered a suicide mission if Sherman had any doubts. He had had none. They were very brave men.

That was why it was so hard to wait while his soldiers were fighting and dying. Yet this was the plan they had all agreed upon, the right course to take, and he had to see it through. His adjutant knocked, then opened the door.

"Admiral Farragut and Captain Dodge are here, General."

"Any more reports from the front?"

"None, sir."

"All right, show them in."

Dodge was commander of USS *Thunderer*, the lead mortar ship. Farragut, as naval commander in chief, had chosen her as his flagship for the beginning of the operation. As usual, this veteran commander would be first into battle. Then, as Sherman started to speak, there was a rapid knocking on the door and the adjutant pushed in, his arms filled with newspapers.

"Captain Schofield in *Avenger* put a raiding party ashore in Fishguard—and they seized these newspapers that had just arrived there by train from London."

Sherman took the *Times* from him and stared at the blaring headline.

INVASION IN THE SOUTH: PLYMOUTH TAKEN

There were other headlines like this. He quickly flipped the pages for word of any troop movements. Yes, plenty, volunteers rushing to the colors, trains diverted for military use, martial law declared. There was silence in the room, broken only by the rustle of newspapers as they all read the first reliable reports of enemy activity. In the end it was Sherman who was the last to drop his newspaper onto his desk.

"We have stirred up a right hornet's nest," he said.

"You certainly have," Farragut said. "It appears that everything is going according to plan."

"Everything," Sherman agreed. "I just wish that there was more word about events in Liverpool and Birmingham."

"Being attacked, vicious fighting, according to this paper," Dodge said.

"Yes, but nothing about diversion of troops." Sherman shook his head. "I suppose that is a lot to ask from any public statements made by their government. There is no reason for the military to confide all of the details of their operations to the newspapers. Quite the opposite is probably true. Well then, to matters at hand. In your last report, Admiral, you said that the fleet was ready to put to sea."

"As indeed it is. The coal bunkers are full, rations and water stored aboard. The troops finished their boarding about two hours ago."

"Then we sail as planned?"

"We do indeed."

"You realize that this final attack will take place almost exactly two days after the landings at Penzance?"

The two naval officers nodded, knowing what Sherman was thinking and, like him, not wanting to speak any doubts aloud. The two-day delay had been deliberate. Two days more for the British to understand what was happening in the west—two days for them to take positive action against the invasion in the south. Two days to rally their forces and dispatch them to the invasion sites.

But this was also two days more for General Grant's men to hold them back.

And four days in all for Generals Lee and Meagher, and their troops, to defend the concentration camps that they had seized. It was all going according to plan. But it was also a plan that might very well send a good number of soldiers to their doom.

"Well then," Sherman said, drawing himself to his feet. "Let the operation begin."

★

As his pinnace brought Captain Dodge back to his ship, he saw another boat pulling away from *Thunderer*'s side. He clambered up the ladder and through the open hatch to find Gustavus Fox, the Assistant Secretary of the Navy, waiting for him.

"This is a pleasant surprise, Mr. Fox."

"My pleasure, Captain. I regret the delay, but there were unexpected difficulties in getting your river pilot here before you sailed. He is here now." He indicated the scowling, gray-bearded man being held by two marines. This was not the time to explain that Lars Nielsen, safely back in his native Jutland and drinking away the money that he had been given, had not been eager to leave Denmark again. A small force had to be quickly organized; a night landing and a sudden scuffle had resolved the situation.

"This a great relief, Mr. Fox. I must say that I was more than a little concerned."

"We all were, sir. I'm glad that I could be of service."

They sailed in daylight. Because of the necessity of keeping well away from the English coast, they were taking a more circuitous route well out into the Atlantic. It was a slow convoy, since they could not proceed at a pace faster than that of their slowest vessel. Some of the converted sailing ships were underpowered and sluggish—as were the newly built sea batteries. Certainly their engines were large enough, but the tons of armor plating, as well as the immense mass of the giant mortars, made for a ponderous weight.

It was an incredible sight—hopefully unseen by the enemy—as, one by one, the ships emerged from the mouth of the river Lee to join the warships already situated at their stations. They formed up as they moved, the cargo ships with their human consignment to the center of the convoy. The mortar ships were circled by more mobile vessels as well because, with their armor shields in place, they were unable to fight in the open sea. But their day would soon come.

On guard to the flanks, before and after as well, were the ironclads.

Some of them had raced ahead and interposed themselves between the convoy and the invisible British shore. This was a busy part of the Atlantic and there were other ships in the seaway. These were shepherded aside by the guarding ironclads, kept safely over the horizon so none of them ever had a glimpse of the bulk of the convoy.

The ships sailed this way until it was dark, then took nighttime stations so that each ship could follow the shielded lights of the ship in line before them. A rainy dawn found them entering the mouth of the English Channel. France to one side, England to the other, both invisible in the mist. Careful navigation had brought them to the right place at the correct time. Ironclads ranging out on the port flank to observe the English coast and assure the accuracy of their position.

General Sherman, on the bridge of USS *Thunderer*, saw that the sea batteries were now ranging ponderously ahead of the rest of the convoy as had been planned. *Thunderer* with her troops and machines would be the first to approach the British shore. The rain was clearing away now and a gray strip of land appeared through the mist off to the left.

England.

If Sherman's calculations were correct they would now be entering the final and critical phase of his combined attacks. Everything that had been accomplished so far had been leading up to this moment. If the British had been caught off guard, as he hoped, their troops and weapons would have been fully committed to the two earlier attacks.

But if they had seen through his plans, then this last assault would be in grave danger. Reinforced defenses might stop his advance; a blockade ship sunk in the river channel would render his assault useless. If he were beaten off, why then, Lee and Grant's soldiers were as good as dead. Without reinforcements and supplies, their positions were doomed. Waiting now for action, he was assailed by doubts; he fought them off. There was no going back.

Was it possible that the British generals had outthought him? Had they somehow divined the true nature of his approaching attack? Did they somehow know where he would strike next?

London.

The heart of the British Empire, the seat of power, the resting place of the crown.

Could the upstart Americans attack and seize this historic city and bring the worldwide empire crashing down?

Yes, Sherman said to himself, walking across the bridge to see the mouth of the Thames opening out before. *Yes,* he said, jaw set. *It can and it will be done.*

IN BATTLE DRAWN

It was a misty dawn and little could be seen through the clouded ports of the Trinity House cutter *Patricia*, now established off Dungeness. Caleb Polwheal had gotten out of bed in the dark, gone into the galley, and made a pot of tea by lamplight. He was master of the first shift, those pilots who would be standing ready at first light to take any waiting ships up the Thames. Taking his cup of tea, Caleb pushed open the door and went out on deck. Out to sea, just visible in the growing light, were the dark shapes of ships, just emerging from a rain squall that had swept by. More and more of them; this was going to be a busy day.

There were warships there as well, a fact made obvious by their menacing guns. Caleb hadn't been informed of any fleet movements, but that wasn't unusual. The navy liked to keep their secrets. The rain was stopping, the skies clearing; he went back into the ship and tapped the barometer on the wall. The glass was rising as well; it promised to be a fine day. When he came back on deck again, the approaching ships were closer, clearer; he was unaware that the cup had dropped from his limp fingers and had broken on the planking.

What ships were those to the fore? High-sided and bulky with black armor. They had an armored bridge right up in the bow; two side-by-side funnels in the stern. He knew the lines of every British ship—and these were not like anything ever seen in the navy. And the ironclads in line behind them, with two two-gun turrets—these were unfamiliar as well. There was nothing imaginably like these in the British navy. If not British, was it possible then that these ships were . . .

An invasion!

Pushing through the door, he stumbled into the bunkroom, shouting the startled pilots awake.

"Get up, get up! Man the pilot boat. We must get to the telegraph station on shore. Contact Trinity House in London immediately. They must know what is happening out here."

When the news of the invasion fleet reached Trinity House, it was quickly passed on to Whitehall and the War Department. Less than an hour after the ships had been sighted, the message dropped onto the desk of Brigadier Somerville. He had been at his post all night, working to coordinate the movement of the regiments and divisions that were being rushed into battle at Plymouth. After he spent some hours reading all the reports from the fighting fronts, it had been obvious, at least to him, that the attacks on the Midlands' concentration camps had been a feint. The enemy there had no escape, so they could be ignored. Eventually they would be captured and reduced—but not now. The real threat was in the south. Trains already going north had to be stopped, diverted, given new destinations. He had been at his post for two days and was wretched from lack of sleep. The Duke of Cambridge had been there almost as long. But he had gone for some rest before midnight and had never returned. Which was fine for Somerville. He no longer had to explain every action to his commander in chief, who at times had difficulty following the brigadier's quick and complex thinking. He seized the sheet of telegraph paper from the messenger, read it in a glance.

Fleet of warships entering the Thames estuary!

Realization struck. Of course—that had been their plan all the time. The other attacks were only diversions. . . . He was scrawling out a message even as his thoughts raced, his pen nib sputtering and spraying ink in

STARS & STRIPES TRIUMPHANT

his haste. He pushed it to one side, mastered himself, and wrote another message. He thrust both of them, the ink still wet, at the messenger who answered his call.

"Take these at once to the telegraph room. This one goes to the commander of the Southampton Naval Station. This other one must go out at once to the commander of Tilbury Fort."

"What fort is that, sir?"

"The telegraph men will know, you idiot. Give that back—I'll write it here. Now *run*!"

Before the man was out of the room, Somerville had forgotten him and was engaged in drafting messages to the armed forces now spread across the length and breadth of England. Changing all their orders. God—how he had been fooled! Then he stopped and drew himself up and took a deep breath. It was thought not action that was needed now.

He wiped the nib of his pen dry and took out his penknife. He preferred old-fashioned quill pens to the new steel ones. He carefully cut a new point on the quill while he ordered his thoughts. The attack up the Thames was surely aimed at London. He realized that his first priority was to look to the defenses of the capital. The household regiments had to be alerted. The Seventh Company of the Coldstream Guards was in its Chelsea barracks—they would be the first soldiers sent to the defense of Buckingham Palace. There were troops in Woolwich Arsenal; they must be sent for at once. Special trains had to be dispatched to Wiltshire for the troops encamped on Salisbury Plain there. The Prime Minister had to be awakened and informed. Thank goodness that it would be the PM's task to inform Buckingham Palace—not his.

He drew over a fresh sheet of paper and began, clearly and slowly, to write out his commands. Only after they were dispatched would he have the Duke of Cambridge awakened. Time enough after the proper orders had been issued to suffer his choleric wrath.

Admiral Spencer knew exactly what must be done as soon as he read the telegram. *Enemy fleet including warships now entering the Thames.* They

were there with only one possible target in mind. London. A strike at the heart of the empire would have a terrible effect if it were successful. It was obvious now that the various other landings and acts of harassment around the country had just been diversions. Ever since the attack on Plymouth every ship under his command had been manned and on the alert.

Now, at last, he knew where they must go. The enemy could get no farther upriver than London Bridge. Undoubtedly their troops would be disembarking there. The household regiments would see to them all right! There would be warships protecting them, he was certain of that. They would have to face the guns of his own ironclads. The enemy was stuck in a bottleneck—and he was going to drive in the cork. There would be no way out for them: they faced only destruction.

General Bagnell ordered the sergeant who had brought the telegram to throw open the curtains, then squinted at the sheet of paper in the morning light. He was still half-asleep and it took him some moments to understand the purport of the message.

An attack.

Even as reality struck home he heard, through the open window, the bugler sounding assembly. The officer of the day would have read the message and have had the intelligence to sound the alarm. The general's servant, who had let the messenger in, was already bringing his uniform. The many parts that formed the military machine were moving into place. Whenever the attack came—they would be ready. He pulled on his trousers and was stepping into his boots when he thought of the late Lord Palmerston. It was through his intervention and enterprise that Tilbury Fort had been rearmed and expanded. As had the many other fortresses that defended England. It was that great man's foresight that might save England yet again.

It was a clear, fine day. General Bagnell stood beneath the flag, on the topmost battlement of the Water Gate, looking downriver at the placid Thames. The curtain walls of Tilbury Fort, to the east and west bastions, were built on arched counter forts, solidly constructed of Portland stone. The stout walls and parapets beyond were made of brick and had been reinforced with dirt ramparts strong enough to resist an enemy siege barrage, while the large guns concealed in the forts returned their fire. And there were the other defenses; the gun lines outside the walls, safe behind their own parapets, stretching out to east and west of the Water Gate. Six-inch and twelve-pounder guns. All manned, all ready.

There was the sound of heavy guns firing downriver. It must have been the batteries at Coalhouse Fort. The thunder became intense—then died away. A few minutes later the enemy came into view. Coming around the bend in the Thames between East Tilbury and Cliffe. Strange-shaped armorclads like black beetles that crawled on the surface of the water. They had high, sloped sides with armor plate covering above that. But no gun ports that Bagnell could see.

"Prepare to open fire as soon as they are in range," he ordered his aide, who passed the message on to the waiting gunners.

The four ships were closer now—but separating. One of them was moving away from the others, toward the gun positions at Gravesend, on the other side of the river. Good, the gunners there would make short work of her—while he could concentrate his fire on the remaining three.

The gunnery officer shouted "fire" and the Tilbury Fort guns roared out. The peaceful surface of the Thames turned suddenly into a maelstrom of waterspouts as near misses crashed into the river. And there were hits—many of them. Solid shot that hammered into the enemy's iron armor.

And bounced away. Bagnell saw the blur of the ricocheting balls as they hummed into the air.

From this distance the ironclads seemed to be unharmed. And something strange was happening to them as they anchored, their chains running out fore and aft. They were facing broadside to the fort with their upper armor moving, apparently rising. No, not rising, opening up as the metal plates that covered the vessels were swung wide.

His cannon were firing again, but the raised plates deflected the cannon-balls as well as did the armor. Then the first ship seemed to shiver and sink deeper into the water, throwing whitecapped waves out in all directions. A dark cloud of smoke welled up and he had a brief glimpse of a large projectile rising high into the air. Drawing a dark line in the sky that ended on the bastion beside the Water Gate. There was an immense explosion, and when the smoke cleared away, to his horror, the general saw that three guns had been dismounted and destroyed, the guncrews obliterated in that terrible explosion. A single shell had wrought this carnage.

And more of the large shells were falling, until there was an almost continuous roar of detonating high explosives. Unlike normal cannon that fired shells directly at a target, these mortars arched a giant missile high into the air, to plunge down almost vertically onto the target below. Battlements and walls that faced the enemy were no defense against this kind of attack.

But General Bagnell was not aware of this debacle. He, and all of his officers, had been blown to pieces by the third shell that had landed on the fort. He did not live to see either the destruction of his fort or the obliteration of the gun emplacements across the river by the fourth mortar ship. In thirty intense, destructive minutes, all of the defenses of the river at Tilbury had been destroyed. Even as the firing ceased, the first of the long line of ships nosed into sight around the bend in the river and moved, unharmed, toward London.

USS *Atlas* had been idling her engines to keep position in the river against the tidal current. When the mortar ships had ceased firing, her captain saw that the boat that had been shielded by the bulk of the *Thunderer* was now pulling away from her flank. Good. Admiral Farragut was transferring his flag to the *Mississippi*—and taking the Thames pilot with him. Everything was going as planned. As soon as the boat reached the ironclad, Captain Curtin ordered the engines slow ahead. Three blasts on her steam whistle signaled the rest of the waiting ships to follow her upstream. As they got under way, USS *Mississippi* surged forward, passing the slower cargo ship and taking her position in the lead. After the successful landings at Penzance, she had proceeded to the mouth of the Thames to join the attacking squadron. Now she raced ahead, guns loaded and ready, to seek out any other river defenses.

Beside Curtin on *Atlas*'s bridge, General Sherman looked at the smoking ruins of Tilbury Fort as they moved slowly by. "Utterly destroyed in less than half an hour," he said. "I have never seen anything like it."

Curtin nodded understandingly. "That is because you are a soldier and see war as something to be fought on land. But you must remember the success of General Grant's mortar ships in the Mississippi at Vicksburg. No railway gun can match one of these sea-battery mortars for size—and no team of horses could ever move one. But put them into an iron ship and you can cross oceans with them. Just as they have done. But it took the genius of a nautical engineer to design and manufacture them as well."

"I agree completely. Mr. Ericsson is an asset to our country—and most certainly will lead us to success in this war. Are you pleased with the ship you command, Captain? This is also his design."

"Not pleased—ecstatic, if you will permit me to use a word with many connotations. I believe that *Atlas* is the most powerful ship that I have ever commanded. With twin engines and twin screws, she is in a class by herself. And like her namesake, she cannot quite carry the world on her shoulders—but she comes mighty close to it."

The Thames curved in great loops as they made their way upriver. As they came into the Dartford reach, there was the flash of guns from the *Mississippi* ahead of them.

"That will be the arsenal at Woolwich," Sherman said. "They have some batteries facing the river there, but nothing much to speak of. Tilbury Fort is the major defense of the Thames, and no hostile fleet was ever expected to get by her armaments or reduce her by siege."

"Perhaps that was true of yesterday's wars," Curtin said. "But not today's."

Mississippi was already at the next bend in the river when they passed Woolwich. A few battered and burning gun emplacements on the shore were all that remained of her defenses.

The Thames here made a great swing around the Isle of Dogs, and when the river straightened again all of the commercial heart of London

WAR'S TERRIBLE DESTRUCTION

opened out before them. There were ships tied up at the docks on both shores, merchantmen from every corner of the empire. Fresh fruit was being unloaded at Limehouse—whence it got its name. Behind *Atlas* the line of black ships followed steadily—an invasion force that was piercing straight into the heart of London.

More firing sounded ahead as the American ironclad began trading fire with the batteries of the Tower of London. But here, as in Woolwich, the defenses were not substantial at all. One of the towers of the famous castle crumbled under the ship's fire.

One by one *Mississippi*'s guns grew silent, their work done, as the shore defenses were battered into destruction. Her funnels were riddled with holes, her boats shot away, but other than that, the ironclad appeared unharmed. Smoke rolled up from her funnels as she gained way, moving ponderously toward the riverbank, letting *Atlas* proceed up the main channel.

The river was clear ahead. Sherman recognized it from the many photographs and maps that he had pored over. On the right was the road along the Embankment, with fine buildings behind it. Beyond the buildings were the Gothic towers of the Houses of Parliament, the main tower with its immense clock face visible far downriver. The hands pointed to noon. Sherman stepped out onto the wing and could hear the deep tolling of Big Ben sounding the hour. It was the beginning of the afternoon of the British Empire.

Atlas's engines were silent as she drifted toward the Embankment, slower and slower. There were hansom cabs and drays on the road there, private carriages and pedestrians. They were fleeing now as the hulking black ship grated against the granite river wall.

Even before she touched, sailors had leaped over the lessening gap, seized the cables passed down to them, and made them fast to the stone bollards of the waterfront. The sudden rattle of rifle fire sounded; two of the sailors twisted and dropped. Bullets clanged against the metal of the bridge, shooting out one of the windows. A line of red-coated soldiers had advanced from Parliament Square. The front rank stopped to fire—just as the bow battery of *Atlas* fired a canister shell. Holes opened suddenly in the advancing ranks of redcoats. Then a dark shadow passed over *Atlas* as *Mississippi* slid by, her guns opening fire as soon as they could bear.

Captain Curtin was out on the wing of the bridge, ignoring the fire from the shore, issuing commands. The moment his ship was securely moored, he ordered the upper ramp to be extended. The outer door swung slowly aside and there was a mighty clanking as the steam pistons pushed the tons of metal out and down. The information that had been passed on by the Russian agents proved to be correct. At this time of day, on this date, at this particular place, where the tidal river rose and fell by a dozen feet, the ramp was exactly two feet above the granite of the river wall. It clanked down into place; metal screeched as the relentless pistons pushed the ramp forward into position.

Inside *Atlas*, on the upper deck, the Gatling carriers were lined up in even rows that stretched from bow to stern. As soon as the great ship had entered the Thames, the tank crews began removing the shackles and turnbuckles that had secured them in place during the sea crossing. Kerosene lamps on the bulkheads provided barely enough light to accomplish this task.

Sergeant Corbett, driver of the lead machine, cursed as he barked his knuckles on the last recalcitrant shackle, pulled it free of the eye inset in the deck, and hurled it aside. As he did this, green electric lights in the ceiling came on, controlled from the ship's bridge.

"Start your engines!" he bellowed. Drivers and gunners, down the length of the columns, jumped to the task. Private Hoobler, Corbett's gunner, ran to the front of their machine and seized the starting handle. "Battery switch off!" he called out.

"Switched off!" Corbett shouted back.

Hoobler braced himself and turned the handle the required four times, grunting with the effort of pumping oil into the engine's bearings and fuel into its cylinders; gunners were selected for their strength of arm as well as their accuracy of fire.

"Battery switch on," he gasped.

"On!" the sergeant shouted back and thrust closed the small bayonet switch on the control panel. He had to raise his voice above the din of the many barking, hammering Carnot-cycle engines that were bursting into life. Hoobler gave a mighty swing of the handle, but instead of starting, the engine backfired. He cried out in pain as the starting handle kicked back in reverse and broke his arm.

At this same moment the bow door opened and the blaze of sunlight revealed him sitting on the deck nursing his wounded arm. Cursing even more vociferously, Sergeant Corbett jumped down and bent over the wounded man; the crooked angle of his lower arm was vivid evidence of what had happened.

The tank deck was now an inferno of hammering exhausts and clouds of reeking fumes. As the landing ramp went down, soldiers rushed forward from the machines to the rear, shouldered the sergeant and his wounded gunner aside, pushed their stalled vehicle aside as well. A moment later the second Gatling carrier rumbled past them and forward onto the ramp, leading the others into battle. Its spiked wheels dug into the wooden planks of the ramp as it gathered speed. Coughing in the reeking fumes, Corbett tore Hoobler's jacket open and thrust the man's broken arm into it for support; the soldier gagged with pain. Behind them the carriers rumbled forward to the attack while Corbett pulled open the access door to the deck and half dragged, half carried, the wounded soldier out into the sunshine. Once he had settled the man against a bulkhead, he turned and shouted.

"I need a gunner!"

His words were drowned out by the roar of a cannon firing close by. He ran toward it, dodged the discarded shell casing that rolled toward him. Called out again just as the gun's breech was slammed shut and the gun bellowed again. One of the two ammunition carriers shouted back.

"I shot one of them Gatlings in training!"

The gun captain seized the firing lanyard. "I can spare one man!" he called back, then fired the cannon again. Sergeant Corbett headed back on the run, with the gunner right behind him. "Get aboard," he ordered. Checked the bayonet switch and, with a single mighty heave, turned over the engine. It started at once, roared and rattled as he jumped into his seat. He looked over his shoulder at the line of vehicles rumbling by. The top deck was now clear of vehicles. Before the carriers from the lower deck could come off the ramp from below, Corbett sped up the engine, eased power to the wheels, and jerked forward. Into the daylight and down the landing ramp he drove into combat.

The bark of his engine joined the roar of the others, echoed out from the interior of the cavernous ship. A steady stream of tanks, the Gatling carriers, rolled out and down onto the riverbank. Followed by more—and yet still more machines. While fore and aft the companionways had been dropped and a tide of blue uniforms flowed down from the ship and onto the English soil.

"Fire!" Corbett shouted as they clattered off the ramp onto the cobbles. His new gunner bent to his sights and cranked the handle of his gun. Bullets streamed out as he swept the gun along the line of red-uniformed soldiers.

The defending troops were mowed down like a field of grain by the rapid-firing Gatling guns. Some of the defenders fired back, but their bullets merely clanged off the armored front shields of the carriers.

On the bridge of the *Atlas*, high above, General Sherman looked down at the surging battle. The enemy line appeared to be broken, the defenders dead or fleeing the blue-clad troops now moving past the slower gun carriers.

"Cavalry!" someone shouted, and Sherman looked up to see the mounted soldiers pouring out of the streets that led to Whitehall and Horse Guards Parade. Brigadier Somerville had done an exemplary job in alerting the defenses. The American soldiers turned to face this new threat on their flank—but the Gatling carriers surged past them. Their exhausts roaring loudly, pumping out clouds of acrid smoke, they surged forward toward the cavalry. Now, with swords raised, helmets and cuirasses gleaming, the horsemen charged at the gallop.

And were destroyed. Just as the Light Brigade had been when they had charged the Russian lines in the Crimea. But here were rapid-firing guns, more deadly at close range than any cannon could ever be. Men and horses screamed and died, wiped out, sprawling unmoving across the road that now ran red with blood.

None survived. General Sherman went down from the ship's bridge to join his staff waiting for him on the shore.

HMS *Viperous*, the pride of the British navy, led the attack. After taking aboard the pilot off Dungeness, she proceeded at a stately five knots into the main channel of the Thames. The other ironclads, in line behind her, followed in her course. Her guns were loaded and ready; she was prepared to take on any Yankee ironclad and give as good as she received. From his station on the bridge wing, the captain was the first to see the waiting enemy as they rounded the last bend in the river before Tilbury Fort.

There were the American war craft, four hulking black ships drawn up in line across the river.

"Fire when your guns bear," he ordered, looking at the enemy through his glasses. He had never seen ships like this before. Armor was all that he could see—with no sign of gun ports at all. There was a mighty roar as the forward gun turret fired; the ship's fabric shook beneath his feet.

Good shooting. He could see the shells explode against the armor of the ship in the center of the line. The smoke cleared, he could see no signs of damage—then a cloud of smoke blossomed up from behind the enemy's armor. He had a quick glimpse of an immense shell climbing in a high arc, seemingly suspended in space before it dropped. An enormous fountain of water sprang up beside the port bow, drenching the foredeck.

Even before the first shell struck, a second was on its way. This struck the *Viperous* amidships, and the tremendous explosion almost blew the mighty ship in two.

Anchored and ready, the mortar batteries were as deadly against the slow-moving enemy as they had been against the fortress on land. Within a minute the mortally wounded iron ship had settled to the riverbed, with shells sending up massive waterspouts around the rest of the attacking fleet as they withdrew out of range.

Sherman's rear defenses were secured. He need fear no attacks from the river as long as the floating batteries were in place.

BUCKINGHAM PALACE ATTACKED

More and still more of the Gatling-gun carriers emerged from *Atlas* and rumbled down the ramp. These had been stowed deep in the ship's hold and had climbed to the disembarking level using a series of interior ramps between decks.

Nor was *Atlas* now the only ship tied up at the embankment. While the ironclads stayed on station in midriver, the transports at the river wall had sent their soldiers charging ashore. Regiments of riflemen were forming up even as the first cannon were being lowered to the Embankment. The horse handlers led their mounts, trotting up to Sherman's staff; he felt better after swinging up into the saddle.

"We've pushed units up these streets toward Whitehall," an aide said, pointing out the positions on his map. "Our men will be taking defensive positions in the buildings on both sides. There'll be no more surprise attacks by cavalry from that direction."

Sherman nodded approval, touched the map. "These troops in Parliament Square must be neutralized. Then the Gatlings can take out these defensive positions in the buildings there."

"We're taking fire from Westminster Abbey," an officer reported.

"Return it," Sherman said coldly. "If that is their choice, I say that our men's lives come before an ancient monument. I want all the defensive positions reduced before we advance to the Mall. It will be a two-pronged attack, there and down this road. Is it really called Birdcage Walk?"

"It is, sir."

"All right. The staff will join the column there—let the attacking units know. Report to me when you are ready."

The sound of cannon, the tearing violence of gunfire, could easily be heard at Buckingham Palace. From the other side of St. James's Park, above the trees, clouds of smoke roiled skyward. Queen Victoria stood white-faced on the balcony, shaking her head in disbelief. This was not happening, could not be happening. Below her there was the clatter of hooves and the scrape of wheels on the cobbles of the courtyard. She was aware of her ladies-in-waiting calling to her, pleading, but she did not move. Even when one of them was bold enough to touch her sleeve.

A man's voice sounded from the door behind her, silencing the shrill voices.

"Come now, Your Majesty. The carriages are here."

The Duke of Cambridge had an urgency in his voice. Victoria's first cousin, he was familiar enough to take her by the arm. "The children have gone ahead. We must go after them."

The children! Mention of them cleared her head and filled her with a certain urgency. She turned from the window and let the Duke lead her from the room. He went on ahead, leaving her ladies to see to her.

He had a lot to do and not much time to do it in. When his servant had shaken him awake that morning, his head was still fogged with fatigue and he could make little of what was happening at first. Warships? The Thames? When he had hurried to his office, Brigadier Somerville made it all too clear.

"The attacks in the Midlands—even capturing Plymouth—that was all a ruse. And it succeeded. They are striking up the Thames, and London is their target."

"Tilbury. The fort there will stop them."

"I sincerely hope so, but we cannot rely on hope. So far everything about this invasion has gone exactly as they have planned. I fear they must have some strategy how they will attack the fort. London must be defended, and I have made every effort to see that is done. The household troops have been alerted and I have sent for reinforcements. Now we must see about saving the government—and the Queen. You must convince her that for her own safety, she must leave."

"Leave? Go where?"

The Duke was being even thicker than usual this morning; Somerville fought to keep the anger from his voice. "Windsor Castle for now. The Prime Minister and his cabinet can join her there. Immediate danger will be averted and further plans can be made once she is safe. She will listen to you. You must convince her that this is the proper course of action. The forces attacking us are overwhelming. If she is seized in Buckingham Palace, why then, this war is over before it has even properly begun."

"Yes, of course." The Duke rubbed his jaw, his fingers scraping over the unshaven bristles. "But the defense of the city?"

"Everything has been done that can be done here. Only the Queen's safety remains in doubt."

"Yes," the Duke said, climbing slowly to his feet. "Call my carriage. I will take the matter in hand."

The hours had passed like minutes in Buckingham Palace. The Duke had had the household cavalry turned out, mounted and ready. The stables behind the palace were stirred to life. Now it was time to leave. The sound of gunfire was louder, closer. Yes, now, the last carriage door slammed shut. With a crack of whips and clatter of hooves they swung out of the forecourt, through the palace gateway, and into Buckingham Gate. Riding west toward safety.

The resistance by the British forces around Parliament Square was dying down. Flesh and blood could not stand against the mechanized attack, the Gatling guns and the decimating volleys of the rapid-firing rifles of the American troops. General Sherman noted the reports as they came in; issued clipped orders. These veterans knew what to do. Within an hour the enemy had been pushed back into St. James's Park and the final assault

OLD GLORY IN TRIUMPH!

was ready to begin. Sherman wrote a last order and passed it to the waiting rider.

"For Colonel Foster at Admiralty Arch. He is to advance when he sees us move out."

During the brief wait ammunition had been rushed to the Gatling carriers. Horses also pulled forward a wagon laden with barrels of liquid fuel to fill their emptying tanks. Sherman read the last of the reports and nodded.

"Sound the attack," he said.

As the bugle notes echoed from the buildings, they were drowned out as the engines of the Gatling carriers roared into life. Clouds of blue smoke rolled across the square from their blatting exhausts as the advance began.

It was attrition and death for the defenders. Armored in the fore, spitting leaden death, the carriers rolled up to the hastily constructed barricades and slaughtered the troops that were concealed there, firing until the ineffective defending fire died away. Willing hands tore gaps in the barricades and the carriers rolled through the defensive lines. There was another cavalry charge down Birdcage Walk by the defenders as Buckingham Palace came into view; it was no more successful than the first and only a handful of survivors stumbled in retreat.

The Gatling carriers rumbled ahead of the troops, pausing only when they reached the palace. A household guard regiment there put up a heroic defense, but their thin steel cuirasses could not stop the American bullets. Through the gates the attackers surged, held up for a moment by defenders within the palace itself. But the withering Gatling fire crashed through the windows on the ground floor, sending a spray of death crawling up to the defenders firing from the floors above. With a roaring cheer the soldiers surged forward into the palace itself.

When General Sherman and his staff rode into the palace yard a few minutes later, the battle had come to a bloody end. Corpses sprawled across the cobbles. Here and there were a few wounded survivors now being tended by medical corpsmen. Two American soldiers, with slung rifles, emerged from the entrance holding between them an elegantly dressed man bearing a white cloth.

"Came walking right up to us, General, just a-waving this tablecloth," the corporal said. "Let on how he wanted to speak with whoever is in charge."

"Who are you?" Sherman asked coldly.

"Equerry to Her Majesty, Queen Victoria."

"That is fine. Take me to her."

The man drew himself up, trying to control his quaking limbs as he faced the armed enemy.

"That will not possible. She is not here. Please call off this attack and the senseless killing."

"Where is she?"

The man stiffened, his mouth clamped shut. Sherman started to query him, changed his mind. He turned to his staff.

"We will assume for the moment that he is telling the truth. Search the palace, speak to the servants, find out where the Queen has gone. Meanwhile I will make my headquarters here."

"Look, General, up there," an officer called out, and pointed toward the roof of Buckingham Palace. Everyone who heard him turned to look.

An American soldier had appeared on the roof and was lowering the flag that flew there. It fluttered down the face of the building and lay crumpled on the stones. Now the Stars and Stripes was going up in its place. A great cheering broke out from the watching soldiers; even Sherman nodded and smiled.

"This is a great moment, a great day, sir," his chief of staff said.

"It is indeed, Andy, it surely is."

A DARING ESCAPE

From his window, facing out onto Whitehall, Brigadier Somerville had an uninterrupted view of the battle for London. Once he had informed the household cavalry and the foot guards, all of the troops defending the city, of the approaching menace, the defense of the city was out of his hands. There was the continuing sound of gunfire from the direction of the Embankment; cannon sounded in Parliament Square. He watched as proud cavalrymen trotted by, helmets and cuirasses gleaming. This was the second time he had seen the cavalry attack the enemy; none had returned from the first wave.

Now Somerville saw the shattered remnants of the last charge returning from battle. It was terrible, but he could not look away. If the finest soldiers in the land could not stand against the enemy—was there any hope for them at all? He saw bloody disaster, death, and destruction. This was the end. A knocking at his door stirred him from his dark reverie. He turned to see Sergeant Major Brown enter and snap to attention and salute.

"What is it, Sergeant Major?" He heard his voice as from a great distance, his mind still dazed by the horrors he had just witnessed.

"Permission to join the defenses, sir."

"No. I need you with me." Somerville spoke the words automatically—but there was a reason. With an effort he drew his thoughts together as an element of a plan began to form. His work in London was done. But, yes, he could still be of value to this war, to the defense of his country. The rough idea of what he must do was there, still not fleshed out, but it held out hope. He knew what he must do for a start. Escape. He realized that the sergeant major was still at attention, waiting for him to finish what he had started to say.

"Stand at ease. You and I are going to get out of this city and join up with Her Majesty's forces where we can do the most good." He looked at the man's scarlet jacket with its rows of medals. He couldn't leave the safety of the building looking like this. "Do you keep any other clothes here?"

The soldier was startled by the question, but nodded in reply. "Some mufti, sir. I use it when I'm not on duty."

"Then put it on and come back here." The brigadier glanced down at his own uniform. "I'll need clothes as well." He took some pound notes from his pocket and passed them over. "I'll need trousers, a jacket, coat. Find something my size among the clerks. See that they are paid for the clothes. Then bring them back with you."

Sergeant Major Brown saluted and did a smart about-face. Somerville automatically returned the salute—then called out to Brown. "That's the last salute for the time being. We are going to be civilians, members of the public. Don't forget that."

When he had given Brown the money, he realized he had very little more remaining in his wallet. He was going to need funds to fashion their escape from the city, perhaps a good deal of them. That was easily recti-fied. He went down the corridor and up a flight of stairs to the paymaster general's office.

The halls and offices were deserted; everyone was either watching from the front windows or had fled to safety. He righted an overturned chair and went across the room to the large safe. The key was on the ring in his pocket; he unlocked it and opened the door. Gold guineas would be best, coin of the realm, and welcome anywhere. He took out a heavy bag that thunked when he dropped it on the desk. He needed something to carry it in. He opened a closet and found a carpetbag behind the umbrellas there. Perfect. He dropped two bags of coins into it, started to close it. Opened it again and took out a handful of coins from one of the bags and put them into his pocket.

He was back in his office before Brown returned, dressed for the street and bearing an armful of clothing. "Not of the best quality, sir, but was all I could find in this size."

"That will do fine, Sergeant . . . Brown. You'll carry this bag. Careful, it has gold coin."

"Yes, sir . . ." He stopped as the rapid firing of a gun sounded through the open window. It was followed by a roaring, racketing sound, something he had never heard before. Somerville and Brown crossed the room to look carefully down into the street. They gaped in silence at the strange contrivances passing by below.

They had wheels—but were not drawn by horses. They were propelled in some internal manner, for clouds of fumes poured behind them, the source of the strange hammering noise. A blue-clad soldier rode in the rear of each contrivance, somehow directing it.

At the front, crouching behind armor plate, was a gunner. The nearest one turned the handle of his rapid-firing weapon and a stream of bullets poured out.

A bullet crashed through the glass just above their heads and they drew back from a last vision of the attacking troops following the Gatling guns.

"They are going in the direction of the Mall," Brown said grimly. "They'll be attacking the palace."

"Undoubtedly. We must wait until the stragglers have passed—then follow them. We are going to the Strand."

"Whatever you say, sir."

"Then we must find a cab. There should still be some in the streets."

They stood in the doorway until the last soldiers had gone by. There were uniformed corpses in the streets now; a cavalryman lay nearby, dead beside his mount, sprawled in the animal's entrails. Like Somerville and Brown, a few other figures scuttled along the pavements to safety. They walked quickly, taking shelter in another doorway when an American cavalryman galloped past. After that it was a hurried dash to the Strand and down it past Charing Cross station. They could see people huddled inside the station, but they did not stop. All of the cabs were gone from the forecourt. They had to walk as far as the Savoy Hotel before they found a cab waiting outside the entrance there. The frightened cabbie stood, holding his horse, his face white with fear.

"I need your cab," Somerville said. The man shook his head numbly, beyond speech. Brown stepped forward, raising a large fist; Somerville put out a restraining hand. "We are going to the docks—" He thought quickly. "Go through the City, away from the river, until you are well past the Tower. You'll be safe in the East End." He dug one of the guineas from his pocket and passed it over.

The sight of the coin did more than words ever could to move the cabby to action. He took it, turned and opened the door for them. "The East End, sir. I'll go through Aldgate, then to Shadwell to Wapping. Maybe to Shadwell Basin."

"Whatever you say. Now go."

The sound of gunfire grew more distant as they went up Kingsway. There were more people here, hurrying through the streets, as well as a few other cabs. The City of London seemed undisturbed, although there were armed guards outside the Bank of England. They reached Shadwell Basin without any incidents and Brigadier Somerville saw, tied up in the basin there, just what he was looking for.

A Thames lighter, brown sail hanging limp, was on the far side of the basin. He called up through the hatch to the cabbie. There were three men sitting on the deck of the sturdy little ship when they alighted beside it. The oldest, with a grizzled beard, stood up when they approached.

"I need to hire your boat," Somerville said without any preamble. The man laughed and pointed with his pipe at the direction of the river. Above the rooftops of the terraced houses the dark bulk of a large ironclad could be seen moving by.

"Guns and shooting. You ain't seeing old Thomas on the river this day."

"They won't shoot at a boat like this," Somerville said.

"Begging your pardon, your honor, but I ain't taking any man's word for that."

The brigadier dug into his pockets and drew out some gold coins. "Five guineas to take us downriver. Five more when we get there."

Thomas looked wary. He couldn't get five guineas for a month's, two months' hard labor on the river. Greed fought with fear.

"I'll take those now," he finally said. "But ten more when we get there."

"Done. Let us leave at once."

Once they were out of the basin, the big sail was hauled up and they made good time through the muddy water. Rounding the Isle of Dogs, they looked back and saw an approaching warship coming down the river behind them. Thomas shouted commands and the sail came down; they drifted close by the docks on the shore there. The ship went smoothly by, the sailors visible on deck giving them no heed. They went on when it had passed, moving quickly and uneventfully until Tilbury came into sight.

"Mother of God . . ." the helmsman said, standing and shading his eyes. They all looked on in horrified silence at the smoking ruins of the shattered fortress. Walls and battlements had been destroyed, dismounted gun barrels pointed to the sky. Nothing moved. Thomas automatically turned closer to shore at the sight of the four hulking black ships that were anchored across the river. The stars and stripes of the American flag flew from a flagstaff at the stern of the nearest warship. Beyond them, in midstream, the masts and funnel, some of the upperworks of a sunken ship projected a few feet above the water.

"Is she . . . one of ours?" Thomas asked in a hushed, hoarse voice.

"Perhaps," Somerville said. "It does not matter. Proceed downstream."

"Not with them ships there!"

"They are not here to harm a vessel like this one."

"You can say that, your honor, but who's to tell."

Somerville was tempted to reason with the man; reached into his pocket instead. "Five guineas right now—and then ten more when we get downriver."

In the end avarice won. The lighter crept along the riverbank, slowly past the ruined fort. The warships anchored in the river ignored it. Then they moved faster once they were past the invaders, swept around the bend under full sail.

Ahead of them, anchored by the channel, was another ironclad, bristling with guns.

"Drop the sail!"

"Don't do that, you fool," the brigadier shouted. "Look at that flag!"

The British white ensign hung from the staff at her stern.

A MONARCH'S PLIGHT

General Sherman allowed thirty minutes to make absolutely sure that the battle for London was truly won. He went carefully through the reports, checking the references on a map of the city spread across the ornate desk. Through the open window behind him he could hear that the sounds of battle were dying away. A rumble of cannon in the distance, one of the ironclads from the sound of it. They were proving invaluable in reducing the riverside defenses. Then the crackling fire of a Gatling gun.

"I think we have done it, Andy," he said, sitting back in the chair. His chief of staff nodded agreement.

"We are still finding pockets of resistance, but the main bodies of enemy troops have all been defeated. I am sure that we'll mop up the rest before dark."

"Good. Make sure that sentries are posted before the men bed down. We don't want any surprise night attacks."

With the city secured, Sherman's thoughts returned to the next and most important matter at hand.

"You made inquiries. Did you find out where the Queen went?"

"No secret of it—everyone in London seems to know, the ones near the palace saw her pass by. Windsor Castle, they all agree on that."

"Show me on the map."

Colonel Summers unfolded the large-scale map and laid it over the one of London.

"Quite close," Sherman said. "As I remember, there are two train lines going there from London." He smiled when he saw his aide's expression. "Not black magic, Andy. It is just that I have been a keen student of my *Bradshaw*—the volume that contains timetables for every rail line in Britain. Get a troop of cavalry to Paddington Station. Seize the station and the trains."

Reports and requests for support were coming in and for some time Sherman was kept busy guiding the attacks. Then, when he looked up, he saw that Summers had returned.

"We're not going anywhere by train for some time, General. Engines and rails were sabotaged at Paddington."

Sherman nodded grim agreement. "At the other stations as well, I'll wager. They're beginning to learn that we make good use of their rolling stock. But there are other ways to get to Windsor." He looked back at the map. "Here is the castle, upriver on the Thames. Plenty of twists and turns to the river before it gets there. But it's pretty straight there by road. Through Richmond and Staines, then into Windsor Great Park."

Sherman looked at the scale on the map. "Must be twenty-five, thirty miles."

"At least."

"These soldiers have had a long day fighting; I'm not going to have them endure a forced march after that. Can we spare the cavalry?"

"We certainly can—now that the city has been taken. And they are still fresh."

"Can we round up more horses?"

"The city is full of them, dray horses for the most part."

"Good. I want the entire troop to take part in this. Round up all the horses you need and harness them to some Gatling guns. We'll move them out when the guns are ready. I'll take command. Make sure the city stays pacified."

"What about the river, General?"

"That was my next thought. There are plenty of small boats in the

Thames that we can commandeer. Put some of our sailors in each one to make sure the crews follow orders. Get a company of troops upriver that way. General Groves will be in command. If he gets there first I want his men to get around the castle but not attack it until he receives the command from me. Whoever is in the castle now—I want them still there when we occupy it."

"Understood."

The cavalry went west at an easy trot, General Sherman and his staff to the fore. Almost as soon as they had passed through Chelsea, where a bitter battle had been fought to take the barracks, all signs of war fell behind them. Distant guns still rumbled sporadically, but they could have been mistaken for thunder. The streets were strangely empty for the time of day, though the soldiers were aware of watching eyes from the passing windows. The only untoward incident occurred when they were passing through Putney.

There was the crack of a gun and a bullet passed close to General Sherman.

"Up there!" one of the soldiers shouted, pointing to a puff of smoke from the window of a residence. One after another the cavalrymen fired, their bullets crashing the glass from the window and sending chunks of frame flying.

"Leave it," Sherman ordered. They galloped on.

It was late afternoon before they passed through Windsor Great Park and saw the crenellated towers of the castle ahead. As they came through the woods, they saw that there were American riflemen who had taken up positions behind many of the trees facing an open green field. A sloping lawn led up to the castle beyond. A major of the Kentucky Rifles stepped forward and saluted Sherman as he slid down from his horse.

"Men all in position, right around the castle, sir."

"Any resistance?"

"They tried some potshots from the windows, but stopped when we returned their fire. We stayed away, like you ordered. Gates closed tight, but we know there are a passel of people inside."

"Is the Queen among them?"

"Don't rightly know. But we rousted out some of the citizens from the

A MONARCH'S PLIGHT

town. All say the same thing, and I think they are too frightened to lie. Lots of carriages came today—and the Queen's was one of them. Nobody come out since."

"Good work, Major. I'll take over from here."

Sherman returned the man's salute, then turned to look up at the grim granite walls of the castle. Should he wait until they could bring some cannon up to batter an opening in them? There were a number of doors and windows; a sudden attack might take the castle by storm. But many good men would be lost if the defenders put up a stiff defense. A moment later the decision was taken out of his hands.

"The big front gate is opening, General," a soldier called out.

"Hold your fire," Sherman ordered.

The gate swung wide, and from inside the castle there sounded the roll of a drum. The army drummer emerged, accompanied by an officer carrying a white flag.

"Bring them to me," Sherman ordered, greatly relieved. A squad trotted toward the two soldiers and accompanied them forward, automatically falling in step with the drumbeat. The officer, a colonel, stopped in front of Sherman and saluted, which Sherman returned.

"I wish to speak to your commanding officer," the British colonel said.

"I am General Sherman, commanding the American army."

The officer took a folded sheet of paper from his belt. "This message is from His Grace the Duke of Cambridge. He writes, 'To the commander of the American forces. There are women and children here, and I fear for their safety if this conflict continues. I therefore request you to send an emissary to discuss terms of surrender.' "

Sherman felt an intense wave of relief—but did not reveal it in his expression. "I shall go myself. Sergeant, pick a small squad to accompany me."

It was a large and elegantly furnished room, awash with light from the ceiling-high windows. A tiny woman sat in a large chair, dressed in black, quite chubby, with a puffy face and perpetually open mouth and exophthalmic eyes. She wore a fur miniver over her shoulders and a white widow's cap with a long veil, as well as a diamond-and-sapphire coronet. The group of ladies-in-waiting around her looked uneasy and frightened. Lord John Russell, diminutive and ancient, was at her side. Along with the uniformed Duke of Cambridge, appearing his usual assertive self.

General Sherman and his party stopped before the waiting group; no one spoke. After a moment Sherman turned away from the Queen and addressed the Duke of Cambridge.

"We have met before," Sherman said.

"We have," the Duke said, fighting to control his temper. "This is Lord John Russell, the Prime Minister."

Sherman nodded and turned to Russell—presenting his back to the Queen. There were horrified gasps from the ladies, which he ignored. "You are leader of the government—while the Duke heads the army. Are you of a like mind that the hostilities are to cease?"

"Some discussion is needed . . ." Russell said. Sherman shook his head.

"That is out of the question. I was instructed by President Lincoln that the war would be ended only by unconditional surrender."

"You presume too much, sir!" the Duke raged. "Surrender is a word not lightly used—"

Sherman silenced him with a curt wave of his hand. "It is the only word that I will use." He turned back to the Queen. "Since you are said to rule supreme in this country, I must tell you that your war is lost. Unconditional surrender is your only option."

Victoria's mouth gaped even more widely; she had not been spoken to in this manner since she was a child.

"I cannot . . . will not," she finally gasped.

"By God—this has gone far enough!" the Duke raged, stepping forward and pulling at his sword. Before it was free of its scabbard, two soldiers had seized him and prisoned his arms.

"Outrageous . . ." Russell gasped, but Sherman ignored them both and turned back to the Queen.

"I will cease all military operations as soon as surrender is agreed. You will remember that you sent the white flag to me. So tell me now, is the killing to stop?"

All eyes in the room were now on the diminutive figure in the large chair. The color had drained from her face and she pressed a black handkerchief to her lips. Her eyes found Lord Russell and sought help. He drew himself up but did not speak. When she turned back to General Sherman, she found no compassion in his grim expression. In the end she simply nodded and dropped back in the chair.

"Good," Sherman said, then addressed himself to the Duke of Cambridge. "I will have the papers for surrender drawn up for you to sign in your capacity as commander of all the armed forces. The Prime Minister will sign as well. You will remain here until that is done." Once again he spoke to the Queen.

"It is my understanding that you have a residence on the Isle of Wight named Osborne House. I will see to it that you are taken there with your family and servants. The war is now over."

As he looked around at the luxury of Windsor Castle and the silent witnesses, Sherman could not hold back a sudden feeling of triumph.

They had done it. There would still be skirmishes, but with London taken and the Queen in protective custody, the war would undoubtedly be over.

Now all they had to do was win the peace.

BOOK THREE
DAWN OF A NEW AGE

★

A COUNTRY DIVIDED

It was a time for confusion, a time for control. The peoples of Great Britain were stunned into inaction by the sudden, earthshaking events, and they appeared to be unable to quite grasp the overwhelming tragedy that had befallen them. Superficially, after two days of uncertainty and near riots, life continued in what appeared to be a normal way. People must eat—so the farmers brought their produce to market. Shops and businesses reopened. The local constables, in a great part of the land, remained at their posts, symbols of law and order. Only in the larger cities was there disconcerting evidence that the world had indeed turned upside down. Blue-clad soldiers patrolled the streets, armed and ready for any exigency. They were there in all of the major train stations, billeted in the police barracks and in hotels, or in rows of neat bell tents in the city parks. At Aldershot and Woolwich, and other army camps, the regular troops were confined to barracks and disarmed, the volunteers and the yeomanry disbanded and sent home.

Cornwall and Plymouth were already occupied and more reinforcements were landed there. Trainloads of troops then went west and north and quietly took over Wales and the northern shires. Only Scotland remained undisturbed—although cut off from all communication with the south. The telegraph wires were down and the trains did not run. Scottish troops remained in their barracks for want of any instructions, while rumors were rife. The English newspapers did not arrive, while the Scottish ones, with access to valid information, had more wild speculation than news.

Martial law had been declared in the land and the national newspapers were the first victims. American officers were now sitting quietly in every editorial office and reading each day's issues with great interest. There was no attempt at editorial censorship—the papers were allowed to print whatever they saw fit. However, if the Americans felt that editorial material was inaccurate, or might tempt the populace to riot, or in any way might affect the new peace, why then, the printed newspapers were simply not distributed. Within a few days the clear message sank home and a blandness and aura of harmony emanated from all their pages.

"You are sure that you are not going too far with this censorship, Gus?" General Sherman asked, slowly turning the pages of *The Times*. He had summoned Gustavus Fox to his office in Buckingham Palace. Fox smiled as he shook his head.

"When war walks in the door, truth flies out the window," Fox said. "You will remember that President Lincoln closed down the strident, dissenting Northern newspapers during the War Between the States. I think that we can be a little more sophisticated now. People will believe what they read in the newspapers. If the populace of Britain reads only about peace and prosperity—and sees no evidence for them to think differently—why then, there will be peace in the land. But rest assured, General, this is only a temporary measure. I am sure that you prefer to operate now in an aura of numbed peace rather than one of disorganization and unrest while your—what shall we call them?—pacification measures go into effect."

"True, very true," Sherman said, rubbing at his beard as he cudgeled his thoughts. Winning the peace was proving to be more difficult than winning the war had been. He had to rely more and more on civil servants and clerks—even politicians—to organize the peaceful occupation of the country. Thank God that martial law was still in place. He accepted advice, even asked for it, but when it came time for firm decisions, he was the final authority.

"Well—let us put the matter aside for the moment. I sent for you because I've had a delegation cooling their heels in a waiting room for most of the morning. I wanted you here when I let them in. I have had a communication from President Lincoln." He held up the letter. "He congratulates us on our victory, and expresses great pride in the armed forces. I'm having this read out to every soldier and sailor who contributed to that victory. Put it into the newspapers, too—if they will print it. He also includes a letter to the British people, and the papers will certainly print that. But first I would like you to read it to these politicos. See what they have to say about it."

"That will be my pleasure, General." Fox took the letter and went through it quickly. "Wonderful. This is just what everyone wants to hear."

"Good. We'll have them in."

The Prime Minister, Lord John Russell, led the delegation; Sherman remembered him from the encounter with the Queen. He introduced the others, mostly members of his cabinet. The only one to make a positive impression on Sherman was Benjamin Disraeli, the leader of the opposition in Parliament. His lean, spare figure was dressed in the most finely cut clothes; there were impressive rings upon his fingers.

"There are chairs for all," Sherman said. "Please be seated."

"General Sherman," Lord Russell said, "we are here as representatives of Her Majesty's government and, as such, have to present certain grievances . . ."

"Which I will hear in due course. But first I have here a communication from Abraham Lincoln, President of the United States. Which will be read to you by Mr. Fox, the Assistant Secretary of the Navy. Mr. Fox."

"Thank you." Fox looked at the angry faces before him, the puckered brows. Only Disraeli seemed at ease, intent.

"This is addressed to the people of Great Britain. As their elected representatives it is only right that you hear it first. Mr. Lincoln writes, 'To all of the peoples of the British Isles. A great war has now been brought to a conclusion. Years of strife between our countries are at an end. Peace has now been declared, and it is my heartfelt wish that it be a long and successful one. To this end I must assure you that we wish to be friends to you all.

STARS & STRIPES TRIUMPHANT

" 'As I write this, I am told that a delegation is now being assembled here in Washington City and that they will very soon join you in London. Their task will be to meet with your leaders to see that the rule of democracy is restored to Britain as soon as it is possible. We extend this hand of friendship with the best of goodwill. It is our fond hope that you will seize it for the sake of our mutual prosperity.' It is signed Abraham Lincoln."

The British politicians were silent for a moment as they thought about the import of the statement. Only Disraeli understood it at once; he smiled slightly and pursed his lips over his steepled hands.

"Mr. Fox, General Sherman, might I ask a small question, a matter of clarification?" Sherman nodded. "Thank you. All present agree with your president, for we all favor democracy. In fact, we enjoy it now under the benevolent rule of Queen Victoria. Why is there no mention of the monarchy in this letter? Is this omission deliberate?"

"You will have to judge that for yourselves," Sherman said abruptly, not wanting to become involved in wrangling at this time. "You must discuss that with the delegation which will be arriving tomorrow."

"I protest!" Lord Russell said, filled with sudden anger. "You cannot trample over our way of life, our traditions . . ."

"Your protest is noted," Sherman said coldly.

"You preach democracy," Disraeli said calmly. "Yet you rule by force of arms. You occupy this palace, while the Queen is banished to the Isle of Wight. The doors of our parliament are locked. Is that democracy?"

"That is exigency," Fox said. "Might I remind Mr. Disraeli that it was his country that originally invaded ours. The war that you started has now ended. Our forces will not stay in this country one day longer than is needed. What Mr. Lincoln wrote seems very clear. With democracy established in Britain, we will welcome you as a partner in peace. I hope that you agree."

"We certainly do not—" Lord Russell said, but General Sherman interrupted him.

"That is enough for today. Thank you for coming."

There were spluttered complaints from the politicians, and only Disraeli reacted calmly. He bowed slightly toward Sherman, turned, and left.

As soon as they were gone, Sherman's head of staff, Colonel Summers, brought in a stack of paperwork needing his urgent attention.

"Any of these important, Andy?" Sherman asked, gazing unhappily at the thick mound.

"All of them, General," Colonel Summers said. "But some are more important than others." He drew out a sheet of paper. "General Lee reports that all enemy activity has ceased in the Midlands. Morale is high—but food is running short, not only for his troops but for the freed Irish civilians as well."

"Have you dealt with that?"

"Yes, sir. Contacted the Quartermaster Corps as soon as his telegram came in. The train with relief supplies should be leaving London now."

"Well done. And this?" He held up the telegram that Summers had just handed him.

"It's from our border guards stationed outside of Carlisle. It appears that they stopped a train, really just an engine and a single car, coming south from Scotland. Occupants were a General McGregor, who says that he is commanding officer of army forces in Scotland. There was also a politician, name of Campbell, says he is chairman of the Highland Council. I contacted the editorial department of the The Times and they confirmed the identification."

"Get them here as soon as you can."

"I thought that would be what you wanted. I had them, and an honor guard, sent south on a special train which will be on its way by now."

"Well done. Any word from General Grant?"

"He reports the occupation of Southampton with no casualties. Had trouble with some of the fleet, but nothing to speak of. He should be arriving in London in about an hour."

"I'll want to see him as soon as he arrives. Anything else here of any importance?"

"Some orders to sign."

"Let's have them. The sooner that I am done with the paperwork, the better."

A CONSTITUTIONAL CONGRESS

John Stuart Mill looked ill at ease. He shuffled through the sheaf of papers on the table before him, then squared the pile and pushed them away. The room was large and ornate, the walls hung thickly with the portraits of long-dead English kings. Outside the tall windows stretched the immaculately manicured gardens of Buckingham Palace. At the far end of the conference table General Sherman signed the last of the orders in the folder, closed it, then glanced up at the clock on the wall.

"Well—I see that our guests are not as prompt as might be expected," he said. "But they will come, be assured of that." He spoke lightly, hoping to alleviate the philosopher's unease. Mill smiled wanly.

"Yes, of course, they must realize the importance of this meeting."

"If they don't—I count upon you to enlighten them."

"I shall do my best, General, but you must realize that I am no man of action. I am more at home in my study than on the debating floor."

"You underestimate your abilities, Mr. Mill. In Dublin you had the politicians eating out of your hand. When you spoke they were silent, intent on partaking of your wisdom. You will be fine."

"Ah, yes—but that was Dublin." Mill sounded distressed, and there was a fine beading of perspiration on his brow. "In Ireland I was telling them what they had spent their lifetimes waiting to hear. I showed them just how they could finally rule in their own land. They could not but be attentive." Now Mill frowned unhappily at more recent memories. "However, my countrymen have taken great umbrage at my presence in Dublin. *The Times* went so far as to call me a traitor to my country and to my class. The other newspapers were—how shall I say it?—more than indignant, actually calling down curses upon my head . . ."

"My dear Mr. Mill," Sherman said calmly. "Newspapers exist to sell copies, not to dispense the truth—or to see both sides of an argument. Some years ago, before I resumed my interrupted military career, I was, for a short while, a banker in California. When my bank fell upon hard times, there were calls to tar and feather me—or, preferably, burn me at the stake. Pay the papers no heed, sir. Their miasmic vaporings rise from the pit and will be dispersed by the clear winds of truth."

"You are something of a poet, General," Mill said, smiling weakly.

"Please don't let anyone else know; let it be our secret."

Colonel Summers knocked discreetly, then let himself in. "Finished with these, General?" he asked, pointing to the folder.

"All signed. Take care of them, Andy."

"The two English gentlemen are here to see you, sir," he said, picking up the papers.

"Show them in, by all means."

When the door opened again John Stuart Mill was on his feet; General Sherman slowly joined him.

"Lord John Russell, Mr. Disraeli," the colonel said, then quietly closed the door and left.

The two politicians crossed the room, as different in appearance as they could possibly be. The aristocratic Russell amply filling his old-fashioned broadcloth suit. Disraeli, the successful novelist, the veteran politician, the man about town, spare and thin and dressed in the most outstanding way. He stroked his small, pointed beard and nodded politely toward Sherman.

"Do you gentleman know Mr. John Stuart Mill?" Sherman asked.

"Only by reputation," Disraeli said, bowing slightly toward Mill, his politician's face empty of any expression.

"I have met Mr. Mill and have followed his public activities. I have no desire to be in his company," Russell said in a cold voice, averting his eyes from the other man. Mill's face was suddenly drawn and white.

"Mr. Russell—I would suggest that you be more courteous. We are here on a matter of some importance to both you and your country; therefore, your ill temper does you no favors, sir." Sherman snapped the words out like a military command.

Russell flushed at the harshness of the words, the common form of address. He clamped his mouth shut and stared out of the window, resentful at being put down by this Yankee upstart. Sherman sat and waved the others to their chairs.

"Please be seated, gentlemen, and this meeting will begin." He waited a moment, then went on. "I have asked you to come here in your official positions. As Prime Minister of the government and leader of the opposition. In those capacities I would like you to assemble a meeting of the House of Commons in Parliament."

With an effort Lord Russell controlled his temper, and when he spoke his words were as cold and emotionless as he could manage. "Might I remind you, General, that the Houses of Parliament have been locked tight—upon your orders, sir."

"They have indeed." Sherman's voice was as flat as the other man's. "When the time comes the doors will be unlocked."

"To both chambers?" Disraeli asked, his voice betraying no evidence of the singular importance of his question.

"No." Sherman's words now had the imperious force of command. "The House of Lords has been abolished and will not reconvene. There is no place for hereditary titles in a democracy."

"By God, sir—you cannot!" Russell said vehemently.

"By God, sir—I can. You have lost your war and now you will pay the price."

Disraeli coughed lightly in the ensuing silence, then spoke. "Might I ask—have all the arrangements been made for the Queen to open Parliament?" Again his voice held no hint of the immense purport of his question.

"She will not. The private citizen Victoria Saxe-Coburg will remain in her residence on the Isle of Wight for the time being. This is a new Britain, a freer Britain, and you gentlemen must learn to accommodate yourself to it."

"This is still a constitutional Britain," Russell broke in. "It is the Queen's parliament and she must be there to open it. That is the law of the land."

"Was," General Sherman said. "I repeat. Your war has been lost and your country occupied. The Queen will not open Parliament."

Disraeli nodded slowly. "I presume that there is a reason for calling this session of Parliament to sit."

Sherman nodded. "There is indeed. Mr. Mill will be happy to enlighten you when he speaks to your assembly. Are there any further questions? No? Good. The Parliament will assemble in two days."

"Impossible!" Lord Russell fought to control his voice without succeeding. "The members of Parliament are spread across this land, dispersed . . ."

"I envisage no problems. All of the telegraph lines are now open and the trains running as scheduled. There should be no difficulty in assembling these gentlemen." Sherman rose to his feet. "I bid you good day."

Russell stamped from the room, but Disraeli held back. "What do you hope to accomplish, General?"

"I? Why nothing at all, Mr. Disraeli. My work is complete. The war is over. It is Mr. Mill who will be speaking to you about the future."

Disraeli turned to the philosopher and smiled. "In that case, sir, I ask you if you would be so kind as to join me? My carriage is outside, my London chambers close by. Any intelligence of what you plan to speak of would be gratefully received."

"Most kind, sir." Mill was unsure of himself. "You must know that people in these isles do not take kindly to my presence."

"Why then, we shall ignore them, Mr. Mill. I have taken great pleasure, even inspiration, from your works, and would deem it a singular honor if you would accept my invitation."

Sherman started to speak—then held his counsel. Mill would have to decide for himself in this matter.

"Most willingly, sir," Mill said, drawing himself up. "It will be my great pleasure."

Only after Mill and Disraeli had left did Colonel Summers bring General Sherman the message.

"This arrived a few minutes ago," he said, handing over the envelope. "The messenger is still here awaiting an answer. He was worried about being seen speaking with us, so we put him in a room down the hall."

"That's very secretive."

"With good reason—as you will see when you read the communication."

Sherman nodded as he read the brief message. "This concerns the emissaries that just arrived from Scotland?"

"It does indeed. A General McGregor and a Mr. MacLaren of the Highland Council. A third man also traveled with them, but he did not reveal his name."

"Getting more mysterious all the time. They want me to attend a meeting after dark at the home of a Scots nobleman. Do we know anything about him?"

"Just his name, the Earl of Eglinton, and the fact that he was a member of the House of Lords."

"Isn't this kind of thing more in Gus Fox's line of work?"

"The messenger was insistent that he must talk to you first on an unofficial basis. I asked him what authority he had. It was then that, ever so reluctantly, he revealed the fact that he was Earl of Eglinton himself."

"More and more interesting. Let's have him in here."

The Earl of Eglinton was tall and gray-haired, with a military bearing that was not reflected in his plain black suit. He did not speak until the soldier who had ushered him in had left.

"It is very good of you to see me, General." He nodded at Summers. "I am sure that the colonel has told you of the need for secrecy."

"He has—though not the reason for it."

The Earl looked uncomfortable, and hesitated before he spoke. "This is—how shall I say it?—a most difficult matter. I would really like to postpone any discussion until after you have met my associates at my home. Mr. MacLaren is the one who will make a complete explanation. I am here as their host—and to explain their bona fides. Nevertheless, I can tell you that this is a matter of national importance."

"Am I to assume," Sherman asked, looking closely at the Earl, "that Scotland is somehow involved in this?"

"You have my word, sir, that it is. I have a carriage with a reliable driver who will be arriving soon. Will you be able to accompany me when I leave?"

"Perhaps. If I do go, my aide, Colonel Summers, will accompany me."

"Yes, of course."

Summers had been looking closely at the Scottish nobleman. "I have a single concern," he said. "That is for General Sherman's safety. He is, after all, commander in chief of our occupying forces."

The Earl of Eglinton's face grew pale. "You have my word that there is no danger or threat of danger, none whatsoever."

"I'll take the gentleman's word, Andy," Sherman said quietly. "I think we had better go with him and see what this is about."

Their wait was not a long one. Just after dark a guard brought the news that the gentleman's carriage was waiting. Sherman and Summers both wore their swords, as they had since the war began. The colonel now had a cavalry revolver in a holster on his belt. The carriage had stopped away from the courtyard lights so they could enter it unseen. As soon as the door was closed, they were on their way. It took only a few minutes to drive to Mayfair. As soon as they stopped, the door was opened and a man looked in and nodded to the Earl.

"You were no' followed," he said with a thick Scottish accent. "Angus there said the street is empty."

They emerged into a mews of carriage houses. The Earl of Eglinton led the way through a gate and into the house beyond. The door opened at their approach and they felt their way inside in the darkness. Only when the door was safely closed behind them did the servant uncover the lantern he was carrying. They followed him up the staircase and into a brightly lit room. Three men stood as they entered. Only when the door had closed did the Earl make the introductions.

"Gentlemen, this is General Sherman and his aide, Colonel Summers.

General McGregor commands all of Her Majesty's armed forces in Scotland. The gentleman next to him is Mr. MacLaren of the Highland Council. And this is Mr. Robert Dalglish, who is chairman of ..." The Earl of Eglinton hesitated before he finished the sentence, looking distraught. Then he pulled himself up and spoke in a firm voice. "Chairman of the National Party of Scotland."

Sherman could tell from the way the three men reacted that this revelation was of great importance. "I am sorry, Mr. Dalglish, but I am not familiar with this organization."

Dalglish smiled wryly and nodded. "I did not think that you would be, General. It is what might be called by some an illegal organization, one that believes in Scottish nationalism. Our precursor was the Association for the Vindication of Scottish Rights. This was a worthy organization that worked for a reformed administration in Scotland. Their cause was a good one— but in the end accomplished little that mattered. We of the National Party have set our sights higher since the conflict with the Americans began. There is much agreement that it is time for a change across the breadth of Scotland. We, and our sympathizers in high places, work for the cause of Scotland's freedom."

Sherman nodded; the reason for this clandestine meeting was becoming clear.

"Gentlemen, please be seated," the Earl of Eglinton said. "That is a carafe of Highland malt whiskey on the table—may I serve you?"

Sherman had a moment to think while the drinks were being poured. He raised his glass then and spoke quietly.

"Gentlemen, shall we drink to the freedom of the Scottish nation?" he asked.

With these words the tension seemed to drain from the air. They were of a common mind, a common purpose. But some matters needed clarification. Sherman turned to McGregor.

"You said, General, that you were commander in chief of Her Majesty's forces in Scotland."

"That was indeed my title. I now prefer to simply call myself commander of the army in Scotland. My troops are all in their barracks—where they will remain until there are further instructions. You of course know that the Scottish soldiers who fought in Liverpool have been disarmed and have returned north."

"What do your officers think of this turn of events?"

"I will be completely frank with you, sir. There are some English officers attached to our regiments. They are temporarily under detention. All of the other officers are with us in this."

Sherman thought about this, then turned to Robert Dalglish. "With the military of a single mind—I think I know how members of your National Party must feel. But what of the rest of the population of Scotland?"

"I of course cannot speak for them," Dalglish said. "But if a poll were taken tomorrow I have no doubt of the outcome. Our people will speak as one. A Scotland free of English influence. The restitution of our soverign right to self-government taken away from us one hundred and sixty years ago when our own parliament was abolished by that blackmailing Act of Union. I am sure that it can be done without violence."

"I am of a like mind, Mr. Dalglish. The United States encourages democracy in other countries, an objective that has succeeded in Mexico, Canada, and very recently in Ireland. What are your thoughts on that?"

Dalglish smiled. "We have representatives now in the Irish republic studying how democracy works there. We want nothing better than free elections in a free Scotland."

"Rest assured, then," Sherman said. "My country will stand by you in this endeavor."

"Let it be swiftly done," Dalglish said with great feeling. "I raise my glass and thank you, General. This is a most memorable moment in the history of my land."

The rains of the previous night had blown themselves out. The dawn of the day of the first meeting of Parliament since the war began bright and clear. The wet streets glinted in the sunlight as Benjamin Disraeli's richly ornamented coach came down Whitehall to Parliament Square. Big Ben struck the hour of eleven as it drew up at the entrance. The footman ran to let down the step, then stood aside as Mill and Disraeli descended. They passed, heads down, before the blue-clad soldiers guarding the entrance.

Parliament was again in session.

The opening was brief, even curt, and the MPs murmured loudly in protest. Lord Russell, in the front row, rose slowly, nodded at the opposition on the opposite benches, ignoring John Stuart Mill completely, although he was just a few feet away.

"Gentlemen, this is a most tragic day." His voice was hollow and laden with portents of gloom. "I know not how to advise you, for too much horror has passed since last we sat. Our arms are broken, our country occupied. Our queen a prisoner in Osborne House." Voices were raised in anger at his words; there were even violent shouts. The speaker banged his gavel repeatedly, calling for order. Russell raised his hand and the protests slowly died away.

"I have been told that the House of Lords has been abolished— hundreds of years of our history wiped out with a stroke of the pen."

The shouting grew in angry volume, feet stamped in rage upon the floor, and they did not stop, no matter how Lord Russell called out to them, the speaker shouting hoarsely for them to cease, banging over and over again with his gavel. Only a few of the MPs were aware that the doors had opened and that American soldiers, rifles at the ready, stood in the opening. They opened ranks to let a general officer through; he marched straight ahead and stopped before Lord Russell and spoke to him. Russell nodded slowly and raised his hands for silence. Slowly and reluctantly the noise abated. When his voice could be heard again, Russell spoke.

"I have been reminded once more that this House now operates under certain restraints. We must let our voices be heard—but we must get on with the matters to hand. If we do not do this, we will be silencing ourselves, even before we have spoken. We owe it to the people of this country, whom we represent, to speak up on their behalf. Terrible events have occurred and we have survived them. But this house must also survive and be heard, for we speak for the nation."

There was a murmur of approval from the members as Russell resumed his seat. The American officer turned and left the chamber, his soldiers following after; the doors were closed. With Russell seated, Benjamin Disraeli, leader of the opposition, rose in his stead.

JOHN STUART MILL—AT BAY

"May I remind the honorable gentlemen of our history. If we forget history we risk repeating it. Once before, this land was riven by violence. A king unthroned, Parliament dissolved. A man who called himself the Protector assumed control of this country and ruled it with an iron hand. But I ask for no latter-day Cromwell now. I ask only that we maintain the rule of law as set forth in the Magna Carta and the Bill of Rights. I ask you to hear what Mr. John Stuart Mill has to say to us."

The silent hatred in the venerable chamber was almost palpable. Mill felt it—but ignored it. He had come here armed with truth, and that was his strength and his shield. He stood and looked around him, standing straight, his hands clasped behind his back.

"I wish to speak to you about the extent that forms of government are a matter of choice. I speak of principles that I have been working up during the greater part of my life, and most of these practical suggestions have been anticipated by others—many of them sitting in this house.

"In your debates both Liberals and Conservatives seem to have differed. But I say to you that a much better doctrine must be possible, not a mere compromise, by splitting the differences between the two, leaving something wider than either, which, in virtue of its superior comprehensiveness, might be adopted by either Liberal or Conservative without renouncing anything which he really feels to be valuable to his own creed.

"I ask you to look upon our own history when you look at the Americans who now move among us." Mill waited patiently until the angry murmurs had died away. "Do not see them as strangers, for they are indeed verily our sons. The truth is that their country has been built upon what were our doctrines. The founding principles of the United States were British ideas of liberty to begin with. They may have slipped from our hands since that time, but they are still enshrined on the other side of the Atlantic.

"That the Americans have modeled their democracy on ours is a fact that should flatter, not incense us. They have an upper and lower chamber of their congress, just as we do. But with a single great difference. All of their representatives are elected. Power flows up from the people, not down from the top, as is our practice here.

"I heard many of you cry out in anger at the decree that has abolished the House of Lords. But the notion that power can be conferred by blood struck the Americans as absurd. Which it is. As that astute Englishman Thomas Paine argued—it is people of high talent, not birth, who should rule the country. For him a hereditary governing class was as absurd as a hereditary mathematician, or a hereditary wise man—and as ridiculous as a hereditary poet laureate."

There were shouts of anger at these words—but also calls to let Mill speak on. Mill took the opportunity to glance at a sheet of notes he had taken from his pocket, spoke again in a loud and clear voice.

"There is one great difference between our two democracies. In America, rule is from the bottom up. Here it is from the top down. It is the monarch who rules absolutely, who even owns the land under our feet. The Queen opens and closes Parliament, which is led by her prime minister. At sea it is the *Royal* Navy that guards our shores.

"In this, America is completely different—it has its constitution, which spells out the people's rights. The closest that Britain has to the Constitution is the Bill of Rights of 1689, which reads, 'And whereas the said late King James the Second having abdicated the government and the throne being hereby vacant, his Highness the Prince of Orange . . .' Now I must draw your close attention to the next words: '. . . *whom it hath pleased Almighty God* to make the instrument of delivering this kingdom from popery and arbitrary power.'

"This is clear enough. Power in this land comes not from the people but from on high. Your monarch rules with her authority, which is on loan from God. She in turn passes her power on to the government—while the people remain its servant."

"You insult us!" an angry member calls on. "You speak not of the power vested in Parliament by our Magna Carta."

Mill nodded. "I thank the gentleman for bringing that document to our attention. But neither the Magna Carta nor the Bill of Rights points out clearly the rights of our citizens. Indeed the Magna Carta is wholly concerned with the relationship of twenty-five barons to the King and the church. And, to the modern citizen, its contents are incredibly opaque. Hear this: 'All counties, hundreds, wapentakes and trithings shall be at the old rents without any additional payment, except our demesne manors.' And this as well: 'No clerk shall be amerced in respect of his lay holding except after the manner of the others aforesaid.' I am sure that all here will agree that this is not a practical guide to good, modern government. I would therefore point out to you a document that is."

Mill took a thin, bound folio from his pocket and held it up. "This is the Constitution of the United States. It endows power to the people—who lend some of this power to the government. It is the most radical statement of human rights in the history of the human race.

"What I sincerely ask this house to do is to read this document, peruse your Bill of Rights and Magna Carta, then consider this proposition. That you then assemble in a constitutional congress to prepare a constitution of your own. A British law for British people. I thank you."

He sat down—and within a moment there were calls and shouts as half of the Parliament rose to their feet and called for attention. The speaker recognized the Prime Minister first.

"I beg to differ from Mr. Mill. He may be English, but he speaks a foreign language—and wants to bring foreign ideas into the rule of this parliament. I say he is not welcome here, nor are his alien kickshaws. Our rule of law was good enough for our fathers, and their fathers before them. It is good enough for us."

There were cries of acclaim at Russell's words and no dissenting voices were heard. Speaker after speaker followed him, most echoing his sentiments, although a very few admitted that constitutional reform might be a topic that could bear possible examination. They were shouted down. Benjamin Disraeli waited until the tumult had lessened before he rose to speak.

"I am greatly concerned that my learned opponent has forgotten his own interest in this matter. Did he not himself attempt to introduce a new parliamentary reform act in 1860 that would have reduced the qualifications for voting in all the counties and towns? I believe that only the late Lord Palmerston's opposition led to the reform's demise."

"I suggested reform," Russell responded. "Not the destruction of our parliamentary heritage." This was greeted with enthusiastic shouts of agreement.

"Well then," Disraeli said, still holding the floor, "let us have a motion considering Mr. Mill's quite intelligent proposals . . ."

"Let us not!" Lord Russell called out. "I shall not be part of a parliament that sits to consider treason. I am leaving—and call upon all like-minded members to join me."

This brought on enthusiastic cheers and a growing rumble of feet as the members rose in great numbers and exited the chamber.

In the end only Benjamin Disraeli and a dozen other MPs remained.

"Not a truly representative portion of the house," Disraeli said quietly.

"I disagree," Mill said. "This is the core of a congress. It will be joined by others."

"I sincerely hope that you are right," Disraeli said with little enthusiasm in his voice. "I am here because I wish to see that the rule of law, and not occupation by a foreign power, be restored to this land. If this congress you propose is the only way—then so be it."

THUNDER BEYOND THE
HORIZON

As soon as the members of the newly established occupying government had arrived from Washington, General Sherman was more than happy to turn over his offices in Buckingham Palace to them. The recently appointed politicians and State Department officials were very welcome to the ornate apartments. Sherman was much more at home in the Wellington barracks, itself no more than a few hundred yards from the palace. The buildings had been standing empty since the guards regiment they housed had been disbanded. A newly arrived regiment of Pennsylvania Rifles had now moved in, and he joined them. When the office walls and the endless paperwork closed in on Sherman he would have his mount saddled, then ride out into Green Park, or St. James's Park, which was just across Birdcage Walk, and let the wind blow the cobwebs out of his brain. The former commanding officer's quarters were spacious and very much to his liking. This officer had left the regimental trophies in their cabinets, the bullet-riddled flags still hung upon the wall. When the occupation was over, their rightful owners would return and find everything just as they had left it. Meanwhile, a silken Stars and Stripes stood proudly on a bronze mount before them all.

The officers' mess was luxurious and comfortable. Sherman was enjoying a late meal there when the guard admitted Gustavus Fox.

"Well, you have been a stranger, Gus. Pull up a chair and sit down. Have you eaten?"

"Much earlier, thank you, Cumph." Since their journey on the *Aurora*, despite their age disparity, they had grown quite close. "But it's my throat that's parched; I could do with a drink."

"Easily done." Sherman signaled to a waiter. "Our departed hosts left behind many barrels of fine ale. I shall join you in a glass. Perhaps we can even toast the Gatling gun. Have you heard the little poem that the gunners recite?"

"I don't believe that I have."

"It goes like this: 'Whatever happens, we have got / the Gatling gun, and they have not.' "

"It only speaks the truth."

"It does indeed. Now—what brings you here?"

"A matter of some importance, I truthfully believe." Fox drank deeply from his glass and nodded happily. "Capital." When the waiter had gone he took a sheaf of papers from his pocket and slid them across the table. "I'll leave these with you. But I can sum them up quite clearly. I have had my clerks going through all the British military files, both army and navy. A good many were destroyed, but the capitulation of the armed forces was so swift that most of them were left behind. However, there were still masses of files burned in the War Department fireplaces. Luckily the navy was not as astute and duplicates of the ones that had been destroyed were found in their files. What you have there are details of a convoy of ships. It is called Force A. They sailed from India some weeks ago."

"India?" Sherman frowned as he pulled the papers toward him. "What kind of a convoy?"

"Troops. Fourteen troop-carrying vessels, most of them liners like the SS *Dongola* and SS *Karmala*. Among the units the Rajput Fifty-first Pioneers are listed. Along with the Second Battalion of North Lancashire Rifles, the Twenty-fifth Battalion of Royal Fusiliers—and more like that. They are accompanied by a number of warships, including the HMS *Homayun*, as well as the armorclad HMS *Goliath*."

"I don't like this at all. A force this size can raise a lot of dander. When are they due here?"

"If they keep to their schedule—in about one week's time."

"Do you think they have been informed about the war—and the occupation?"

"I am sure of that. As you know, most of the British navy that was at sea did not return to port. More than one ship fled Portsmouth to escape capture. Some of them surely knew about this convoy and would go to join it. Also, the convoy will have stopped at coaling stations en route, which would have been informed by telegraph of world events. We can be sure that they know exactly what has happened here."

"You're in the navy, Gus. Any idea of what we should do?"

Fox raised his hands in surrender. "No, sir! This is well out of my league. But I did send Admiral Farragut a copy of these shipping movements and asked him to join us here."

"A wise move. He is a sound tactician."

While the waiter was refilling their glasses, Sherman read through the papers that Fox had given him. Then he had the waiter bring him a pencil and made some notes on the back of one of those sheets. When he spoke again his voice was grim.

"That is a sizable infantry force that is coming our way. I doubt if they will have the strength to retake this country from us, but there will still be some terrible battles if they manage to get ashore. If they do, there will surely be risings as well from demobilized British soldiers. This is not what we want."

Admiral Farragut was of a like mind when he joined them. "Bad news indeed. I've sent orders to all our ships to refuel and stand ready."

"What do you plan to do?" Sherman asked.

"Nothing—until we have worked out where the convoy is headed. They will not go to the assigned ports that are in these orders, you can be sure of that. They will know by now about the occupation and the commanding officer of the troops will plan accordingly. I think the decision must be yours, General, because this is a military matter. Their army commanders will be planning a landing—or landings. Their navy will act as an escort and provide fire to cover any landings."

"That was my thought as well." Sherman finished his ale and rose. "Let us take this discussion to my office and consult the maps there."

The map of the British Isles was unfolded on the desk below the oil lamp. General Sherman studied it thoughtfully.

"Any ideas, Gus?" he asked.

"None! I have no intelligence of their destination and am no tactician. I will not attempt to even guess."

"Very wise. Which leaves the responsibility to me. First—let us limit the possibilities." He tapped on the map. "I think that we can eliminate landings in the north and west. Scotland and Wales are too distant from the seat of power. Cornwall is the same as well. We must look to London."

"They will not attempt to come up the Thames as we did," Farragut said. "It is common knowledge that our floating batteries are still stationed there. But here to the east, in the Wash, there are protected waters where landings are possible. Or farther south, perhaps, at the port of Harwich."

Sherman shook his head. "Again—too far from the center. Harwich is a better possibility, it is surely close enough to London. But we would be warned if they landed there and could easily mass the troops to stop them. Therefore I believe that it is the south coast that we must worry about. They will know that we have seized Portsmouth, so they will not come ashore there. But here, farther east along the south coast, it is very different. Flat beaches, shallow waters, easy access from the sea. Brighton. Newhaven. Hastings." He ran his finger along the coast.

"Hastings, 1066," Fox said. "The last successful invasion before ours."

"I can station a screen of ships across the mouth of the English Channel," the admiral said. "From Bournemouth right across to the Cherbourg Peninsula. The Channel can't be more than eighty miles wide there. A force the size of this one coming from India would be easily spotted as it approached. But, of course, if they do go west to Cornwall or beyond, we will never see them. Their troops would be well ashore before we knew anything about it."

The ticking of the clock could be clearly heard in the silence that followed. This was a command decision—and General William Tecumseh Sherman was in command. The burden of decision rested upon his shoulders alone. His commander in chief was on the other side of the Atlantic and could not be consulted in time. It was indeed his sole judgment. He glanced up at the clock.

"Admiral, can you meet me here at eight o'clock in the morning to discuss your orders?"

"I shall be here."

"Fine. Gus, I want your clerks to rake through the files. Get me the strengths of all the units listed in these orders. I will also want that by eight in the morning at the latest. Earlier, if you can manage it."

"I'll get onto it right now."

"Good. On your way out, tell the officer of the day to send for my staff. It is going to be a long night."

Dawn was just breaking when a haggard-eyed Fox brought the files with the strengths of the various military units that were in the approaching convoy. The staff officers moved aside when he came in and handed the papers to General Sherman.

"They are all here, General. All of the troops listed as being in the convoy. I wish I could be as sure of the accompanying naval vessels. Here are the original manifests, but any number of ships could have joined the convoy since they sailed. The route and dates of the convoy were well known throughout the fleet. Any or all of the British ships that escaped capture could be with the convoy now."

"Excellent. Now I suggest that you get some rest. You have done all that could be done."

Sherman himself looked as alert as he had the evening before. A seasoned campaigner, he was used to days and nights without sleep. By eight o'clock, before Admiral Farragut arrived, the plans were well in hand. Once the orders had been written, the staff officers dispersed to implement them as soon as possible. Sherman was alone, looking out the window at the park when the admiral came in.

"It is done," Sherman said. "Orders have been issued and the first troop movements will begin this morning."

"To . . . where?"

"Here," Sherman said, slapping his hand down on the map of the south coast of England. "They will try to land here—they have no other choice. But our troops will soon be digging in all along this coast. From Hastings to Brighton. The heart of our defenses will be at Newhaven Fort, right here. Some of the guns there were damaged, but they have all been replaced by now. That coast will soon be bristling with American might. Any attempts to land will be blasted from the water. But I hope that disaster will not happen. It must be averted."

"How do you plan to do that?"

"I will be able to tell you when I join you. When do you estimate that it is the earliest that the convoy will arrive?"

"They may be slower than anticipated, but in any case they cannot get to the Channel any faster than was originally planned. Three more days at the earliest."

"Good. You will post your ships at the Channel mouth, as you outlined last night. I shall join you in two days' time. Will you have a ship for me in Portsmouth?"

"The *Devastation* just came in from patrol and is refueling in Southampton. I'll telegraph orders for her to await you there, then she will join us in station. I sincerely hope that you are right in your summation of the situation, General."

Sherman smiled wryly. "Admiral, I *have* to be right or we are lost. If the British army from India gets ashore, it will be a ragtag, murderous invasion with no guarantee of a successful outcome for either side. I have issued my orders. What happens next is up to the enemy."

As soon as it had been deemed safe, John Mill's daughter, Helen, had joined him in London. Through an agent she had found a most attractive furnished house to rent in Mayfair, on Brook Street. She knew how important a warm home environment was for Mill and she bent every effort in that direction. The strain of the work that he was doing was very great indeed, and he walked now with his shoulders bent, as though he were carrying a heavy load. As indeed he was. He was in his sitting room, still in sleeping cap and dressing gown, enjoying his morning tea, when Helen brought in a copy of *The Times*.

"I am almost afraid to read it these days," he said, touching the newspaper gingerly with the tips of his fingers.

Helen laughed as he squinted at the first page. "It is not really that bad. They are actually weighing arguments pro and con concerning the proposed constitution—instead of thundering away, all barrels blazing, the way they did in the beginning." She reached into the pocket of her dress and took out some envelopes. "Your Mr. Disraeli was here even before the morning post and left these off for you."

"Wonderful! I shall put the newspaper aside with pleasure. He promised me a list of possible members for the proposed congress—this will hopefully be them." He quickly read through the papers. "That is a familiar name. Charles Bradlaugh?"

"You must remember him, Papa. The founder of the *National Reformer* and a great pamphleteer."

"Of course—yes! A committed republican and a freethinker. I can hear the wounded cries now if we permit an atheist to join our congress. Indeed, we must have him. I will get an invitation off to him today. Ah—and here is Frederic Harrison as well. A gentleman well-known to the working classes as possessing a practical knowledge of how the trade unions operate. Disraeli strongly advises that he be present, and I can only agree."

With Disraeli's aid and political know-how, a list of members for a constitutional congress was slowly being assembled. There were veteran politicians and reformers like William Gladstone, as well as up-and-coming politicians like Joseph Chamberlain. Although the newspapers sneered at the very idea of this congress and the political cartoonists had a field day at its expense, a possible panel was slowly being formed. Now it was only a matter of fixing a date that would be suitable for all parties concerned. What had seemed like a novel invention at first soon began to take on the appearance of respectability.

WAITING FOR DESTINY

Three days had passed since the USS *Devastation* had joined the squadron that stretched across the mouth of the English Channel. This was the proper place to intercept any ships entering the Channel where it joined the Atlantic Ocean. The northernmost ship in the line cruised within easy sight of Portland Bill. South of it, using just enough power to breast the incoming tide, rode USS *Virginia*. Beyond this ship, almost on the horizon, another American ironclad was just visible. The line of warships now reached from within sight of the English coast right across the Channel as far as Cap de la Hague on the tip of the Cherbourg Peninsula. Every ship in the squadron was in sight of at least two others. When the British came—*if* they came—there was no way that they could escape observation.

If they came. This little word echoed over and over in General Sherman's brain as he paced the flying bridge of the *Devastation*. When they had joined the squadron they had taken up station next to Admiral Farragut's flagship, USS *Mississippi*, at the center of the line. She was still in position next to them, steaming as slowly as they were.

Sherman once again found himself standing at the rail, looking east across the empty sea. Would the convoy come? Had he been wrong in his assumption that they would attack the south coast of England? For the thousandth time he tracked the logic that had led him to the inevitable con-clusion that this was what they would do. He still believed they must strike at this coast, but three days of waiting had left his theory hard-pressed. As he turned away he saw that a small boat was pulling away from the *Pennsylvania*. He realized suddenly that it must be noon—that was the hour appointed for his meeting with the admiral. They would discuss tactics yet again, and the state of the squadron, and Farragut would stay for luncheon. Sherman's eyes strayed once more to the empty horizon, before he left the bridge and went to wait for the admiral on the deck.

"Still fine weather," Farragut said as they shook hands. Sherman only nodded and led the way below. There was nothing they could say that had not been said often before. Sherman took the carafe from the sideboard and held it up.

"Will you join me in a sherry before we dine?"

"An excellent thought."

Sherman had just poured out the drinks when a seaman burst through the door.

"Captain's compliments." The words rushed from his mouth. "The lookout reports ships to the southeast."

The sailor had to move swiftly aside as the two officers rushed past him. By the time they had reached the bridge, the line of ships could be seen on the horizon. Captain Van Horn lowered his telescope. "The leading ship is an armorclad—you can tell by her upper works. And there is more smoke from ships still not in sight. Eight, ten of them at least."

"Is this it?" Sherman asked.

Van Horn nodded firmly. "Without doubt, General. There could be no other force that size at sea."

"Follow General Sherman's orders," Admiral Farragut said as he turned away. "I must return to my command and issue the signal to assemble all our force here."

"I want you to approach those ships as soon as the admiral's boat is clear. And do it slowly."

Van Horn nodded. "Slow ahead. Five knots, no more."

"Would you also have that flag hung in the bow," Sherman said.

The captain's orders were relayed to the deck and two sailors ran forward with a bundle of cloth. Grommets had been attached to the corners of one of the tablecloths from the officers' mess. It was quickly fixed to a line and run up the bow mast. The approaching ships could not miss seeing the white flag. Nor the Stars and Stripes flying from the masthead.

When they had halved the distance to the approaching convoy, the captain stopped the engines. They drifted slowly to a stop, rolling in the light seas. The brisk westerly wind caught the improvised flag and it flapped out for all to see.

"If they should open fire?" Captain Van Horn asked brusquely.

"They won't," Sherman said firmly. "It would not be gentlemanly. And they are certainly aware of the other ironclads behind us. They will know what that means."

If Sherman had any doubts about the wisdom of meeting the enemy like this, he did not express them. Twice before in his life he had ended conflict with a flag of truce. He had every faith that he could do it once again.

The leading ships could be seen quite clearly now; black armor and menacing guns. Signal flags had been run up and it appeared that the convoy had slowed. However, one of the ironclads had drawn away from the others and approached the American ship.

"*Defender,*" Van Horn said, peering through his glass again. "Main defenses six hundred-pounders, the new modified *Warrior* class."

The British warship was coming right toward them, smoke pouring from its funnels, a bone in its teeth. As it drew closer it could be seen that its guns were trained on the American ship. When it had closed to within two hundred yards, it turned and slowed, presenting its starboard side. And as it turned, its guns turned as well, keeping trained on the *Devastation*.

"Has the boat been lowered?" Sherman asked.

"In the water as you ordered."

Without another word Sherman left the bridge and scant moments later had climbed down into the waiting barge. Eight oars dipped as one and the craft shot swiftly across the water. As it approached the black flank of the British warship, it could be seen that a boarding ladder had been lowered over the side. Sherman climbed it as swiftly as he could. As he pulled himself up onto the deck, he found an army officer waiting for him.

"Follow me," the man said abruptly, and turned away. Two sailors armed with muskets fell in behind them as they walked to the companionway. In the wardroom below, two army officers were waiting, both general officers. Sherman came to attention and saluted. They returned the salute in the British manner.

"We have met before, General Sherman," the first officer said.

"Yes, in Canada. You are Brigadier Somerville."

Somerville nodded slowly. "This is General Sir William Armstrong, commander in chief of Her Majesty's forces in India."

"Why are you here?" Armstrong asked brusquely, barely controlling his anger at meeting the man who had conquered his country.

"I am here to save lives, General Armstrong. We know the size and strength of your command from the documents that we seized in London. You will see behind me a major force of ironclads that will not permit you to pass peacefully, should you attempt to enter the Channel. They will avoid your warships, wherever possible, and concentrate on sinking your troopships. Should any of the transports succeed in passing our forces by, I want to inform you that the entire southern coast of England is now defended by American troops and guns. Any boats that attempt to land troops will be blown out of the water."

"How do you know what we plan to do?" Armstrong snapped, cold anger in his voice.

"It was what I would have done, General. It was the only possible option."

"Do we have your word that your troops are stationed here?" Somerville asked coldly.

"You have my word, sir. We have had a week to prepare our defenses. Newhaven Fort has been rearmed. The Twentieth Texas has dug in behind the shore at Hastings and are supported by five batteries of cannon. Do you wish me to list the defenders in the other positions?"

"That will be sufficient, General. You have given us your word." Somerville's voice was uneven as he spoke; his shoulders slumped. He had tried; they all had tried.

But they had failed.

"Return the Indian troops to India," Sherman said. "If they come here they will only die. The fleet and the guns are waiting."

"But my country!" Armstrong said, his voice rough with anger. "You have conquered, destroyed—"

"Conquered, yes," Sherman snapped. "Destroyed, no. We only want peace and an end to this reckless war between our nations. Even now your politicians are meeting to found a new British government. When they have done that and the rule of law has been restored—we look forward to returning home. We want peace—not continued conflict. When you rule your own country once again, we will go. That is all that we want."

"And we must believe this?" Somerville said, bitterness in his voice.

"You have no choice, General, no choice at all."

"Take this man outside and hold him there," Armstrong ordered the armed sailors standing by the door.

Sherman shrugged off their hands when they reached for him, turned, and left; the door closed behind them. In the corridor he looked coldly at the sailors; they shuffled their feet and did not meet his gaze. They had heard what had been said inside. The taller of them, a petty officer from his insignia, looked around then spoke quietly.

"What's happening ashore, sir? We hear but little, the worst kind of scuttlebutt."

"The war is over," Sherman said, not unkindly. "Our troops won the day. There were deaths on both sides, but there is peace now. If your politicians agree, there will be a lasting peace in the years to come. If we can leave your country with that peace guaranteed—we will do just that. That is our desire, just as it must be yours."

Sherman heard the door open behind him, turned, and entered the saloon.

"You have reached a decision," he said. It was not a question.

"We have," General Armstrong said, bitterness in his voice. "The Indian troops will return to India. You can guarantee them a safe passage?"

"I can. What of the British troops? Will they surrender?"

"Terms must be discussed first."

"Of course. And your navy ships?"

"That you must discuss with the admiral commanding. I cannot speak for him."

"Naturally. I feel that you are making a wise decision."

"Not wise, but the only possible one," Somerville said, resignedly. General Sherman could only nod in agreement.

At last the long war that had begun when the Confederate representatives had been taken from a British ship, which had spread from America to Mexico and Ireland, which had ended here in England, was over.

DAWN OF A NEW DAY

"**T**here is a gentleman at the door to see you, Father," Helen said. "He sent in his card."

John Stuart Mill took the card, held it to the light. "Ah, Mr. William Gladstone. He has had my letter, then, and responded accordingly. Please show him in."

They shook hands warmly when Helen ushered Gladstone in, for this was a meeting that both men greatly desired.

"I came as soon as I had your communication. Unhappily I was out of the country for the last parliamentary session and I do regret missing it. I have had mixed reports from my colleagues—but all of them tell me that, if you would excuse the expression, the fur did fly."

Mill laughed aloud. "It surely did." He warmed to the politician and was pleased. This was a most important encounter.

"Mr. Gladstone," Helen said. "Would you take tea with us?"

"I would be delighted."

"Please be seated," Mill said. "This is a meeting I have long desired. I have read your political writings with great interest, great interest."

"You are kind to say that."

"It is but the truth. You were responsible for the Railway Bill of 1844 that opened up third-class travel for all in Britain. It was only due to your insistence that trains now stop at every station in the country. I admire your interest in the ordinary folk of this land."

"Indeed they do interest me—for they are citizens just as you and I are."

"They are, without a doubt, but that is not a popular point of view. I also note that although you have always rejected the idea of parliamentary reform, you spoke up in favor of it when Edward Baines introduced his reform bill. You argued that it was manifestly unfair that only one-fiftieth of the working classes had the vote."

"That is indeed true—and it is perhaps the main reason that my views on reform changed."

Mill leaned forward, his voice tense with the grave import of his question. "Then I take it that you are in favor of universal suffrage?"

"I am indeed. I believe that every man in this land should have a vote."

Helen had opened the door and carried in the tea tray; she could not help but overhear these last words. "But, Mr. Gladstone, to be truly universal, should not suffrage include women as well as men?"

Gladstone was on his feet as he spoke, bowed graciously, and smiled. "My dear Miss Mill, your father has written of the aid you have given him in his writings. Now, having met you, I can surely believe that. Yes, I do agree that someday the vote must be extended to women. But the longest journey begins with but a single step. This is a conservative country and we will be hard-pressed to obtain universal male suffrage. But I promise that when the time is right, the vote will be extended to be truly universal."

Helen smiled, and responded to his bow with a gracious curtsy. "I shall hold you to your word, sir. Now—let me pour your tea and then leave you gentlemen to your discussions."

Gladstone sipped his tea and nodded toward the closed door. "Your daughter is a jewel, Mr. Mill. I hope that you will not be offended when I say that she has a mind like a man's."

"I understand your meaning, sir, though Helen might take some offense."

"None intended! I meant simply that I can see why you value her contributions to your labors."

"I do, greatly. She is the one who convinced me that a universal ballot must also be a secret ballot for general elections. This will prevent working-class people being influenced in their vote by watching employers and landlords."

"That is indeed a cogent observation. I had not considered that aspect of the vote, but now that I have thought it out, I can see that it will be of utmost importance."

"But you do realize that a secret ballot with all men eligible to vote— might be the very force that changes this country forever?"

"In what way?"

"Now, as you well know, sovereignty in Britain does not rest with the people, but with the Crown-in-Parliament. This parliamentary sovereignty is the British concentration of power. This means that Parliament is supreme and nothing can stand before it. Not the will of the people—not even the law. If a statute blocks the will of the government, why, ministers can simply change it. Even if that obstacle is common law evolved over the centuries."

"Unhappily, that is indeed true."

"But if power flows upward from the people, this would not be possible. The people must elect their representatives to work the common will. If they do not—why, they will be ejected from power. That, and the checks and balances of the judiciary and a supreme court, will be the force to ensure that the will of the people will be sovereign. Not hereditary lords or a hereditary monarch. Not even God can alter that."

"You believe then that disestablishmentarianism is to be intended?"

"I do. There shall be no ordained church ruled by the monarch. As in the American constitution, there should be no established church at all. In fact, there must be a strict separation between church and state."

Gladstone put his teacup down, nodded, and sighed.

"This may prove a bitter pill to feed to the people of this island."

"Strong medicine is sometimes needed. But with your good grace, Mr. Gladstone, and the others in our constitutional congress, the will of the people could become the law of the country."

"A noble ambition—and hopefully a possible one. I am your man, Mr. Mill, behind you every step of the way."

★

The crew on duty aboard the newly launched USS *Stalwart*, named for the dauntless warship sunk during the battle for Ireland, looked on with interest as the magnificent steam yacht came up the Solent and slowly passed them by. Their work was to guard the city of Portsmouth, and the great naval station there. But they could see no threat in this well-turned-out little ship that was flying the royal ensign of Belgium. They would have found no menace there—even if they had not received strict orders to let the vessel pass undisturbed. In the last of the evening sun, the yacht passed through Southampton Water and into Cowes Roads. After rounding the Isle of Wight, it drifted gently up to the fenders on the dockside in Cowes. Its arrival must have been expected, because a carriage was there, waiting.

Others besides the carriage driver had been expecting the trim vessel's arrival. There was another yacht tied up farther down the docks. A yacht as well turned out and gleaming as the royal Belgian one.

On the bridge of the *Aurora* two men stood, watching the other vessel's arrival. They were both dressed in well-cut broadcloth suits, but each had the bearing of a military man.

"So far, Count, your information seems to be more than accurate," Gustavus Fox said.

"It should be," Count Korzhenevski said, "since I paid a good deal in gold for it. Belgium is a small country, its politicians notoriously penurious. However, one or two of them know that my agent there pays well for sound information. They queue up to be bribed. You have alerted the navy?"

"As soon as I got your message and arrived here. That yacht is not to be approached, searched, or troubled in any way. Free to come—even freer to leave."

"I am glad of that," the Count said, looking through his glasses again. "But one does wish that they could be a little more discreet. That is the fifth large trunk that has been loaded aboard from that dray."

"The German nobility has never been known for its intelligence."

"Quite." The Count squinted at the sun setting behind the rolling hills. "It will be dark soon."

"Not soon enough. The quicker this escapade is over and done with, the happier I will be."

"Do not despair, dear Gus." The Count laughed and pulled at his arm. He snapped a quick command in Russian to the officer on watch. "Come below and share a bottle of champagne. We shall be called as soon as there is any activity on the pier."

In Osbourne House there was a great stirring when the Belgian Foreign Minister, Baron Surlet de Chokier, was admitted. The Queen was waiting, wearing black traveling dress and fussing over her younger children. The Prince of Wales, known to all the family as Bertie, stood to one side; Alexandra, his bride of two years, also beside him. They were a contrasting pair: she was slight, and very attractive. Young though he was, if the pudgy Bertie had ever had any charm, it was long since gone. Blackbearded and potbellied, he was already going bald. He looked on, apparently bored, when the Baron spoke to the Queen.

"It has all been arranged, Your Majesty. King Leopold was immensely concerned with the safety of you and your family, and indeed was most relieved when you accepted his offer of sanctuary. The yacht is tied up and awaiting only your presence."

"It will be safe?" Victoria sounded lost, unsure of herself.

"I assure Your Majesty that Belgium will provide a safe haven for you, far from this devastated, war-torn country. Your bags are being loaded. We only await your royal presence."

The Queen looked down at the children, wrapped warmly in jackets, and then at Bertie and the bare-armed Alexandra.

"You'll get a chill," she said firmly.

"Not really, Mama," Bertie said, a sly smile on his lips. "I think that Alexandra and I will be quite safe here in Osbourne House."

"But—we planned. For all our safety . . ." Then Victoria's eyes widened and she gasped. "You are not coming!" Her voice was shrill, angry. "You will remain here, behind my back? We are the Queen. You have been talking to the monarchists, haven't you? Behind my back!"

"Of course not, Mama," he said. But there was little reassurance in his voice and the tiny smile belied the meaning of his words.

"You want me gone!" she screeched. "With me in Belgium, you want the crown for yourself!"

"Don't excite yourself, Mother, it does you ill. You will enjoy Belgium, I am sure."

In the end Bertie excused himself and left, waving the shocked Alexandra after him. It was some time before the horrified ladies-in-waiting could convince the Queen that she must go on the yacht—if only for the sake of the children. Weeping and distraught, she eventually entered the carriage, hugging the crying children to her.

Aboard the *Aurora*, over half of the bottle of vintage champagne was gone before Gus and the Count were summoned on deck once again. Although the lamps on the dock had not been lit, the waning moon cast enough illumination for them to clearly see the arrival of the carriages. Dark figures, one after another, emerged and were hurried up the gangway. Even as the passengers were boarding, a cloud of smoke issued from the little vessel's funnel and floated across the harbor. Soon after that the lines were taken in and the yacht puffed out into the Solent. Minutes later the *Aurora* moved slowly in her wake. They sailed past the anchored naval vessels and out into the ocean. The Belgian yacht continued away from the shore a good few miles before she altered her course to the east.

"She is now out of British territorial waters and well on her way to Belgium," the Count said happily. "Now—let us finish that bottle since this necessitates a little celebration."

Once in the salon, he poured their glasses full, raised his on high. "This calls for a toast," Korzhenevski said. "Did your American schools teach you about Bonnie Prince Charlie?"

"Not really. We are not a country that goes in much for British history."

"A serious lapse. One must always know one's adversaries. It seems that in Scotland they toasted the deposed prince as 'the King over the water.' "

"That has a nice ring to it." Gus raised his glass as well. "Shall we drink, then, to the Queen over the water?" They touched glasses and drank deep.

"Did they really think that we wanted to keep her here?" Gus mused. "King Leopold has done us an immense favor. Too bad we cannot thank him."

Although it was after dark in England, it was still early afternoon in Washington City. President Abraham Lincoln looked wearily at the papers that cluttered his desk, then pushed them away. He pressed the electric button that summoned his secretary. John Nicolay poked his head in through the door.

"Take these away, John, if you will. I can't bear the sight of them. I foolishly thought that with the coming of peace, there would be a vast diminution in the paperwork. There is, if anything, a good deal more. Away with them."

"Just as you say." He squared the sheets into a neat pile, then took more folded papers from his pocket. "I was just going to bring this in. The morning report from the War Department."

"Ah, the military mind. Their idea of what constitutes morning sure stumps me. Anything there that I want to hear?"

"Mostly passing on reports from London. The constitutional congress is still meeting, and they expect to have a document that they can vote upon by this time next week."

"Sure are taking their time."

"Our Continental Congress took a lot longer to draw up the Constitution."

"Indeed they did. I stand corrected. Any more?"

"Yes. A report from General Sherman. He will be in Edinburgh by now with his commission. The terms of the separate peace with Scotland are all agreed and will be formerly signed now."

"So the Scots will have their own parliament. That will not go down well with the English."

"That the Scots do have—and no, it did not go down very well at all south of their border. The English newspapers are incensed and predict riots and blood in the streets."

"They always do—but thankfully it never happens. Sherman is too good a soldier to permit anything like that to take place. Like it or not, they have had peace thrust upon them."

"There is also a confidential report from Gus Fox that Queen Victoria is about to be secretly smuggled out to Belgium."

"God bless Gus! I don't know how he managed it, but that is the best news ever. Without her presence in the country, the monarchists will have no rallying point. I would be more than delighted if they vote this constitution in, then elect a representative government so I can bring the boys home."

"There have been no difficulties on that score from the soldiers, Mr. President. Since General Sherman has been slowly reducing the occupying forces, any of them who want to return home have already done so. There have not been many volunteers. Seems their pay goes a lot further over there. They like the public houses and the women. Only complaints I've heard mentioned are about the weather."

"Well, an army that only complains about the rain must be in pretty good all-around shape. Anything else?"

"That's all for today. Except Mrs. Lincoln says that she wants you on time for lunch today."

Lincoln looked up at the clock and nodded. "Guess I better get down there. I want to keep peace in the world."

"That you have done, Mr. President," Nicolay said, suddenly serious. "Your first term began with a war—as has your second one. But peace rules now, and may it do so forever."

"Amen to that, John. Amen."

Peace at last, Sherman thought. The agreements signed and sealed. And now a separate peace agreement with Scotland. Great Britain had reluctantly been reduced in size. Still, it meant peace in his time. The victory was well worth the battle. But there had been too many stuffy rooms of late—and even stuffier politicians. He walked across to the windows and opened them wide, breathed deeply of the cool night air. Below him were the lights of Edinburgh, with the Royal Mile stretching away down the hill. He turned around when there was a quick knock on the door.

"Open it," he called out. The sergeant of the guard looked in.

"General Grant is here, sir."

"Fine. Show him in."

Grant, smiling through his great black beard, crossed the room and took Sherman by the hand.

"Well, it is all over, Cumph. You really won this one."

"We all did. Without you and Lee and Meagher—not to mention our new navy—I could have done nothing."

"I admit, we surely all did our part—but we can't forget that the strategy was yours, the combined arms and the lightning war. At times I feel sorry for the British soldiers; they must have felt like they were trampled by a stampeding herd of buffalo."

"Perhaps they were. Our American buffalo just stomped them down and kept on galloping."

Grant, running his fingers through his beard, nodded agreement. "I doubt if they appreciate it—but it was the best thing that ever happened to them in battle. They took casualties, yes, but not nearly as many as they would have suffered had there been a long war of attrition. Now England, along with Ireland, is at peace and being dragged into being a democracy. And from what I have seen these last weeks, the Scotch seem to be tickled pink to have their own country again."

"They are a fine people, and like the Irish they now feel indebted to the United States. I feel a certain pride in having people like them on our side. And something else they have—the best-tasting whiskey that I have ever drunk. I have one of their malts here if you would like to join me in a celebratory drink?"

"Just a single one will do me fine. I think of all those years of falling into bed dead drunk every night and feel no wish to return to that condition."

"You won't. You have changed too much during these years of war. That man who needed drink to get through the day is long gone. But you are right. One will surely be enough."

There was a bottle of Glen Morangie and glasses on the sideboard;

Sherman poured the drinks and raised his glass. "A toast, then. Something fitting."

"All I can think of is peace in this world—and heaven in the next."

"Amen to that."

General Sherman sipped at the fine whiskey, then turned to the open window to look out at the land that had produced it. General Grant joined him, seeing the sparkling lights of the great city of Edinburgh, then beyond it the dark countryside. A peaceful vista, and their thoughts were at peace as well. But out there, beyond Scotland, was the English Channel. Traditional waterway and barrier that had kept the warring nations of Europe at bay for almost a thousand years. And beyond this barrier was a continent perpetually in turmoil, still wanting to settle its countries' differences by force of arms.

"There is still a lot of trouble brewing up out there," Grant said, his words echoing Sherman's thoughts. "Do you think that those people, all those Europeans with their frictions and feuds and long memories of war and revolution—do you think that they can keep the lid on all their troubles?"

"I certainly hope that they can."

"Haven't done too well in the past, have they?"

"Indeed they haven't. But perhaps they will do better in the future." Sherman drained his glass, put it down on the table beside him. "Still, they will have to be watched. My appointment by the President was to keep America free. We have all traveled a long and bitter road to assure that freedom. Our country must not be threatened ever again. Nor will it ever be, not while I have a breath in my body."

"I am with you there, Cumph, we all are. Peace is our aim—but war is our trade. We don't want it. But if it comes we can lick it."

"That we surely can. Good night, Ulysses. Sleep well."

"We all shall sleep well. Now."

SUMMER—1865

THE UNITED STATES OF AMERICA
Abraham Lincoln *President of the United States*
William H. Seward *Secretary of State*
Edwin M. Stanton *Secretary of War*
Gideon Welles *Secretary of the Navy*
Salmon P. Chase *Secretary of the Treasury*
Gustavus Fox *Assistant Secretary of the Navy*
Judah P. Benjamin *Secretary for the South*
John Nicolay *First Secretary to President Lincoln*
John Hay *Secretary to President Lincoln*
William Parker Parrott *Gunsmith*
John Ericsson *Inventor of USS* Monitor

UNITED STATES ARMY
General William Tecumseh Sherman
General Ulysses S. Grant
General Ramsay *Head of Ordinance Department*
General Robert E. Lee
General Thomas Francis Meagher *Commander of the Irish Brigade*
Colonel Andy Summers

UNITED STATES NAVY
Captain Schofield *Captain of USS* Avenger
Admiral David Glasgow Farragut *Naval Commander in Chief*
Captain Raphael Semmes *Captain of USS* Virginia

Captain Sanborn *Captain of USS* Pennsylvania
Captain Dodge *Captain of USS* Thunderer
Captain Curtin *Captain of USS* Atlas
Captain Van Horn *Captain of USS* Devastation
Commander William Wilson *Second Officer of USS* Dictator

GREAT BRITAIN

Victoria Regina *Queen of Great Britain and Ireland*
Lord Palmerston *Prime Minister*
Lord John Russell *Foreign Secretary/Prime Minister*
William Gladstone *Chancellor of the Exchequer*
Benjamin Disraeli *Leader of the Opposition*
John Stuart Mill

BRITISH ARMY

Duke of Cambridge *Commander in Chief*
Brigadier Somerville *the Duke's Aide*
General Bagnall
General Sir William Armstrong *Commander in Chief of Her Majesty's Forces in India*

BRITISH NAVY

Admiral Spencer
Lieutenant Archibald Fowler *Lieutenant HMS* Defender

BELGIUM

Ambassador Pierce *American Ambassador to Belgium*
Leopold *King of Belgium*
Baron Surlet de Chokier *Belgian Foreign Minister*

IRELAND

Jeremiah O'Donovan Rossa *President of the Republic of Ireland*
Isaac Butt *Vice-President of the Republic of Ireland*
Ambassador O'Brin *Irish Ambassador to the United States of America*

Thomas McGrath *Irish Intern in Birmingham*
Patrick McDermott *Irish Intern in Birmingham*

RUSSIA
Admiral Paul S. Makhimov *Admiral Russian Navy*
Count Alexander Igoreivich Korzhenevski *Captain of the* Aurora
Lieutenant Simenov *First Engineer of* Aurora

SCOTLAND
General McGregor *Commander in Chief of Her Majesty's Forces in Scotland*
Mr. MacLaren *of the Highland Council*
Robert Dalglish *Chairman of the National Party of Scotland*

9/14

DEMCO